AN ITALIAN DREAM

KATE FROST

Boldwood

First published in Great Britain in 2022 by Boldwood Books Ltd.

Copyright © Kate Frost, 2022

Cover Design by Alexandra Allden

Cover Photography: Shutterstock

Every effort has been made to obtain the necessary permissions with reference to copyright material, both illustrative and quoted. We apologise for any omissions in this respect and will be pleased to make the appropriate acknowledgements in any future edition.

A CIP catalogue record for this book is available from the British Library.

Paperback ISBN 978-1-80280-452-2

Large Print ISBN 978-1-80280-451-5

Hardback ISBN 978-1-80280-450-8

Ebook ISBN 978-1-80280-454-6

Kindle ISBN 978-1-80280-453-9

Audio CD ISBN 978-1-80280-445-4

MP3 CD ISBN 978-1-80280-446-1

Digital audio download ISBN 978-1-80280-447-8

Boldwood Books Ltd
23 Bowerdean Street
London SW6 3TN
www.boldwoodbooks.com

For my friends.
For your strength and courage through heartache.
You know who you are.

1

STELLA

Stella Shaw had a secret. More than one, actually, but this secret was monumental and exciting, despite her nervousness that it was also new and daunting. Things like this didn't happen to someone like her.

She'd been building up to this moment for weeks, going through a whole gamut of emotions, wanting to tell her best friend her news. And now, if it wasn't for the warm bubbling water in the hot tub, her palms would be sweating like crazy.

Fern was looking content, resting back against the side of the tub, gazing up at the night sky. Stella couldn't help but smile at Fern in her bobble hat and bikini, the water glowing azure blue around them as the steam rising into the chilly air was snatched away by the darkness.

A spa weekend at Aqua Sana in Wiltshire had been a ruse for them to spend time together – Stella's treat. She'd said she'd won the weekend, but that wasn't the full truth. Fern had happily gone along with it; it wasn't as if she treated herself often.

Stella steadied her breathing and gazed up at the lights in the surrounding pine trees twinkling like hundreds of dancing fireflies.

A short distance away, along a lit wooden walkway, the Forest Spa glowed invitingly. Apart from the nerves, she was feeling properly relaxed. She turned her focus to Fern.

'I need to tell you something.'

Fern looked across the hot tub and frowned. 'OMG, you're not pregnant, are you?'

'What? No. As if!'

'Just checking.'

'I am so done with having kids.' Stella gave Fern a knowing look. 'And I'm not engaged either. I promise.'

'Okay then...' Fern said slowly, her beautiful blue eyes fixing on Stella's face. 'I'm out of guesses.'

Stella took a deep breath and released a foggy plume into the January evening. 'I bought a Lottery ticket on a whim. I'd had a knockout appraisal at work and got a bottle of prosecco and a ticket on the way home to celebrate. Turns out I got pretty lucky.' At the fluttering in her chest, she breathed deeply again. 'And won.'

'Are you serious?' Fern bobbed upright in the water. 'How much?'

'A million.'

'*You've won a million?*'

Stella laughed at Fern's high-pitched exclamation and nodded. 'I really have. I've won a million on the National Lottery. Well, a bit more than that actually.'

Fern squealed with delight and threw her arms around Stella, the movement splashing water over the side of the hot tub.

'This is amazing!' Fern released Stella and readjusted her bobble hat.

'It sounds crazy, I know, but I just didn't know how to tell you.' They'd been best friends since the start of secondary school and had gone through so much together. Apart from Stella's eighteen-year-old daughter, Chloe, Fern was the only person she trusted with the news. Not her sister and certainly not her parents, not that she saw much of them anyway.

'This is what the spa weekend has been all about?'

Stella nodded. 'I wanted us to do something special.'

'I'm over the moon for you.' Fern squealed again and looked at Stella with a mix of wonder and shock. 'It's a lot to take in though.'

'Tell me about it!'

Fern shook her head. 'What are you going to do with a million pounds?'

Stella rested her arms along the edge of the hot tub and looked at Fern thoughtfully. 'I've been thinking about that a lot. Well, how to spend some of the money. It's a huge responsibility and I want to make good choices.'

'Hold on.' Fern frowned. 'When did you actually win?'

'October. Well, that's when I claimed it. I didn't realise I had a winning ticket for nearly four weeks.'

'How on earth have you kept this to yourself?'

'I wanted to tell you, I really did, but it's been a lot to process, to suddenly have this life-changing amount of money. I had to open a new bank account, have a chat with the Lottery people, then meetings with legal and financial advisors. A life coach too. There's been loads to think about. And if it makes you feel any better, I only told Chloe at the beginning of the week and I've not told Jacob yet because he'll immediately tell his dad, particularly if I ask him not to. I can't be dealing with that right now. I don't want my whole life turned upside down. That's why I opted for anonymity. I didn't want my name and face to be splashed everywhere or to deal with the fallout from that. Going public felt complicated. Although keeping it secret has thrown up its own issues. I'm so relieved to have finally told you.'

'I'm so glad you have.' Fern reached across the bubbling hot tub, put her hand on Stella's and grinned. 'I think this calls for champagne!'

It was rare for them to spend the whole weekend together. With Chloe away at Kingston University studying drama and Stella's thirteen-year-old son Jacob at his dad's every other weekend, Stella had plenty of time to focus on herself, to go out and enjoy life, but it was a different story for Fern. Young motherhood, raising twins, plus twenty years of marriage to Paul, had taken its toll on her once vivacious, fun-loving friend. On the cusp of turning forty, it was good to see her letting her hair down and enjoying herself for once.

They'd left early that morning, driving just over an hour from Nailsea to Aqua Sana in Longleat Forest. The laughter they'd shared on the drive had taken Stella back to their teens when they'd both had no responsibility and little to think about beyond where they were going out. They'd often drive into Bristol together, leave the car at a friend's, go to a nightclub in town and crash back at the friend's – unless one of them pulled and ended up somewhere else for the night.

With shrieks and giggles, they climbed out of the hot tub and braved the cold, throwing on their white robes and dashing in flip-flops along the wooden walkway inside, past the pool area to the alpine steam room. Stella imagined the heat cleansing her pores, drawing out all the badness. She imagined it tugging at her regrets too, trying to cleanse her past. Would she change anything if she could go back? Probably. Actually, scratch that. Definitely.

When it came to relationships, Stella's love life had been chequered to say the least. While Fern had got pregnant at the end of the summer after their A-levels, Stella had headed off to Cardiff University to study business management and enjoy student life to the full. Yet, a couple of years later, she'd followed in Fern's footsteps when an ill-fated fling at university resulted in Chloe being born not long after she graduated, but she did graduate. She and

Gary made the best of it, getting hitched, moving to Bristol and muddling along together for a couple of years before divorcing when Chloe was two.

With no choice but to move back in with her parents, who she'd had a difficult relationship with even before she disappointed them with an unplanned pregnancy, it was the push Stella needed to work her arse off for herself and Chloe, find an entry-level job in marketing that utilised the skills she'd acquired at uni and move out. Somehow she'd managed to juggle work and school runs, relying on childminders and friends such as Fern to enable her to make a success of single motherhood.

Then she'd met Rhod and had fallen for his charm and good looks. Life had been sweet for a while. They'd got married and Jacob had come along. Five-year-old Chloe had doted on her baby brother. They were a family for a few years, just like Fern, Paul, and their girls, Ruby and Amber, were, until the cracks in Stella and Rhod's relationship became insurmountable. History repeated itself and she found herself divorced and a single mum for the second time, although both Chloe and Jacob's dads remained supportive fathers.

Stella shifted uncomfortably on the curved tiled bench and not just from the overpowering heat of the steam room. Life was good, so much better than when she was married, but she couldn't help but feel a failure when she thought back on past relationships, however strong she was for going it alone again. She knew she had a confidence and an outgoing personality that overshadowed Fern, but before Fern had got pregnant, *she* was the one who used to light up a room, who everyone noticed – men in particular. As sweat poured down her face and between her bikini-clad breasts, Stella contemplated their differences. Fern was a natural beauty with large doe eyes, full lips, lush porcelain skin and delicate features. They were both blonde, although Stella had a little help from a

bottle with her choppy ice-blonde shoulder-length hair, while
Fern's was a natural honey-blonde, long and wavy. They were both
slim and had kept in shape, although Stella was curvier, something
she'd embraced as she'd got older. Her outlook on turning forty
was: bring it on! Her motto was 'work hard, play hard', but she
knew Fern wasn't relishing the idea of the big four-zero. Stella
looked at her now, resting back with her eyes closed, her long hair
scrunched up in a band, golden tendrils framing her flushed face.
She wasn't one for rocking the boat, opting instead for a quiet life
and making do with her lot. In Stella's eyes, her best friend
deserved more.

With an excited Fern asking Stella a barrage of questions about
the Lottery win, they moved from the heat of the steam room to the
extreme cold of the ice cave, which left them refreshed and
giggling. Stella relished the warm softness of her fluffy robe as they
finally relaxed in the Scandinavian Snug and began to thaw out.
They sat on the deep padded seating, their legs curled beneath
them, snuggled under cosy blankets. An artificial fire glowed and
crackled in the centre of the room, and the numb icy feeling
dispersed as the warmth enveloped her.

'This is the life.' Stella sighed.

Fern raised her eyebrows. 'And something you can get used to.'

Stella silently acknowledged that what was a treat for her, must
feel like a total treat to Fern. It could be her reality whenever she
wanted from now on.

'The first thing I want to do is go on holiday,' Stella said,
smoothing her hand down the soft fur blanket across her lap. 'I was
thinking the last two weeks in May to celebrate our fortieth birthdays. Me, you and our girls for most of it. Jacob can come out with
his dad for a bit over half-term. Paul too if he fancies it. We've never
done a proper girls' holiday.'

'We have.'

'A caravan in Wales when the girls were young doesn't count.' She gave Fern a stern look, then giggled. 'It was fun though. It'll be like old times... except in luxury.' She placed a hand on Fern's. 'And it's on me.'

Fern's eyes widened. 'Oh Stella, you can't go spending all your money on us. This weekend is more than enough.'

'I want to do this. And it's a celebration for *us* turning forty!'

Fern shook her head. 'It doesn't have to be a joint thing – my birthday's six weeks after yours.'

'So? I want this to be a birthday celebration for both of us – to kick-start our forties in style.' Stella grinned and drummed her feet in excitement on the smooth wooden floor. 'It will be so much fun. Our forties are going to be the best decade of our lives.'

Stella noticed Fern's smile wane a little. They'd recently talked about their impending forties and she knew Fern was uncertain about heading into a whole new decade. Both of them had spent their twenties raising children and while Stella still had Jacob at home, that part of Fern's life was over. At twenty, Ruby and Amber were adults and had left home, not really needing their mum any more. She knew Fern was floundering, and with good reason. Stella tried to encourage her to do things that would make her happy, whether that was to go out more or by giving her the confidence to pursue long-held ambitions. Fern was most definitely stuck in a rut. Stella hated seeing her this way, particularly when Paul continued to live his life as he'd always done...

Stella placed a warm hand on Fern's arm. 'One other thing, though. Please don't tell anyone. I'll break the news to Amber and Ruby, but don't tell Paul yet.'

'I won't, don't worry.' Fern looked at Stella intently. 'When are you going to tell everyone though? It's not like this is something you can keep secret forever. As soon as you start spending, people will start asking.'

'I know.' Stella acknowledged that she was normally careful with her hard-earned money. Splashing out on things wouldn't go unnoticed for long. 'I just need more time to think it through. I don't want to be rash and have regrets. I also don't want people crawling out of the woodwork as soon as they know I have money. I'm only telling the people I absolutely trust at the moment, and that's a pretty small circle: just you and Chloe. I trust Jacob, I just don't trust his dad to not blab to everyone.' She raised an eyebrow. 'Come on, let's get changed and go celebrate.'

* * *

After a boozy dinner of moules mariniere and poulet Breton, which involved much flirting – on Stella's part at least – with the young and rather good-looking waiter, they headed arm-in-arm, tipsy and giggling, back through the forest to their luxurious woodland-themed two-bedroom apartment which was nestled among the trees.

Stella uncorked a bottle of champagne and, with a pop and a cheer, she poured them each a glassful.

'To being forty and fabulous.' She clinked her glass against Fern's.

'And to friendship.' Fern tapped their glasses together again and they each took a sip. 'So, where do you want to go on holiday?'

'I have no idea.' Stella laughed. 'I'm so used to having to think about the cost. I don't want to spend ages travelling, so perhaps Europe.' She swirled the champagne around her glass. 'Somewhere beautiful and inspiring. Fitting for a fortieth. Preferably with good-looking men.' She winked. There'd been plenty of men after Rhod, even another brief engagement, but no one she'd truly connected with.

Fern laughed. 'Maybe Italy.' She wrinkled her pretty nose. 'Spain? There are so many places. Could island-hop in Greece.'

'That's it! I know how we can decide where to go!' Stella plonked herself down on the sofa, splashing champagne on her skirt. She waved her hand, put the glass down and picked up her phone. 'Let's look up the most beautiful islands in Europe.' She thumbed the search into Google. 'Write each of these down on a separate piece of paper.'

Fern grabbed a notepad and pen from the desk.

'Ready?' Stella said as she scrolled through a post with jaw-droppingly beautiful island views. 'Santorini, Ibiza, Capri, Madeira, Rhodes, Corsica, Mykonos, Sardinia, Hvar, Malta and Sicily. That'll do.' She took the pad from Fern, tore off the eleven sheets, folded each piece of paper in four and dropped them into an empty mug. She held it towards Fern. 'Go on, pick one.'

Fern shook her head and pointed her champagne glass at Stella. 'Uh-uh. No, you should. This is your treat, remember. I want you to be happy with the choice. Plus, you're the lucky one.'

Stella stuck her hand in the coffee cup, mixed the paper up and pulled one out. With butterflies in her stomach, she unfolded it.

'Ah!' She looked up at Fern and grinned. 'Capri. We're going to Capri!'

They hugged each other and danced around the room. Stella felt giddy with excitement, as if the years had melted away and they were eighteen again, celebrating after a night out.

'I know nothing about Capri,' Fern said breathlessly as they collapsed back on to the sofa and grabbed their drinks.

'That's what's so exciting – all I know is it's off the coast of Italy and is supposed to be a totally glamorous place where rich people go.'

'That'll suit you perfectly!'

Stella reached for her phone and googled Capri. 'An island in the Bay of Naples famed for its rugged landscape, upscale hotels and shopping,' she read. 'Ooh, designer labels and limoncello. Apparently Sophia Loren and Mariah Carey own villas there. I think I chose well!'

They clinked their champagne glasses together and chatted until late, getting more and more excited about an island that sounded better and better the more they read about it.

At just gone midnight, they headed to bed to try to get some sleep before their final day of pampering with Elemis face and body treatments booked in the morning. It was a weight off Stella's mind to have told Fern about her Lottery win, and it had been nice, really nice, to see her relaxed and laughing for once, but there was still much they needed to talk about. Much that she needed to tell Fern. But with a sleepy head fuzzy from wine and champagne, that would have to wait. They'd get their birthdays out of the way first and start the next decade of their lives afresh. She bit her lip; she knew it wasn't going to be as straightforward as that.

Before closing the curtains on the night, Stella gazed out through the window to the moonlit forest with its spindly tree trunks and skeletal branches ebony against the clear, deep indigo sky. It was still hard to believe the Lottery win had happened to her. The money wouldn't change her, she was sure, but she did now have the opportunity to turn her life on its head.

2

FERN

Stella dropped Fern back home at 10 p.m. on the Sunday evening with a hug and the promise of speaking soon. The house was dark, with only the hallway light on a timer.

Fern waved and closed the door behind her. It had been exhausting being happy for Stella, and although she was truly over-joyed for her friend, Stella's win and excitement accentuated her own jealousy. Fern knew she'd always been a smidge jealous of her best friend. She'd always questioned that feeling. She had a comfortable life. Her husband Paul had his own successful construction business and she didn't have to work, she just chose to, to do something for herself that gave her a small income. Unlike Stella, she didn't have a career, just a handful of part-time jobs that she'd flitted between over the years. She now worked as a sales assistant in a home furnishing shop. She'd never been driven by money or wanted to pursue a career like Stella had, working her way up from a marketing assistant to a global strategist – to be honest, she wasn't actually sure what Stella's job even entailed. They were worlds apart in that respect. Fern had always muddled along, trying to be happy with her lot.

Fern silently repeated, *I am happy with my lot.*

She left her bag in the hallway and poked her head into the living room, just in case Paul had fallen asleep on the sofa, but it was empty, the TV off, the blinds still open.

The house was too quiet without the girls. Even after two years, she still hadn't got used to it. Straight after her A-levels, Ruby had gone to the University of Birmingham to do nursing. She was the studious one, while Amber had travelled around Asia and Australia before starting a business with marketing degree in London. Whereas Ruby would come home as often as possible, Amber tended not to come back in the holidays if she could help it. Fern missed them both, but she certainly missed the easy-going relationship she'd once had with Amber. The whole of Fern's adult life had revolved around them, so it still felt strange to only have herself and Paul to think about, although he was out so much of the time, it was just her rattling around in the detached house they'd worked hard for, building Paul's business from scratch.

Stella would have gone home to an empty house too, although normally Jacob would be there. He'd still be at his dad's and Stella was going to pick him up tomorrow after school. At least she didn't have a completely empty house. She had a good few years to go before Jacob fled the nest.

A pang of jealousy hit once more as her thoughts returned to Stella. Surely it was only natural to feel envious of her best friend's good fortune? Their friendship had survived into adulthood and they'd supported each other as young mums. Even though Paul had stood by Fern when she'd got pregnant with Amber and Ruby at eighteen, it was Stella who she'd relied on for emotional support as they navigated their way through parenthood. Stella was the one person she trusted to always be there for her. She was over the moon about her win. The jealousy was a perfectly normal response and she would not begrudge Stella this stroke of good luck. She absolutely deserved it.

Fern switched on the kitchen light. Her heart sank. She'd only been away since yesterday morning yet dirty plates, bowls and mugs were piled next to the sink. A loaf of bread was left on the side, crumbs scattered across the worktop. A pan with congealed fat was on the hob. The smell of cold bacon hung in the air. She wrinkled her nose and opened the dishwasher. Empty, as she'd left it.

She messaged Paul.

Home safely. Thanks so much for leaving all the washing up...

He probably wouldn't even check his phone if he was out with his mates. He probably wouldn't get her sarcasm either. She assumed he was at the pub. He was usually out somewhere – at football or in the gym. She knew she should leave the mess, but she also knew he wouldn't do it when he got home and he'd be straight out to work first thing in the morning, so she'd end up doing it anyway. She pulled on rubber gloves. She hated coming down to a messy kitchen.

Fern stacked the dishwasher and started to wash up what was left. She gazed out of the window into the garden. The kitchen only pooled enough light for her to just make out the patio. It had been a grey, miserable January day, but that hadn't mattered in the warmth of the spa. It had felt like a dream, having sweet-smelling oil worked into her aching shoulders and swimming in the warm water of the outdoor pool as she'd floated on her back, gazing up at the lead-grey sky. It had been a real treat and something that Fern wouldn't normally do because she'd either have to save up for it or ask Paul to pay. She could only dream of having the kind of financial freedom that Stella now had. But it wasn't just financial freedom that was playing on her mind, it was the idea of any kind of freedom.

A familiar tightening in her chest brought her back to the present; back to the tedium of real life. She breathed long and deep, pulled off the rubber gloves and dried the few things on the draining board.

If Stella was sensible with the money, she wouldn't need to work again. The possibilities were endless, although a minefield too with two exes, two sets of ex in-laws, not to mention extended family and friends to consider. Fern wasn't even sure if she'd want to win that amount of money and she didn't have the complicated love life that Stella had. After all, she'd been with Paul since they were seventeen, more than two decades of her life.

The front door slammed. Keys crashed to the floor. Paul swore. Without even seeing him, she could tell he was drunk.

'Fern, babe?'

'In the kitchen!' She sighed and finished wiping over the surface.

'Didn't think you'd still be up.' He sidled behind and slid his arms around her. He smelt of lager and cigarettes.

'Well, hello to you too.' She wriggled away from him. The last thing she wanted was to start an argument, so she decided not to point out that she'd cleaned up his mess, but she wasn't in the mood for his drunken antics. 'I was just about to go to bed. Do you want a coffee to sober yourself up?'

'Nah, I'm fine.'

She raised an eyebrow but didn't say anything. He'd be the one to suffer in the morning. He looked as if he was struggling to keep his eyes open and he had at least two days' worth of stubble grazing his jaw. He'd probably been out the night before too. Despite his tiredness, he flashed her a cheeky grin. Even after twenty years, he'd managed to keep his laddish good looks.

'You had a good night then?' she asked, softening a little.

'Just a quiet one with Gaz and Martin.' He poured himself a glass of water. 'You go; I'll be up in a minute.'

'Remember to turn off the light.' She left the kitchen, collected her overnight bag from the hallway and went upstairs.

With the girls away, their four-bedroomed house felt too big. Empty-nest syndrome was a strange old thing. She felt as if she was floundering with no real purpose, although it was evident from tonight that she still had a man-child to look after. Apart from the briefest of spells after turning eighteen, she'd never known a care-free adulthood and now she did have the time to focus on herself and what she wanted to do, she was at a complete and utter loss.

She lived for the girls, but the girls didn't need her any more. They were grown women, with their own hopes and dreams. She was close to Ruby and they'd message each other and chat often, but it was a different story with Amber, who only seemed to communicate with her when she needed something.

Fern sighed. With no holiday planned yet with Paul, a luxury holiday with Stella to celebrate their fortieth birthdays would be something to really look forward to, as well as time with Amber and Ruby. Perhaps it would be a way to reconnect with Amber and understand why their relationship had become so strained. It wasn't just with her; it was Paul too. Amber had been just as sullen and distant with him over the past eighteen months or so and Fern had no idea what they'd done to upset her.

She undressed and slipped into her pyjamas. Her skin still felt smooth and soothed after the spa weekend. She unpacked her washbag and went into the en suite. She'd treated herself to an expensive cleanser and used it to remove what little make-up she had on.

Paul thumped upstairs. The bedroom door banged against the wall. He grunted.

Why he thought it was a good idea to get plastered on a Sunday evening, she had no idea. In the bathroom mirror, she caught him grinning at her from the open en suite door. She dropped the dirty cotton wool pad into the bin.

He staggered towards her and dipped his hands beneath her pyjama top as he nuzzled her neck. 'You smell lush.'

'I've been pampered all weekend, that's why.'

'Oh shit, yeah. Nearly forgot.' He chuckled.

Not nearly forgot, Fern thought, *you did forget*. His drink-addled brain stopped him from walking straight, let alone remembering where she'd been for the last thirty-six hours.

'You had fun?' He worked his hands upwards, finding her bare breasts and giving them a squeeze.

She frowned at him through the mirror. He grinned back.

'Yeah,' she said. His hands were finally caressing instead of squeezing. 'It was a lot of fun and relaxing, just what I needed. Stella too.'

'Uh-huh.'

She knew he wasn't really listening.

'Come to bed,' he said, removing his hands.

'I will in a minute.'

He disappeared into the bedroom. She heard him hopping about, trying to take off his jeans. She knew there'd be a pile of dirty clothes left next to the bed for her to tidy up in the morning.

Fern squeezed the toothpaste onto her toothbrush and started cleaning her teeth. It was hard keeping a secret from her husband. Not that he was in any fit state to listen to her tonight. The Lottery win was huge news, particularly as he'd known Stella for as long as he'd known Fern. They'd all grown up together; rather too quickly in Paul and Fern's case. And tonight it sounded as though he'd been out with Gary, Stella's first ex-husband. He knew both of her ex-husbands: Chloe's dad Gary and Jacob's dad Rhod. Stella had been clear with Fern that she didn't want either of them to know about her Lottery win yet, so it would be best for Paul not to know either. There was no way he'd be able to keep that sort of news to himself. She would respect her friend's wishes.

'Stella's invited me and the girls on holiday with her, you too if you can make it for the last few days,' Fern called from the en suite. She spat into the sink, rinsed her toothbrush and put it away. 'An early fortieth celebration. Is that okay with you? Her treat from the bonus she got at work…' Her voice trailed off as she emerged from the bathroom to find Paul half propped up in bed with his eyes closed and his mouth gaping open, a fluttering snore telling her he was well and truly asleep.

Fern sighed and slipped into bed next to him. He'd managed to take his T-shirt off but was just in his boxer shorts. She wasn't sure if she was upset or relieved that he was asleep and sex was no longer a possibility. The conversation about the holiday to Capri would also have to wait.

She turned away from him and snuggled beneath the covers, curling her hands around her pillow. It was at night, in the dark quietness of their family home, that her mind wandered and discontentment crept up on her, filling her head with worry and anxiety. Recently, there had been many times when she'd cried herself to sleep and she had no idea why, but tonight her head was filled with thoughts of the holiday in May and the beautiful island of Capri…

3

STELLA

Stella got back to an empty house too, not that she minded in the slightest. Jacob was at his dad's and Chloe was at university, but she liked the space and time to herself, plus she knew she could have company if she wanted.

She dumped her bag at the bottom of the stairs, switched on the living room lights and closed the blinds. The kitchen was spotless, as she'd left it. She filled the kettle before deciding she wanted something stronger than a cup of tea. She poured a generous amount of Baileys into a glass and popped in a couple of ice cubes.

To say she was proud of her house and how hard she'd worked over the last few years to be able to afford it, was an understatement. It wasn't detached or as big as Fern's, but it was all hers. Selling the house she'd shared with Rhod had broken her heart. But becoming a single mum for a second time had made her more determined to make a success of herself. After her second divorce, she'd taken risks, swapping her comfortable marketing manager job for one in a fast-growing digital company that had quickly expanded internationally. She'd become laser focused on her ambitions and she'd achieved everything she set out to, enabling her to afford her three-bed semi on a nice road in Nailsea. She didn't want to settle for nice any longer though. She didn't need to. Everything was going to change; she was well aware of that.

She rattled the ice around the glass. She'd gone through all sorts of emotions over the past three months, and keeping the news to herself had been hard, but right. There were too many people who would try to lay a claim, too many people who would come crawling back, after their share of her riches. She was also aware of how the money would impact Chloe's and Jacob's lives. She loved them to bits and was immensely proud of the young adults they'd become, but she didn't want to spoil them or for their outlook on life to dramatically change because of her new-found wealth. The weight of responsibility lay heavy on her shoulders.

After the initial thrill, the reality of winning all that money gave her palpitations. Keeping quiet about her win to friends and family had been tough, but it allowed her the time to process the enormity of it without people interfering. She could only imagine how everyone would chip in about how *they* thought she should spend her money. Chloe had already talked about moving house – to one with a pool. Stella could almost hear the ka-chings going off in Chloe's head as she'd talked about buying clothes, going on holiday and paying off her student loan. Sure, Stella could be a little frivolous, but she needed to be cautious and careful and invest in their future. The win needed to impact Chloe and Jacob positively, that was Stella's main concern.

She wasn't sure how long Chloe would be able to keep a Lottery win a secret. Fern she could trust completely. She didn't have to worry about her telling Paul. How Fern had stuck being married to Paul for so long, she had no idea. She bit her lip and stared out over the dark garden. Stella did know why, because Fern didn't know anything about what Paul got up to, or if she did, she hid it well. She seemed content enough to make do with her lot. She'd compromised massively, perhaps to the extent of her own happiness over that of her family. Stella partly admired that, but at the same time, she felt sorry for her.

Two weeks in Capri, celebrating their birthdays, would be a highlight for them both, some real sunshine in their lives, a chance to reconnect with themselves and spend proper time together. Stella would often invite Fern out in Bristol with her work friends, but Fern would always say no, giving the excuse of clubbing not being her thing any longer. Stella understood that she was married, but there was no harm in living a little. And it wasn't as if Paul didn't go out partying.

Stella was aware of the differences in their lives; Fern had been married with kids for half her life now, while she was single yet again and making the most of the freedom. That was exactly what she had: freedom. Over the years, Fern's life had become so... vanilla. Stella wanted to do everything she could to inject fun and sparkle back into it. A holiday would be good for them all. It was the least she could do to treat her best friend. Paul wouldn't say no; he wouldn't dare. And if he had an issue, then she'd have words. He wouldn't have a leg to stand on. It was about time he did something nice for Fern.

Stella downed her Baileys and switched on her phone. She'd purposely left it off all weekend. Jacob was with his dad and at thirteen he really didn't want her calling him before bed to wish him goodnight. There was a missed call from Thierri, a guy she'd seen out in town a few times now. They'd chatted, snogged a bit, swapped numbers and he'd been chasing her for a proper date. She also had messages from Rhod and her colleagues Annie and Louise. They were good friends, but she hadn't known them for as long as she'd known Fern.

Not only had the spa weekend served the purpose of finally telling Fern about her Lottery win, but it had been good to spend quality time with her. They'd been friends for nearly three decades, their lives entwined in so many ways. They lived close to each other, and with the girls being a similar age and having gone to the same school they'd never drifted apart. Both she and Fern had strained relationships with their own families, which made their bond even stronger. They'd always been there for each other.

That thought left a bitter taste in her mouth, knowing what she'd done. Stella pushed away the troubling thought, stacked the empty Baileys glass in the dishwasher and switched off the kitchen light. It was too late to sit and watch crappy TV.

She lugged her bag upstairs and unpacked. The king-size bed looked welcoming but lonely. She didn't necessarily want company, but with Jacob at his dad's for an extra night and no school run to fit in before work in the morning, it didn't have to be the usual early to bed Sunday evening. Thierri wasn't exactly the drop-dead-gorgeous man she was perhaps hoping to stumble across in Capri, but he wasn't bad-looking either. She had no doubt that, given the chance, he'd happily warm her bed. There was always the option of phone sex. She could close her eyes and listen to his sexy French voice, deep and lilting...

She pressed his number and let the phone ring.

* * *

Stella loved having the focus of a holiday and the joint birthdays to plan during the long dull days of January. Chloe was beyond excited and was adamant that it was fine to miss two weeks of university, saying, 'It's only my first year and I haven't got many lectures anyway.'

Stella set up a WhatsApp group called Capri Baby! and broke the news about her Lottery win and the holiday to Amber and Ruby. She trusted Ruby more than she did Amber and Chloe – of the three girls, Ruby had always been the more serious, sensitive and studious.

It was no surprise when Ruby turned down the offer of the holiday because she was on a nursing placement, but Stella made her promise to come out for a few days for the birthday celebrations at the end of the two weeks.

As predicted by Fern, Amber jumped at the chance of an all-expenses-paid holiday – whether she could afford to take time off from her business degree or not, her focus at university was about having fun rather than working hard. Not that Stella blamed her in the slightest. She was certain that if things had worked out differently for Fern and she hadn't discovered that she was pregnant after starting university, she would have behaved exactly the same.

Jacob was already spending the May half-term with his dad and Rhod was more than happy to have him for an extra week. Unsurprisingly, he didn't argue when Stella offered to pay for their flights to join them at the end of the holiday. And when Fern asked Paul if he wanted to come to Capri with Ruby for the last few days, due to work commitments, and to Stella's relief, he declined. For the best part of two weeks, Stella was going to get the girls-only holiday she craved. She couldn't wait.

4

FERN

A freezing miserable winter morphed into spring, bringing with it a flurry of activity in preparation for the impending holiday to Capri. Stella had organised everything, from booking the flights and accommodation to keeping her and the girls updated via their WhatsApp group.

Fern went along with the joint birthday plans, but as she wasn't actually turning forty until July, she wanted the focus of the celebrations in Capri to be on Stella. With the holiday being paid for by Stella, she agonised over what to get her for a present. Fern didn't have much spare cash and she didn't like asking Paul for money, particularly when she wanted it to be something special just from her. In the end, by saving up a little extra each month, she bought two things: a silver friendship bracelet to give Stella on her birthday in Capri, plus a colourful print of iconic Bristol sights by a local artist for when they returned. She hoped it would remind Stella of all the things they'd done together and the happy times they'd shared over the years: taking the girls and Jacob to the Bristol International Balloon Fiesta, a fish and chip cruise on *The Matthew* for a friend's wedding reception and the distant memory of boozy nights out on the harbourside. Ideally, she would have loved to have created something herself, but she hadn't really drawn since her teens. Her desire to do a creative course such as the graphic design degree she had once hoped to pursue was a distant dream and her passion for art had diminished over the years, along with her confidence.

With the start of May, the countdown to the fourteenth was on, and Fern's excitement was mixed with guilt that Paul would be working while she was away having fun. She knew she shouldn't think like that, but still…

'Are you absolutely sure you don't mind me swanning off for two weeks?' Fern asked at breakfast.

'Course not.' He looked at her across the kitchen table, a piece of toast in his hand, a mug of tea in the other. 'Stella's doing well for herself though.'

'Yes, she is,' Fern said calmly. It didn't sit comfortably with her not being able to tell Paul the truth, particularly as the girls knew. 'You're going to be okay on your own?'

He shrugged. 'I'll be working most of the time.'

'The freezer's full – I cooked a batch of chilli. There's a couple of different curries too. The recycling schedule is pinned to the fridge and I've marked anything important on the calendar.'

'Thanks, love.'

'And if you're able to drop Ruby at the airport on the twenty-seventh to save her getting a taxi, that'll be great. I know the flight's super early.'

'It's fine, don't worry.' He downed the tea, dumped his mug and plate next to the sink and left her with a peck on the cheek.

One week to go and the excitement grew as Stella teased them by adding a couple of images in their WhatsApp group of a sparkling pool and a sun-drenched terrace of the villa they'd be staying in. Haircuts and waxes were booked, and Paul told Fern to treat herself to a new bikini and a couple of summery outfits. By the time the holiday dawned, Fern felt more optimistic and uplifted than she had in a very long time.

Fern woke before the alarm on the morning of the holiday with excitement and nerves twisting her stomach. Paul was snoring next to her, in just his boxer shorts with the bed covers thrown off. She lay on her side and gazed at him for a while, considering whether to run her fingers through his chest hair, to kiss him awake for morning sex. Perhaps she would have done a long time ago. She couldn't remember the last time he'd woken her like that either. Once the girls were older, and particularly now they'd left home, there was more time and opportunity to do things like that, to put the spark back in their marriage, but she had zero desire and she was unsure why. She slipped out of bed instead and went into the en suite to get ready.

Amber had arrived home the day before, and after her shower, Fern knocked on her bedroom door to make sure she was awake.

Paul needed to leave for work early. He said goodbye to Amber and gave Fern a kiss. It was an odd thing; she was used to him working a lot, getting home late, and when the girls were younger, she'd go away with them for a long weekend and Paul would have weekends away with his mates too, yet they'd never spent as long as two weeks apart. Fern pulled him close and hugged him tight. He hugged her back and laughed.

'You silly mare; you're only going for a couple of weeks. You have a nice time.' And that was it, he was out of the front door without a backwards glance.

Fern went upstairs to their bedroom to double-check she had everything. She felt silly for feeling uncertain about going away

without him. It was just two weeks. Anyway, she wasn't going to
have time to miss him. Halfway across the room, she stopped, a
thought hitting her. Would she actually miss him? She found
herself continually being annoyed by Paul, only little things, but
lots of little things had grown into a bigger problem. He was always
too busy to talk. It never seemed the right time to bring up her
concerns and upset him, because she knew she would.

'Mum! Have you got a spare toothpaste you can chuck in for
me?' Amber's voice carried up the stairs, tugging her from her
worries.

'I'll check!' Fern called back.

She riffled in the cupboard under the sink and found another
toothpaste. She closed the en-suite door and took one last look
round the bedroom. She was sure the bedding wouldn't be changed
or the bed made until she returned.

She sighed and jogged down the stairs to join Amber and wait
for Stella. At the sight of their suitcases and bags lining the hallway,
her excitement and anticipation returned.

Amber was waiting in the front room, perched on the arm of the
sofa, scrolling on her mobile.

Fern glanced at her watch. 'Stella and Chloe will be here soon.
You sure you've got everything?'

'Yes, Mum.' Her tone was frosty.

'I'm only checking because you've already asked me for one
thing.' Fern sighed as she handed her the toothpaste. She didn't
want to feel as if she had to tiptoe around Amber. She hoped the
holiday would bring them closer together but witnessing Amber's
coolness with both her and Paul since she'd got home the day
before, she wasn't feeling optimistic.

Amber was, in Fern's mind, dressed more for a night out than
for a long journey. Although, to be fair, with a stack of bangles on
her arm, gold-coloured sandals, a short skirt and a crop top that

showed her slender tummy, she looked ready for a day of shopping in Capri. Her make-up was flawless and her long blonde hair tousled. Fern had gone for comfort over style, with slim-fitting capri-style trousers and a pale-blue short-sleeved blouse. She looked and felt very middle-aged as she gazed at her slim and sparkly grown-up daughter.

Tyres crunched on the gravel driveway. Clasping her phone, Amber raced to the front door and yanked it open. Fern followed and they stood on the doorstep together as a taxi pulled up and Stella got out with a wave. Fern's heart dropped as she realised she was way off the mark with her choice of clothes. Stella managed to look both summery and glitzy with a floor-skimming leopard-print maxi skirt and a black top with capped sleeves that showcased her tanned arms. Fern was pretty certain the whole outfit was brand new and the tan was out of a bottle, but she couldn't deny just how good she looked.

Amber squealed with excitement as she greeted Chloe on the path, which only highlighted her cool reserve around Fern. She sighed again. Chloe looked like a typical eighteen-year-old with cut-off jean shorts and a tight T-shirt with some logo Fern didn't recognise emblazoned across it.

Stella reached Fern and hugged her. 'You look gorgeous.'

'So do you.' The squeals of delight from Amber and Chloe continued, but Fern acknowledged she was just as excited. She gripped Stella's hand. 'I've been looking forward to this for so long.'

'And I can't believe it's finally happening!' Stella beamed. 'Right, everyone got everything? Let's get going!'

* * *

Stella had pre-booked the Aspire Lounge at Bristol Airport, so after checking in and being whisked through security, they relaxed in comfort with a glass of champagne and tucked into complimentary Danish pastries. While Fern and Stella flicked through magazines and chatted, the girls went off to do some duty-free shopping. They'd maxed out their baggage allowance and Amber's hand luggage in particular was heaving; Fern had no idea how she was going to lug shopping around too.

It was still only mid-morning by the time they settled themselves on the plane. Somehow they managed to stow their bags and rucksacks in the overhead lockers and beneath the seats. Amber and Chloe were sitting next to each other directly in front of Fern and Stella. Fern could hear them giggling together, their chatter a hundred miles an hour. With their long blonde hair and only a couple of years between them, they could easily be mistaken for sisters. Despite Amber and Ruby being identical twins, personality wise they couldn't have been more different, and Amber had always got on better with Chloe.

The flights from Bristol were no frills with a budget airline, but that certainly hadn't put a dampener on anyone's spirits. Fern relaxed back in her seat, trying to let the worries of everyday life wash away. They were headed for Naples, a city famous for pizza, Mount Vesuvius and notorious for pickpockets – Fern had done her research. But it would only be a place they'd briefly see on their way from the airport to the port and the hydrofoil to Capri. For the next couple of weeks, she could forget about everything and relish the opportunity of an all-expenses-paid holiday, time with her best friend and their daughters. Refresh and rejuvenate, that's what she needed – much like that spa weekend.

The plane took off, juddering upwards. Fern gripped the arm rests and willed it into the air, her panic easing when they had climbed high enough for the plane to level out. Since when had she been a nervous flyer?

The airport and the grey muggy day were left behind as they

reached the Bristol Channel, drifts of white cloud distorting the view of Clevedon Pier as they turned towards Portishead and then Capri.

Soon enough, they'd left England behind and the flight attendants had come by with the catering trolley.

Stella knocked her mini bottle of prosecco against Fern's and swigged straight from it. 'I am planning on having as much fun as I possibly can this holiday.'

Chloe groaned from the seat in front. Fern imagined her and Amber rolling their eyes.

Fern drank to that. She was planning on having fun too, but probably not in quite the same way as her single and newly minted best friend.

'Honestly,' Stella said, lowering her voice, 'I feel like this is our chance to make up for lost time. I don't regret having Chloe young and I'm sure you wouldn't change having the twins for the world, but we both missed out on stuff.'

'Even if I hadn't got pregnant at eighteen, we still wouldn't have had this type of holiday.'

'Yeah, yeah, I know. We'd probably have gone clubbing in Ibiza or got into a bucketload of trouble in Magaluf. So, in many ways, this has worked out for the best.' Stella sipped her prosecco. 'We're still young enough to enjoy all the delights Capri has to offer.' She looked at her with a knowing smile.

'You're not looking for love, are you?' Fern asked.

'God, no. I'm done with relationships and all that. The last thing I want is to share what I have with someone else. A fling, mind...' She winked and gave a throaty chuckle. 'But honestly, Fern, this is *our* time. Forget about our lives back home: exes, husbands, men in general. We deserve this. *You* deserve a break and to think about yourself rather than everyone else for once.'

Fern couldn't argue with that. Time had run away with her. It was hard to comprehend that two decades had gone by in what felt like a heartbeat. To an eighteen-year-old being forty seemed ancient, and yet here she was, soon to pass that milestone. It wasn't that she minded getting older – in many ways, she was more comfortable with herself now than she had been in her twenties post-pregnancy, but she felt adrift, uncertain of her place in the world. There was a lot she needed to figure out.

* * *

They landed in Naples and, with all their luggage, Fern was relieved that Stella had booked a private transfer to the port. Their driver, Fabrizio, greeted them with a jolly *'buongiorno'* and a dazzling smile, and even with the bustle of people streaming from the airport into the warm and sunny May afternoon, Fern acknowledged the relaxed change of pace and the butterflies in her stomach.

With their bags and suitcases safely loaded in the sleek minibus, they set off. Fern gripped the seat in front as they sped along the road, squeezing past other vehicles, Fabrizio navigating his way through the packed and rather run-down streets with traffic in all directions, while shouting down the phone in mind-bendingly fast Italian.

'My wife, she is pregnant,' he called over his shoulder by way of explanation. 'She want gelato. Always gelato.'

Fern's heart pounded. She noticed both Amber and Chloe holding on for dear life too. Even Stella looked stressed, her lightly tanned face pinched into a frown. The combination of the prosecco on the plane, the humidity, the busyness, the noise of cars beeping and screeching left Fern buzzing but eager to reach their destination and enjoy two weeks without having to work, look after the house or spend it with Paul. She got a stab of guilt at that thought.

Treating herself was a rarity and being in Italy was exactly that, a complete and utter treat. All thanks to Stella.

They were all relieved when they made it in one piece and Fabrizio unloaded their luggage. With his help, they dragged their suitcases to the Mollo Beverello part of the port in search of the pre-booked hydrofoil for the forty-five-minute trip to Capri.

Fern stopped for a moment, taking a breath after a whirlwind journey. The gentle sun warmed her shoulders and voices sprinkled the air with Italian and English. Somewhere out there past the hydrofoils lining the dock and across the sparkling sea was their destination: the beautiful island of Capri.

After thanking Fabrizio and safely stowing their luggage, Fern finally felt able to relax. And they did, in the small bar area, with an espresso and a cornetto, an Italian pastry that looked a little like a croissant. The hydrofoil left the port, cutting across the impossibly blue water of the Bay of Naples and leaving behind the city and Mount Vesuvius's domineering presence. Although Fern was fascinated by the idea of visiting Pompeii and witnessing what the volcano had preserved from Roman times, she was quite glad to be heading away from the noise and craziness of Naples.

Fern felt her stomach lurch even though the water was far from choppy. She left the others in the bar area and found an empty seat. She breathed slow and steady, willing the nausea to ebb away.

'Are you okay?'

A voice next to her made her realise she had her eyes closed. She opened them and glanced to her left.

The elderly woman sitting at the end of the row had a warm, welcoming face with rosy cheeks and deep laughter lines. Wisps of white hair had escaped from a floral headscarf and her hands were clasped over the bag in her lap.

Fern smiled. 'Just feeling a little seasick.'

'I'm sure it will pass. It won't be much longer now. Is this your first time to Capri?' The woman had a twinkle in her eye. 'I like to ask and see people's expressions as we near the island. It's quite magical.'

'Yes, first time to Italy actually, although it's a place I've always wanted to go.' It beat the caravanning holidays she'd had when the kids were young and then a couple of all-inclusive holidays to Spain because Paul only ever wanted to go to places where he'd be able to watch the football. 'It's pure chance that we're coming to Capri. I understand it's a pretty glamorous place that the rich and famous visit.'

'Oh, it's certainly glamorous, but there's a whole other side to it too. Such a visual and emotive place. I love it.'

'You've been before then?'

The woman nodded. 'A few times over many years, yes.' She held out her hand. 'I'm Edith by the way.'

'Fern,' she replied, shaking Edith's hand.

'What a beautiful name.'

'Thank you. I hated it as a kid but have grown to love it over the years.'

'I think nature-inspired names are wonderful. If I'd had children, I'd like to have named them things like River, Rowan, Clementine or Ocean.' She chuckled. 'They'd have hated me for it, I'm sure, so just as well I didn't have any.'

Fern couldn't tell if there was a hint of regret in her voice or not. 'My daughters are called Ruby and Amber, so are in keeping with my name, but more beautiful, I think.'

'They certainly are. Gorgeous names.'

'Are you having a holiday on Capri or just a day trip?'

'I'm here for two weeks on an art retreat.'

'Really? That sounds wonderful.'

'You're an artist too?'

'Oh goodness, no. I like the idea of a retreat though and being creative.'

Edith nodded thoughtfully. 'You're here with your family?'

'One of my daughters, plus my best friend and her daughter. A once-in-a-lifetime holiday – for me anyway. You're travelling on your own?'

'I am,' Edith said. 'My friend was supposed to be coming too, but things fell through at the last minute, so it's just me.' She smiled but it seemed forced.

'I'm sorry.'

'Don't be, I wouldn't miss this for the world. I've been looking forward to it for a long time. I'm passionate about Italy – one day I'll pluck up the courage to move here. I said I would when I retired, and now, nearly ten years later, I still keep putting it off. A yearly holiday keeps me going.'

'Just to Capri?'

'I've been all over the place, but Capri and the Amalfi Coast keep tugging me back. I've been on this retreat a couple of times before and it's just magical. I vowed to return, so here I am. Two weeks of being immersed in sketching and painting with the most generous host, luxurious accommodation, beautiful views, sumptuous food...' She smiled. 'You get the idea.'

'That sounds incredible.'

'It is.' She looked at Fern with a furrowed brow. 'There is a room all paid for and going spare if you fancy it...' She shook her head. 'Goodness, you're with your daughter and friend, very silly of me to even suggest it.'

'Not silly at all, and an incredibly kind offer. I'd jump at it given a chance, but like you said, I'm here with my friend and our daughters.'

'I understand, but you'd be more than welcome to come along for the day or even an overnight stay if you fancied doing something different to the usual sightseeing. Your daughter too. It seems such a shame for my friend's spot to go to waste. The retreat's called Il Ritiro d'Arte in Anacapri in case you're interested. All levels of experience are catered for, I promise.'

Fern quite liked the idea of flexing her creative muscles. It had been a long time since she'd drawn or painted. She missed it. Arranging the shop window at work was about as creative as she got these days. She smiled warmly at Edith, realising that her seasickness had subsided. 'That's really very kind of you; I'll bear it in mind.'

Edith fumbled in her bag, pulled out her purse and passed her a business card. 'Left over from my working days; it has my mobile on there if you want to get hold of me. I would be delighted to have the company.'

5

FERN

Fern's eyes widened at the sight of Capri looming green and rocky. Predominately white buildings studded the steep hillside that rose from where the hydrofoil had docked.

Amber and Chloe were walking ahead, dragging their suitcases along the marina. Fern paused and turned back to wait for Stella to catch up. Beyond the stream of the other tourists disembarking, the sea glistened all the way to the flat plain of Naples and the volcano which dominated the horizon.

Fern caught sight of Edith and smiled.

'I hope you have the most wonderful time,' Edith said, slowing as she reached her. 'Remember my offer. *Arrivederci.*' And she was off towards Marina Grande with a wave.

Stella finally caught up with Fern. 'Who was that you were talking to?'

'A really lovely lady. She was supposed to be coming here with a friend but has ended up on her own. She was inviting me on the artist retreat she's going to.'

Stella laughed. 'And I was imagining we'd get propositioned by some sexy young Italians, while you manage to attract the attention of an old lady.'

Fern shook her head. 'She was just being nice and chatty. She seemed quite lonely.'

Stella walked on, leading them to where a porter holding a handwritten sign with her name on it was waiting to take their luggage on ahead to the villa.

There'd been constant chatter throughout the journey from Amber and Chloe, but there was silence as, relieved of their suitcases, they took an open-top taxi away from the glittering sea up the narrow winding road past walled villa gardens spilling over with bright pink bougainvillea. It was quite something to see the girls entranced by the island.

After being dropped off not far from the main piazzetta at the top of the hill, they walked the rest of the way along a road with breath-taking views on one side and gated villas hidden by trees on the other. It was the peace that Fern noticed the most, particularly after the craziness of Naples. She had expected a vibrant bustling island filled with wealth in its shops, cafes and bars, yet away from the piazzetta with its crowds of summery-looking people, she could only hear birds singing in the trees. The drone of a helicopter reminded her she was on an island of the rich and famous. She glanced up at the helicopter; just a dot against the clear cyan sky.

Stella seemed to know exactly where she was going, proudly announcing, 'This is it,' when they reached an entrance with Villa Giardino etched into a plaque in the centre of double gates.

The villa itself was hidden by a forest of cypress, oak and olive trees. Glimpses of honey-coloured stone emerged from among the Mediterranean foliage. Fern had done her research on the island, but Stella had kept where they were staying a surprise. It was even better than she'd anticipated.

A paved path meandered through the garden. It was late in the afternoon and the constant chirrup of cicadas kept them company. Fern walked behind the others, soaking up the gentle heat, the glossy leaves, the flash of orange from a fluttering butterfly and the sweet scent of flowers, which all had an immediate calming effect. This was absolutely the break she needed.

Set beneath a pillared porch, the front door was large, wooden and grand. The door swung open and they were greeted by a smiling Italian woman looking smart in black trousers and a cream blouse with her dark hair neatly tied back.

'*Benvenute*! I'm Violetta. Welcome to Villa Giardino.' Violetta had a light accent and a welcoming smile as she ushered them inside. 'I'm the housekeeper and will be looking after you during your stay.'

They followed her into a large bright entrance hall with an ornate staircase that curved up to the first floor. Sunlight flooded through the skylights, the double height making the entrance hall impressively grand.

'You must be tired from travelling.' Violetta offered them each an ice-cold flannel for their hot faces and hands, which was as deliciously cool and lemon-fresh as the home-made lemonade she handed them as they returned the flannels.

'Your luggage has already arrived and been taken to your rooms. Would you like me to show you around or are you happy to explore on your own?'

Clutching their drinks, Amber and Chloe were already poking their heads into the rooms off the hallway.

'I think exploring on our own will be fine,' Stella said.

Violetta nodded. 'I'll give you some time. How about drinks on the terrace in an hour?'

'Sounds perfect.'

She nodded her approval and left them.

Stella turned to Chloe and Amber. 'To stop any arguments, I've already decided who's having which bedroom. You two are upstairs, Chloe in The Silver Room and Amber you have The Gold Room. Fern and I are on the ground floor.'

The girls were already off, taking the stairs two at a time.

Fern and Stella finished their drinks and explored the spacious ground floor. Stella had refused to say how much she was paying for the place, but it was majestic and Fern could imagine how expensive it was. It was a traditional seventeenth-century villa with ornate tiled floors and antique furniture, combined with modern touches in the widescreen TV in the large and bright living room and the all-important air con and Wi-Fi.

The inside and outside flowed together beautifully, with large French windows allowing light to flood in, while patio doors opened onto the landscaped gardens. Shafts of sunlight streaked in, so different to the grey and humid day they'd left behind.

Fern and Stella grinned at each other as they discovered the dining room, with a large circular table laid out with silver cutlery, the textured wallpaper shimmering gold in the sunlight streaming through the windows. Fern was in awe; she'd never been anywhere quite so beautiful. The location was perfect, within walking distance of the bustling Piazza Umberto, but tucked away in achingly beautiful and peaceful surroundings.

'Come on,' Stella said, running her fingers across the cut glasses on a drinks' tray in the corner. 'Let me show you your room.'

Stella led Fern back across the villa to The Green Room and smiled as Fern's jaw dropped open in disbelief. The room was spacious, airy, and flooded with light. Green, turquoise and burnt-orange patterned floor tiles were offset by the white walls which added to the cool calmness. The king-size bed looked invitingly large and comfortable, piled high with sumptuous pillows.

With tears in her eyes, Fern grabbed Stella and hugged her. 'Thank you, Stella, I mean it. This is unbelievably generous of you.'

'It's my pleasure,' Stella said, looking bashful while batting away her thanks. 'I'll let you unpack.'

Fern spent the next twenty minutes putting away her clothes. Laughter filtered from somewhere upstairs, unmistakably Amber and Chloe. Fern had missed that joyous sound. When Amber was home, she rarely seemed happy around her, and laughter was a distant memory. It reminded her of the girls growing up and simpler, happier times.

She perched on the end of the bed and messaged Paul.

We're here safely. The place is stunning, will send pics. Amber is beyond excited. Hope you've had a good day. Xx

She dropped her phone on the forest- and bird-patterned bedspread. The sense of calm the room evoked was immense. From the nature-inspired decor and furnishings to the flood of sunlit green through the open French doors, she could see where it got its name.

On the dressing table was a new, tropical leaves print washbag filled with make-up and toiletries, including an Acqua di Parma shower gel and body cream. She ran her fingers over the typed note:

A little something special for you. Love Stella xx

It was more than a little something. Gratitude rushed through Fern, for the thoughtful gift and for being in a place like this, where money wasn't an issue and she didn't have to think about anything. The idea of being able to truly relax was seeping through her, the general aches and tiredness from a long journey beginning to disperse.

Fern changed out of her trousers into a long white maxi skirt. She put on her sunglasses, slipped her feet into sandals and went out of the French doors onto a private terrace which was dappled with sunlight. Nestled in the L-shaped wall and screened by trees was a shady reading spot with a large rattan chair and oversized cushions that invited her to sink into their depths. To the front of the patio, a wooden table with two chairs overlooked the gardens. Fern glimpsed the glistening turquoise water of a pool and the deeper blue of the sky beyond.

She left the terrace and wandered into the sunshine. The inside of the villa had blown her away, but the garden was idyllic. Yellow inflorescences hung from the branches of holm oaks and the bright yellow flowers of broom splashed colour along the path that led to the pool. Birdsong danced on the light breeze, while a gentle warmth caressed her, helping to dispel her worries even further.

Fern pushed her sunglasses down her nose and looked over them. The pool was large, curved and perched right on the clifftop, with a view that could only be described as magical. Her initial impression of Capri was of glitz and glamour, but this oozed sophistication. There was a quiet beauty in the craggy green-clad cliffs jutting out of the sea, the town glittering in between.

Everything was so far removed from her life back in England. Her detached house seemed luxurious, but it was nothing remarkable, in a nondescript town. Much like her life really; she had nothing interesting to talk about beyond her kids. Her grown-up children. Life had always revolved around them and she needed to find her way again. Forge a path of her own away from Ruby and Amber. Branch out from being a housewife with a part-time job that she didn't really care about. She needed to become more than just Paul's wife and Ruby and Amber's mum. As clichéd as it sounded, she needed to find herself. Wasn't this the perfect opportunity? It was also a chance to reconnect with Amber, and reclaim a relationship with her built on respect and love.

6

STELLA

The villa was everything Stella had hoped for and more. A sense of peace washed over her as she explored the ground floor with Fern, discovering the fresh, airy rooms. Doors and windows were flung open, letting sunshine and the breeze drift in. The white walls and high ceilings added to the peace, while green and blue dominated outside. The sound of Chloe and Amber's laughter drifted from upstairs; there was a giddiness to it that made them seem much younger than they actually were.

Stella's room was the smallest, but it was still a decent size. She'd chosen it because it was tucked out of the way on the ground floor, just a short stroll from the pool. It was called The Blue Room and was ocean-themed, cool and soothing, with blue and white floor tiles in a repeating pattern that added colour and interest.

Stella spied Fern exploring outside. She'd changed into a long white summery skirt. It swished against her legs as she walked past the open doors of Stella's room. Stella noticed the contentment on Fern's face before she disappeared. She loved how the villa and grounds were sprawling with lots of hidden areas, an easy place to get lost in or to find a bit of peace and quiet. She knew it was just

what she needed to get her head straight about everything, and she
wanted Fern to be happy, *really* happy for once.

Stella stood on the threshold of the terrace and relished the
warmth of the sunlight caressing her bare arms. She sighed. There
was so much that she needed to talk to Fern about, but that could
all wait. For now, they simply needed to enjoy the island.

This is the life, she thought.

* * *

Stella joined Fern on the pool terrace and they sat in
companionable silence, soaking up the view. Violetta brought out a
tray with glasses and a jug of cloudy lemonade and set it on the
large table.

'Would you like dinner served out here later?' she asked.

'Yes, that would be perfect, thank you,' Stella said.

Violetta nodded and returned to the villa with the empty tray.

Fern raised an eyebrow. 'Don't tell me there's a chef too?'

'Violetta's making pizza.' Stella grinned. 'She's our fairy
godmother for the next two weeks. I thought it would be far more
relaxing eating here this evening. There's plenty of time for
exploring and dining out.'

Stella poured the lemonade and handed Fern a glass.

'We're so going to get spoilt here.'

'That's the idea,' Stella said. With each sip of the zesty and
refreshing drink, she felt her troubles fade away. The gentle caress
of the breeze and the late-afternoon sun helped too, if only for a
short while. It was always when she was alone at night that her
head would fill with shame and guilt. Secrets would twist and turn
inside, worries would attack and she'd often struggle to sleep.

Fern looked thoughtful too; Stella wondered what she was
thinking about. She tried to shift her own thoughts to something

more positive. She was proud of the life she'd created for herself as a single working mum. Her semi-detached house was her haven, but it was nothing compared to this. The worry that had ebbed away returned, making her start, but for a different reason this time. She gripped her glass tighter. The reality was: this could be her life; a place like this could be her reality. Winning the Lottery had given her the possibility of freedom but also a load more worry to heap on top of the worries she already held.

Amber and Chloe's laughter reached them before they appeared along the path beneath the trees, stirring Stella from her thoughts. They'd changed into their swim things and she had a brief stab of envy at their youthful energy. *Not that I'm old*, she told herself, but donning a bikini without the fear of revealing stretch marks had got harder over the years. She knew Fern would roll her eyes and say that she had nothing to worry about. Stella looked after herself, but there was always an annoying thought that she wasn't slim or young enough any longer. Not that she'd ever had any complaints about her body, and if she had, she'd have told the bloke in no uncertain terms where to go.

Stella noticed Fern's eyes trailing over the girls too. She wondered if she was feeling the same. She was aware that Fern's confidence had nosedived over the years. In their teens, Fern had had an ease with her body and sexuality that Stella had tried to emulate, but growing up fast had put an end to her friend's exploits.

She sighed as the girls joined them, all slender fake-tanned limbs and new bikinis on beneath their sheer and floaty beach cover-ups.

'Chloe's been admiring the view,' Amber said with a gleam in her eye. She dumped her towel on the table and flopped into the chair opposite.

'I have not!' Chloe whacked Amber's arm.

'If you say so.' Amber turned to Stella. 'The gardener's a young, hot, dark-haired Italian.'

'There's a gardener?' Fern asked.

'Uh-huh.' Amber nodded. 'He only needs to be topless to be a walking cliché.'

'Oh God, that's all we need, you two getting lovestruck – just leave him be, yeah?' Stella shook her head as Amber and Chloe peeled off their cover-ups and padded over to the pool. She leaned closer to Fern and lowered her voice, 'Sounds like I might want to keep him all to myself.'

Fern shook her head. 'The hormones are raging and I'm not just talking about the girls – feels like I'm with three giddy teenagers, rather than grown women.'

'To be fair, Chloe is still a teenager.'

'Yeah, but at her age, I'd given birth to twins. Hard to believe when you realise how young I actually was when you see how young Chloe, Amber and Ruby seem to us now.'

Stella certainly didn't want history to repeat itself or for Chloe to shoulder the responsibility of having a baby at such a young age. No, she wanted her youth to remain carefree. She watched them dive into the pool, their splashing and shrieks filling the stillness of the early evening.

Fern reached across the table and gripped Stella's hand, pulling her attention away from the girls. 'This is all wonderful, Stella. I mean it, it really is, thank you.'

A lump formed in Stella's throat. 'I know, it's idyllic. It surpassed my imagination.'

'Mine too,' Fern said with a wobble. 'And it's more than about you paying for it. You've been so thoughtful with the gifts in the room. Just really lovely and kind. You always have been the best friend.'

'I really haven't.'

Fern's eyebrows furrowed. 'What are you talking about? You've always been there for me. Through everything.'

A wave of emotion pulsed through Stella. 'This is material, nothing meaningful, just something I wanted to do for you.'

'Yes, it may be material, but you've put time and thought into it as well as money. That means a lot.'

Stella watched Fern sipping the lemonade, looking content as she gazed out over the pool. They'd been through so many ups and downs over the years, and Stella was well aware that she'd led a more exciting life than her long-time friend. Perhaps this time away would change that for Fern.

Stella sighed. 'We've been here less than two hours and I'm already questioning why on earth I'd want to return to England.'

Fern looked at her. 'You'd like to live somewhere else?'

'Somewhere other than Nailsea?' Stella laughed. 'Um, yeah. It's a no-brainer.'

'Except you have Jacob back home.'

'Oh, I know. I may have financial freedom, if you want to call it that, but I have responsibilities.' She swept her hand towards the tropical gardens. 'But a place like this makes me realise what I could have.'

The thought was there about what might be possible even with a thirteen-year-old. It wasn't as simple as what she wanted to do, though; she had a son and daughter to consider, exes who would weigh in. But this place had already sparked a desire to change her life beyond all recognition.

'What about your job?' Fern asked as if reading her mind. 'Are you going to carry on working?'

'That's a big question. It feels like I've been handed an opportunity – I *have* been given an opportunity – to take my life in my hands and do what I want. I like my job though, I love going to work and feeling as if I've accomplished something, paid for things myself, like the mortgage and being able to raise Jacob on my own. I don't need Rhod's financial help – I mean, it helps and it shouldn't be just me shouldering everything, but I've never wanted to feel like I have to rely on him. And now of course...' She watched Chloe and Amber giggling together as they looked in the direction of the pool house. She wondered if the fit gardener was there, catching their flirtatious attention. She turned back to Fern. 'I want more from life. I know there's the saying that money doesn't buy happiness, but...' She gestured around them.

'Well yes, this place must be worth millions.' Fern smiled, closed her eyes and lifted her face to the retreating sun. She opened her eyes again. 'But you're happy, aren't you? I mean, before you won?'

'Yes, life was fine...' Laughter erupted from Chloe as she splashed about with Amber. That's what Stella wanted: youthful energy and the ability to not have to worry about anything. 'The money will certainly make life easier,' she said instead. 'But perhaps the things I want are the things that money can't buy.'

Fern pushed her sunglasses into her blonde hair and frowned. She always had been pretty and Stella still envied her friend's delicate features, which often made her seem fragile, but gave her an understated beauty that Stella could only dream of. She'd not yet resorted to any cosmetic help, but she was a fan of fake tan, hair extensions and getting her nails done on a regular basis. Fern always looked good, even with her hair tied in a bun, no make-up on and wearing jogging bottoms and an old T-shirt.

Stella finished the rest of her lemonade and decided the subject needed changing. 'Amber said you'd cooked meals for Paul for while you're away...'

'Yes, I did.' There was a defiance in Fern's voice and the colour of her cheeks deepened. 'It's not a bad thing, although I'm sure Amber told you with complete disdain.'

'He's a grown man, Fern. You don't need to look after him.'

'I know, but it's what I've always done. Looked after him and the girls.'

A melancholy threaded through her words. Stella was conscious that she needed to tread carefully.

'You should think about yourself for once,' she eventually said.

They both fell silent. Stella poured more lemonade and watched Fern as she gazed across the pool to the green-clad hillside, hazy in the softening light.

Chloe and Amber emerged from the pool and dripped water onto the stone paving. They continued to laugh together as they headed towards the pool room to dry off. *Or more likely to harass the poor gardener*, Stella thought.

'I feel like I'm drifting.' With the girls' chatter now distant, Fern's voice was loud in the quiet of the pool terrace. 'I don't know, the girls were my anchor when they were growing up. They were my focus, my reason for getting up in the morning...'

Stella turned sharply. 'Surely they weren't your only reason? You've got friends, you've got me, Paul, a beautiful home, other family...'

Fern snorted. 'You know I rarely see my parents or brother, and I don't have a career.'

'You work though.'

'Yes, a part-time job that I drag myself to and spend the whole time wishing I was somewhere else.' Fern waved her hand. 'I'm being unfair. It's not a bad job, and I like the people I work with, but the girls in the shop, they're so much younger than me. It's the sort of job that's fine in your early twenties, not your late thirties. But in my early twenties I was dealing with toddler tantrums. I don't feel I have any purpose beyond looking after my family.'

'Which you have done, amazingly well. But you've got to stop mothering Paul.' Stella realised she'd said the wrong thing the second it was out of her mouth.

Fern's face clouded. 'You think I mother him?'

'I, um, I didn't mean it to come out quite like that.' She could have said it in a better way, but she was telling the truth. Maybe Fern needed to hear this. The way she treated Paul was doing her no favours, and as for the way he treated her... well, Stella was all too aware of how wrong that was.

'It's the only thing I know how to do,' Fern said quietly. 'That's all I've been for twenty years – a mum, a wife. I've lost my identity and who I am, so I'm very sorry if the way I do things is not to your liking.'

Stella knew she'd hit a nerve but pressed on gently. 'I'm trying to get you to think about yourself, that's all. Put yourself first for once.'

'How did that work out for you?'

It was Stella's turn to be taken aback. 'Yeah, I'm not proud of two failed marriages and countless failed relationships, but I certainly wasn't going to allow myself to be walked all over just to stick with an unhappy marriage.'

'Is that what you think my marriage is, unhappy?' Fern visibly bristled.

'Well, are you happy?' she said softly.

'I'm not unhappy.'

Her voice was filled with such sadness that Stella reached out and hugged her. As she held her close, Stella's heart battered her chest, knowing what she knew. Fern was right to not feel content. She deserved so much more.

7

FERN

Fern was relieved when Stella swiftly moved the conversation on from how Fern was feeling to the more upbeat and less emotional topic of what they were going to do for the next few days. With the arrival of the girls, who had changed into shorts after their dip in the pool, and Violetta with the pizza, the tension dispersed. They remained sitting out on the terrace drinking Aperol spritz until late in the evening. Capri twinkled in the clear dark night, and beyond Marina Grande, the moonlight reflected onto the velvety black sea.

Maybe it was the combination of the food, the alcohol, the company and the setting, but Fern went to bed feeling happier than she had in a long time, the unsettling conversation with Stella forgotten as she slipped beneath the covers.

Birdsong woke her the following morning. She had no idea of the time and didn't care one jot. She stretched out in the large bed, feeling refreshed after a comfortable and peaceful sleep. Sunlight filtered through the trees, sending a warm glow across the terracotta tiled terrace outside. In Fern's eyes, staying in a place so idyllic felt as if there was no reason to stray far, but the island begged to be explored and Stella had booked an afternoon boat tour.

She yawned and reached for her mobile. There was a long message from Ruby and one from Paul replying to the one she'd sent yesterday telling him that they'd arrived safely.

Great.

That was it. Sent at 2 a.m., she noted. Presumably after he'd got back from the pub, although it seemed particularly late. She sighed and put her mobile back on the bedside table. She couldn't be bothered to send a reply.

* * *

It was late by the time they'd all dragged themselves out of bed, showered, dressed and had a leisurely breakfast of sfogliatella, a delicious, sweet ricotta-filled pastry, washed down with fresh orange juice and an obligatory cappuccino. They made their way down to Marina Grande and took the boat tour to the Blue Grotto.

Amber and Chloe sat together and Fern envied the easy way they chatted, with laughter sprinkling their conversation. Obviously they were friends, but if it had been Ruby here instead of Amber, she would have had no issue chatting to her mum too. It always felt as if Amber tried her hardest to avoid talking to her. Fern sighed. At least she had Stella's company and the sun on her shoulders.

The wooden rowing boats, filled with tourists clutching cameras and iPhones, crowded together outside the cave entrance and the Italian skippers called across to each other. The queue for the boats to take them into the illuminated sea cave wasn't long, but so far, at least from the outside, it wasn't quite the magical place Fern had been expecting.

They reached the front of the queue quickly enough though. The skipper of their boat was jovial, his accent thick, his voice loud as he helped them onboard. Stella was squashed next to her, with Chloe and Amber in front. Fern was aware of the other boats bobbing on the water, waiting for their turn to enter the cave.

As requested by the skipper, they laid back in the boat as he pulled them through the cave entrance, the damp darkness all-encompassing. Then they were inside and the shouts and bustle from outside faded away. The cave walls were highlighted by the azure water shimmering around them, the only sounds an ancient Italian song mixing with the splash of oars and hushed voices.

Fern's head filled with memories of holidays with her own family when she was a kid, fighting with her older brother and listening to her parents argue, and then her experience of family holidays in her twenties when the twins were young. It had always felt like an effort, wrangling toddlers and dragging disinterested children around castles and museums. Paul had always seemed like he'd rather be somewhere else too.

She watched Amber now, gazing open-mouthed, soaking up the magic of the vividly blue water as their boat circled the cave. Silver streaks danced beneath the surface and cool water splashed onto Fern's arm. Enclosed in the glowing darkness, it felt mystical and otherworldly, a place that had been here for centuries, untouched and separate from the outside world.

It was soon over and they were back outside, blinking in the brightness of the day, the sea clear and blue but nothing like the blueness of the water in the grotto. After being unsure how the cave would live up to her expectations, Fern was actually sorry to leave, but the promise of a relaxing evening eating and drinking back at the villa was enough of an enticement.

* * *

After the boat tour, they had dinner cooked by Violetta out on the pool terrace. They'd been lucky with the weather earlier, but now white clouds scudded across the sky, briefly extinguishing the sun and sending the temperature plummeting before the sun reappeared. They pulled on cardigans and sipped glasses of chilled white wine, while chatting together as Violetta grilled pezzogna, a local red seabream, on the barbecue and served it with rosemary potatoes, olives and verdure grigliate. For a few minutes, munching and nods of appreciation were all anyone managed.

They'd just finished eating when Fern's mobile rang and she was stunned to see Paul's name on the screen.

'Hey, this is a surprise,' she said, wandering away from the others towards her room. 'I didn't think you'd call.'

'Yeah, sorry. Didn't mean to disturb you.'

'You're not; it's nice to hear from you.' She closed her bedroom door behind her.

'I was just wondering if you knew where my shirt is? The smart navy one with the white buttons. I want to wear it for a meeting on Monday.'

'You're phoning me because you can't find your shirt?'

'And to see how you're all getting on.'

Fern clenched her jaw. That was an afterthought, she was sure.

'How's Capri?' he asked.

She sighed. 'Beautiful. The villa is just incredible. I'll WhatsApp you a couple of pics.'

'Stella's really splashed out, huh?'

'A once-in-a-lifetime holiday. Why not?' She kept forgetting that Stella's Lottery win wasn't common knowledge. Although she understood her reasons, it still amazed her that Stella was able to keep the news secret.

'About the shirt...'

'I have no idea, Paul. Anything that was in the laundry basket has been washed, ironed and put away. If you left it somewhere else, then you'll just need to look around.'

There was silence. He was probably looking for it and couldn't manage to hold a conversation at the same time. She hated the way he often made her feel like this – angry and unappreciated.

'What's the meeting for?' she asked.

'A possible new client with plans for new builds and existing renovations that could potentially keep us busy for the next five years.'

'That sounds great.' Fern sat on the end of the bed and gazed through the French doors at the gentle evening light filtering through the leaves. 'If you can't find that shirt, then the dark grey or the burgundy one you wore for Gary and Kim's wedding are both smart. You look good in them.'

'Yeah, thanks. I'll see what I can find.' There was rustling in the background. 'One other thing – when are you back?'

Fern sighed again. 'On the thirtieth. I marked it on the kitchen calendar. Why?'

'Dave's finally decided on his stag do. The first weekend in June in Newquay.'

'Are you asking or telling me you're going?' She knew which one it was.

'I've already said I'm going, just didn't know if you'd still be away or not.'

'We're here for two weeks, not three, so I'll be back. If there's anything else going on, I'll have marked it on the calendar.' *The one you don't bother looking at,* she thought.

'Ah, bugger. I've found it.'

'The shirt?'

'Yeah, under a pile of stuff on the chair. Arse. I'll have to wear one of the other ones instead.'

Yes, cos you couldn't possibly wash, dry and iron it yourself, Fern thought with bitterness as they said goodbye. It crossed her mind that Stella might have had a point – perhaps she did mother him...

8

STELLA

After just one day trip, the girls were already moaning. Stella had flashbacks to when Jacob was six and Chloe a pre-teen and the effort it had been to keep everyone happy when they went out. That age gap was difficult when both kids wanted vastly different things. Now Chloe was an adult, the last thing Stella was going to do was force her to come out.

Chloe and Amber decided on a lazy day by the villa pool, followed by an evening exploring the rich nightlife of Capri. Fern was keen to go to Villa Jovis, a Roman villa built for Emperor Tiberius. As they set off, Stella wondered if the tension between Amber and Fern the day before had instigated the day apart. No harsh words had passed between them, but it was noticeable how they hadn't really talked to each other at all.

Stella also acknowledged the harsh reality that even though the girls had been more than happy to come on holiday with them, spending all their time with their mums was vastly uncool. Stella had stopped going on holiday with her parents as soon as she was old enough to be left on her own and the idea of her ever going out with them for something beyond a meal was foreign. She spent little enough time with them now, let alone when she was a wayward teen. Why should it be any different with Chloe, just because she thought of herself as a cool young mum?

It was an unseasonably warm spring day. Stella had to admit it was refreshing to head out of the touristy heart of Capri town along the Via Tiberio. Ugh, that thought made her feel like a middle-aged tourist, which was so not how she wanted to be perceived. Wouldn't staying at the villa, topping up her tan and having a dip in the pool have been preferable? She shook the thought away; she was spending time with her friend exploring the island – nothing wrong or middle-aged about that.

The walk was long but eventually worth it, even if her feet were aching and sweat stung her eyes. Perched on a hillside looking out towards the Bay of Naples where Mount Vesuvius dominated the skyline, Villa Jovis had a prominent position. The walls of the villa had crumbled, but the footprint was there, remarkably evident considering it had survived since the first century B.C.

Stella smiled as Fern gave her interesting titbits as they wandered around – she'd obviously read up about the place. Tiberius' Leap, rumoured to be where Emperor Tiberius had chucked unfortunate servants and guests off the cliff to their death, was the one that stuck with Stella. She could think of a couple of exes she wouldn't mind doing that to...

'I bet they had some wicked parties here,' Stella said as they wound their way back up through the ruins. With its idyllic setting, it wasn't hard to imagine how luxurious a place it would have been for a powerful emperor of Rome.

'A tonne of debauchery, for sure.' Fern flashed her a knowing grin. 'You'd have loved it.'

'Yeah yeah, I don't deny it; *Spartacus* is my favourite series ever. What's not to love about sexy, semi-naked gladiators? Apart from all the blood and guts, ancient Rome is my kinda vibe.'

Fern laughed. 'I prefer *Bridgerton*.'

'Ha ha! Of course! The Duke.' She almost said that Fern deserved to be treated as well, but she held her tongue. Paul was certainly no Duke of Hastings.

They paused on the top walkway of Villa Jovis to catch their breath. A light breeze kissed their hot skin, welcome after the climb.

'Sightseeing always makes me feel so... adult.' Stella sighed as she gazed over the sprawling ruins to the sea glinting in the sun.

'What are you talking about?' Fern frowned. 'You are an adult.'

'I know, but I think it stems from being forced on day trips by my parents when I was, like, fourteen. I hated being dragged to some boring castle or cathedral when I wanted to spend time with my friends. I can see it with Jacob now, rolling his eyes at the mere mention of going somewhere with me. I don't know, doing stuff like this makes me feel old.'

'Well, we're certainly not teenagers any longer.'

'That we're not.'

Even though the words were true, they hurt. Perhaps without being conscious of it, Stella was struggling with the idea of turning forty. Even winning the Lottery couldn't change that stark fact. She couldn't rewind time, however much she wanted to. But their youth... She wished she could recapture it, at least the essence of it, the feeling of freedom that being young offered.

'Remember back in the day when we'd go clubbing all night and not drag ourselves out of bed until the middle of the afternoon,' Stella said, thinking back to a time that felt distant, almost as if it had happened to someone else.

'You still go clubbing, Stella.'

'Yeah, I know. It's just not the same. Back when we were seventeen, we didn't have to think about anything else. We lived just for us and for the weekends. We were selfish and self-centred and I know now how much of a nightmare we were for our parents, but those days...' She gazed wistfully across Villa Jovis before turning back to Fern. 'Do you still think about our life back then?'

'Sometimes, but it feels a lifetime ago...'

'It is more than half our life.'

'Yeah. Saying it like that really doesn't help.'

The earlier heat had dissipated and the sun was gentle, pleasantly warming Stella's shoulders. She looked out at the same view that emperors of Rome had gazed upon centuries before, wanting to give Fern the opportunity to say more; she sensed a sadness whenever they talked about the past.

Stella decided to give her a verbal nudge. 'What are you thinking?'

'Honestly? If I'll ever be that happy again.'

'Oh hun, don't feel that way; you've got loads to look forward to.'

'What? Like getting older, becoming a grandparent? Muddling along like I am now?' Fern shook her head. 'It's not that I want to go back to that part of my life. And even if I could, doing anything differently would mean not having Ruby and Amber.' She sighed. 'Despite getting pregnant young and how my life has turned out, I wouldn't change them for the world.'

'I know you wouldn't.' Stella put her hand on top of Fern's, where it rested on the crumbling edge of a wall. 'Come on, let's go get a drink. Or a gelato.'

* * *

The long walk was made slightly easier with a stop-off at a gelateria, where they enjoyed a cooling ice cream: a zesty Caprese lemon flavour for Stella and a smooth and sweet mulberry flavour for Fern. Stella was relieved when they finally made it back to the villa, albeit hot, sweaty and tired.

A bottle of sunscreen and empty wine glasses littered the table outside, and damp towels were strewn over the backs of chairs. Stella bit her lip and imagined just how good an evening Chloe and Amber would have.

By the time Stella and Fern had both showered and changed, the pool terrace was dusk-tinged. As well as stopping for gelato earlier, they'd eaten a huge lunch in a restaurant in Capri town, so apart from munching on a fruit platter and drinking gin and tonic, they decided to forgo going out again to eat. Stella's legs ached and she was enjoying finally feeling cool and comfortable, soaking up the view.

Fern called it a night early and headed to her room with her Kindle. Stella stayed outside a while longer, listening to the chattering insects in the undergrowth as darkness took over. What would the girls be up to now? Actually, she didn't want to know. It might have been a long time ago, but she remembered all too well how she'd behaved at their age.

She poured herself another gin and tonic and retreated inside. It was still early, so she propped herself up against a pile of pillows in her room and rang Jacob.

'Hey, Mum.'

Even though he was safe at his dad's and she'd messaged him every day, it was good to hear his voice.

'Hey there. You're having fun with your dad?'

'Yeah, s'all right. He's taking me and Ethan out for pizza after school tomorrow.'

'Wow. A proper Monday night treat. Lucky you.'

'Yeah, we had a Sunday roast at Granny and Grandad's today.'

'I bet that was nice.' And she meant it too. Although she and Rhod hadn't worked out, she missed her parents-in-law. In many ways, she'd got on better with them than she did with her own parents. It was silly, she knew, to be envious of the relationship

Jacob had with them. They'd all managed to remain civil and friends after the divorce, but she missed the closeness that they'd had as a family. She wondered if anything would change once they knew about her Lottery win.

Jacob was telling her about a film he'd watched. She tuned back in, keen to listen when he was actually willing to talk.

'Are you looking forward to half-term and coming out here?' she asked.

'Yeah, gonna miss football though.'

'I'm sure you can watch it out here if you have to.'

'No, Mum,' he huffed. 'Not on the telly. The actual tournament. I would have been picked for the team.'

'Ah, I'm sorry, buddy. I'm sure there'll be another chance.' Stella sighed. Even a few days on Capri couldn't trump football, but then again, she'd booked Capri completely with herself in mind. She'd been certain that Chloe would love it too. But Jacob... 'I'm looking forward to seeing you. We've got a private pool and the place is amazing, so hopefully that'll make up for missing football.'

'Is there a TV in my room?'

'Not that you'll want to spend any time inside watching TV, but yes.'

They chatted a little more, but Jacob was obviously distracted. She imagined him holed up in his room on his Xbox only half listening to her. She wrapped things up, promising to give him a call in another couple of days.

'Bye, Mum.'

'Love you.'

Stella put her phone on the bedside table and rested back on the pillows. Jacob was at that tricky age. She could sense his internal battle of still needing his mum while not actually wanting anything to do with her. It had been similar with Chloe at thirteen. She'd been the same with her own parents. The trouble was, that distance had continued into adulthood; she wasn't close to them and couldn't see a way of regaining the closeness they'd had when she and her sister had been growing up. She didn't want it to be the same with her own children. Her older sister hadn't disappointed their parents like she had, with drink and drugs in her teens, an unplanned pregnancy, two failed marriages, countless unsuitable (in their eyes) relationships and two children by two different dads. The list went on and on. She'd stopped caring what they thought long ago and only made an effort to keep in touch for Jacob and Chloe's sake.

It had been good to hear Jacob's voice, even if talking to him had made her think about things she didn't want to be thinking about. She snuggled beneath the covers. Fern had been the one who'd wanted an early night. She was a homebody; she enjoyed going out for a meal or to the cinema, but that was as exciting as it got. Stella was a night owl and rarely went to bed this early.

Where would Chloe and Amber be now? she thought. She was insanely jealous and would have loved to have gone out with them. She needed to persuade Fern to have a proper night out. Stella needed her fun-loving friend back again.

Annoyed by the troubling thought that she was getting old, she closed her eyes, tried to empty her mind and willed herself to sleep.

* * *

Stella woke with a start. Even in a villa this size, it was hard not to miss the thump of the large wooden door slamming shut. She'd left the blinds open and a glimmer of moonlight filtered through the trees outside the patio doors. Stella heard Chloe and Amber giggling together, followed by lots of shushing as they clattered across the entrance hall to the stairs. Lying there listening, Stella suddenly felt very awake. They sounded happy and tipsy. Oh, to be young. The voices faded as bedroom doors closed.

It was just gone 1.30 a.m. Apart from Chloe and Amber returning, it was utterly peaceful, far enough away from the centre of Capri town to be undisturbed by music and voices from the bars and restaurants. Fully awake now, she stared in annoyance at the shadowed ceiling, her mind whirring. Her thoughts returned to what she'd been thinking about earlier. She'd have loved to have gone out with them tonight, but she knew they didn't want her tagging along. Should going clubbing really be her scene any longer? The years had flown by. Her twenties were a fading memory, and when she did go out, she was conscious of being older than most of the people she was out with. Was it desperate to be clinging on to her youth, still wanting to enjoy the things she'd done when she was a lot younger? With Chloe at university and Jacob at his dad's every other weekend, she was able to go out and enjoy herself without being plagued by guilt. She felt young. She *was* free and single. Why the hell could she not enjoy herself?

Sleep must have eventually overtaken Stella's thoughts, although she woke early with a foggy head. It was strange how she'd coped with broken sleep in her twenties with two babies, yet in her late thirties being woken in the middle of the night left her feeling groggy. Or perhaps it was from too much gin and tonic the night before. Either way, being here with an eighteen- and a twenty-one-year-old was making her feel her age.

She showered, did her make-up and dressed in a maxi dress, another new one from her pre-holiday shopping spree. She felt the pressure of her Lottery win more at home than she did here. It felt okay in a place like this to splash out. At home, she was conscious of how the money would change her life and the impact it would have. She also had the stress of having kept it secret from almost everyone.

By the time she emerged, the table on the pool terrace had already been laid for breakfast. She was even up before Fern. She settled herself in one of the chairs that faced the pool. There was never time to contemplate anything at home; life was constantly busy, with work, socialising, the kids... Here, she felt relaxed and spoilt, something she could get used to.

'*Buongiorno*,' Violetta said as she appeared on the terrace and set a caffe latte in front of Stella, along with a plate of fresh bread rolls and little pots of jam.

'Oh, that's a lovely sight.' Stella smiled.

Violetta nodded. 'I bring more when everyone else is up.'

'Thank you.'

'You'll be eating out today?'

'I think that's the plan. Anywhere you can recommend?'

Violetta suggested a few places and left her to drink her coffee. Stella relished the peace. Hands down it beat sitting in her kitchen munching marmite on toast and burning her mouth on a scalding coffee before sitting in rush-hour traffic heading into the centre of Bristol.

Voices from somewhere in the garden made her turn. She was surprised when Amber and Chloe wandered onto the terrace instead of Fern.

'Didn't think I'd see you two quite so early.' Stella peered at them over her sunglasses. 'I won't say bright cos you both look like shit.'

Chloe pulled a face and Amber sank down in the chair opposite, her fake-tanned face somehow managing to look pale. Sunglasses shaded her eyes and she was either pouting or trying hard not to puke. Stella had a sudden wave of relief at not being the one to suffer the after-effects of a night out. *Focus on the positives, eh*, she thought wryly.

'We wanted to ask you something,' Chloe said with excitement as she grinned at her mum.

'Oh God, here we go.'

'No, it's something great, isn't it, Amber?'

'Yep, although it would still be great in a couple of hours. You didn't need to drag me out of bed,' Amber groaned.

'We met some guys last night,' Chloe continued, ignoring Amber's obvious lack of interest.

'Oh really,' Stella scoffed.

'No, it wasn't like that. We just chatted to them most of the evening. Had a few drinks, went dancing. They took us to this totally amazing proper local place with live music. It was like the best night out ever, wasn't it, Amber?'

Amber grunted.

Stella raised an eyebrow. 'Do you actually remember anything?'

'I drank a few too many limoncello cocktails...' Amber mumbled.

'So that's a no then.'

'*Mum*,' Chloe said, trying to regain her attention. '*I* didn't drink as much as Amber and remember everything. They were super nice and they've invited us on their yacht.'

Stella raised an eyebrow. 'You're not going to go sailing on some strange bloke's yacht, Chloe.'

'Not just us.' She gestured between herself and Amber. 'They invited all of us. You, me, Amber and Fern.'

'Huh, they did, did they?' Stella held Chloe's gaze. 'And do you know what any of them do for a living?'

'Yeah, they're millionaires, sailing around the Med,' Amber piped up.

Chloe glared at Amber before turning back to Stella and smiling sweetly. 'There are two brothers, their cousin and a friend. Vincenzo, who I was mostly talking to, is an investment banker.'

'Obviously Italian.'

'Don't say it with so much disdain, Mum.'

'They're hot Italian millionaires,' Amber said with a real sense of interest in her voice.

'You are so not helping,' Chloe hissed.

Stella laughed. 'I'm beginning to like the sound of them. Did they invite you sailing with them before or after you snogged them?'

'There was no snogging.'

Stella turned to Amber and raised her eyebrows.

'Chloe's telling the truth. Zero snogging. It must have all been down to our natural charm.'

'Anyway.' Chloe shot a warning look at Amber. 'I told them you'd say no without meeting them first.'

'Well, that's true.'

'So I've arranged for me and you to meet them after lunch today.'

9

FERN

Fern was the last one to breakfast and joined the girls as they attempted to rid their hangovers with strong Italian coffee. Stella had gone inside to finish getting ready.

Chloe filled her in on their night out with the Italian millionaires. It sounded like a good evening, but witnessing Amber's sullen expression and washed-out face, Fern couldn't help but worry about what today would bring. She was rapidly regretting her and Stella's decision for each of them to spend the day with their girls. It had seemed like a good idea, a chance to bond and try to bridge the gap that had widened between them.

Yesterday had been refreshing to spend the day with Stella and really talk, even if casting their minds back to their youth had brought with it the usual worries and regrets. The way Fern thought about things was as if her life was over. She knew deep down, with the girls having left home, she was at a crossroads. She was only thirty-nine, the big fortieth birthday a few weeks away. Lots of women were only just starting a family at this age. Did it really matter that she'd done things the other way around? Her life was not over. Somehow she needed to believe that. She needed to believe that she could find a renewed passion in everything: a career, herself, her marriage...

Facing up to reality and the barrage of thoughts about her future was painful but helpful. Perhaps the same would come of spending the day with Amber. Stella would have a far easier time with Chloe as they, at least, seemed to like spending time together. She hoped a gentle walk, fresh air and some food would improve Amber's mood.

Stella breezed across the terrace in a floaty maxi dress and sandals, looking ready for a day out.

'Have you got everything?' she asked Chloe.

Chloe nodded, downed the rest of her coffee and picked up her bag.

'We'll see you back here later.' Stella squeezed Fern's shoulder as she walked past. '*Ciao*,' she called, before disappearing round the side of the villa with Chloe.

Fern sighed and thanked Violetta as she began to clear away the breakfast things.

'We could just stay here,' Amber muttered as Fern stood up.

'There'll be plenty of time to lounge about here. It'll be fun to explore, I promise. Go get your bag.'

Amber stalked off and Violetta met Fern's eyes. She gave her a knowing smile. 'My daughter is nearly thirty and still sometimes behaves like a teenager.'

'Great,' Fern said with a wry smile. 'I have a few more years of this then.'

As she retrieved her bag and sun hat from her room, she vowed to make the best of it. Amber couldn't continue to be angry with her forever. Maybe today was the chance to understand what was actually going on.

* * *

Amber remained silent and sullen as they walked. It was hard to tell if she was just hung-over, but with vibes of annoyance emanating from her, Fern decided not to even attempt mindless chatter. Instead, she relished the peace while enjoying the gentle warmth and the sights. The island was blooming. Bright pink bougainvillea decorated walls, the lemony scent of myrtle filled the air, and the late-spring flowers nestled crimson, plum and white among fronds of green.

Fern liked that the villa was away from the busy centre of the island. The road wound past lush gardens and hidden villas, then suddenly the view would open up, sweeping down to Marina Grande and out to the Bay of Naples. She didn't mind walking in silence, but they couldn't not talk to each other all day, so eventually she decided to instigate a conversation.

'It'll be nice to see Ruby next week, even for just a couple of days, won't it?' Fern hoped that Ruby was a safe subject, but then immediately felt bad for thinking that she'd have preferred Ruby's company to Amber's.

'She's a nutter for not coming out for the whole two weeks.'

'She's doing a nursing degree – it's not that easy to drop everything.'

'You mean unlike me.'

Fern silently cursed that she'd already said the wrong thing. 'I didn't mean it like that, but yes, there is a difference between doing a vocational course such as nursing and working on actual wards, compared with studying something like marketing. Also, Ruby didn't take a year out like you did.'

'To go travelling. It's not like I bummed about wasting my time.'

Fern shook her head at how defensive Amber was. 'You're taking everything I say as if I'm having a go at you. I'm really not.'

Amber huffed and picked up the pace. More whitewashed buildings lined the road now they were close to the piazzetta. Fern bristled inside at the anger Amber seemed to be directing towards her and had done for quite some time. She had no understanding of what she'd done to upset her, but she was determined to find out. She caught up with her daughter.

'Where are we going?' Amber muttered. 'It feels like we're walking aimlessly.'

'Isn't that the joy of being in a place like this, getting to explore and discover hidden gems?'

Amber rubbed her forehead. 'If I didn't have a hangover, maybe.'

Whose fault is that? Fern refrained from saying it out loud. It would only upset her even more. 'We're going to Giardini di Augusto,' she said instead. 'Hopefully the stunning gardens and views will be worth it.'

'Great,' Amber said with sarcasm.

Fern accepted that she wasn't going to win with Amber today. At least it wasn't far from their destination now, and after they'd explored, perhaps a boozy lunch and some shopping would cheer her up. She loved Amber, but it didn't mean she had to always like her. She reminded herself that today was about rebuilding bridges. However hard it felt, surely it was a positive thing to be spending time with her?

They left behind the quiet roads for pedestrian lanes filled with tourists. A narrow paved lane wound past cream-coloured buildings and a restaurant with a small outside seating area. Tall stone walls lined each side and the sun glinted through the trees. Amber seemed more interested the further they walked; it was hard not to be buoyed by glimpses of blue sky and hot pink flowers against creamy stone walls while the delicious smell of coffee permeated the air.

The path opened out on to a small, paved area where a throng of people stood chatting in front of a low stone wall. Fern gazed past in wonder, taking in the different greens and the snatches of fuchsia and burnt-orange flowers decorating the gardens below. They went through a gate and down a handful of steps lined with miniature domed hedges. Olive trees and the darker evergreen of cypresses dominated the horizon.

'Worth the walk?' Fern glanced at Amber as they followed the path beneath a leaf-covered pergola.

'Yeah, it's not bad.'

That's an understatement, Fern thought as they continued on in silence. At least there was enough beauty surrounding them to focus their attention away from each other. Fern was frustrated that trying to start a conversation with her own daughter had become this difficult. *Oh well*, she thought, *if it's going to be difficult, might as well say what I think.*

'You really want to go on this yacht with—'

'I know exactly what you're going to say.' Amber stopped and held up her hands. 'Just don't. Stella's going to meet them today. She's not young and impressionable like me and Chloe...'

'I wasn't going to say that.'

'Well, whatever you were going to say,' she said, sounding even more annoyed, 'Stella will suss them out. I know you don't like the idea of it.'

'I like the idea of sailing along the Amalfi Coast, just not with people you met while drunk in a bar.'

'It wasn't like that. We talked for most of the evening.'

'Oh well, that's okay then.' Now Fern couldn't keep the annoyance from her voice. She was deemed to be the bad guy because she was the one being sensible, questioning the idea of them swanning off with a bunch of Italian blokes. She was also worried that although Stella was older and should therefore be more sensible, she was likely to throw all caution to the wind and say yes because she craved adventure.

Amber walked ahead, along the shady path, overtaking strolling couples and avoiding groups of people coming from the other direction. Tall pines cast shadows across the path as they strained to reach the light. The air was perfumed with flowers and pine, and a citrus scent drifted on the breeze.

Fern sighed and picked up the pace. Even with surroundings this beautiful, it seemed as though Amber would have preferred to stay back at the villa sunbathing on the pool terrace. So much for a lovely mother-daughter day out.

'*You* just don't know how to have fun,' Amber said the moment Fern caught up with her.

'What? Of course I do. I'm having fun right now.'

'Great, if you consider this to be fun.' Amber crinkled her nose. 'I'm talking about being spontaneous and saying yes to an amazing opportunity. Living the millionaire lifestyle while we're here. I bet you anything Stella will meet them today and say yes. She knows how to live.'

Not knowing how to respond, Fern pursed her lips and walked away. A viewing point overlooked the sea. She leaned on the railing and gazed out. It was true; Stella did know how to live. She was always up for a good time, while Fern preferred a quiet night in to going out. Her confidence had diminished over the years; her spontaneity too, but then that hadn't been surprising as a young mum of twins. Fern sighed. Did Amber see in Stella what she wished for in a mum?

Fern tore her eyes away from the view. Amber was sitting on a bench scrolling through her phone, oblivious to the beauty around her.

She breathed deeply, walked across the path and joined her. Changing the subject and focusing on food would be the best thing.

'What do you want to have for lunch?' she asked brightly.

Amber glanced up from her phone and shrugged. 'Pizza and ice cream.'

'Great, let's find somewhere before it gets too busy.'

Amber stood up and tucked her phone away in her bag. They didn't say much else as they walked back towards the piazzetta. Amber was hard work and Fern didn't want the holiday to be like that. How refreshing would it be to walk the winding tree-lined paths without a grumpy Amber. Time to herself was what she craved. It had taken being here to realise that.

* * *

They found a restaurant with a free table not far from the piazzetta and had a Neapolitan pizza each and shared a bottle of white wine after Amber insisted her hangover would be cured with more alcohol.

Fern's mobile buzzed. She glanced at the screen – finally, a reply from Paul about the photos she'd sent him yesterday.

Looks bloody lovely. Stella has gone up in the world. By the way, wore the grey shirt, meeting was great thanks.

A thank you as well. Blimey, the meeting must have been a big deal. She switched off the screen, looked up and met Amber's cool gaze.

'Who was that?' she asked.

'Just your dad.'

'Oh.' She swigged her wine and took another slice of pizza.

Fern had been aware of the tension for a while, but spending time alone with Amber made it apparent how much the divide between them had grown. With a second glass of wine poured, Fern decided to bite the bullet and ask her outright.

'What's your problem with me?'

Amber looked at her from beneath long black lashes. 'What are you talking about?'

'Oh, don't give me that. Everything I say, everything I do, annoys you. I'd like to understand what I've done.'

'You haven't done anything.'

'Really? It doesn't seem that way.'

Amber clenched her jaw. She glanced away. 'Can we pay and get out of here?'

'Of course, but you're still going to answer my question.'

Fern caught the attention of a waiter and they settled the bill.

It was good to escape back into the sunshine. She'd begun to feel hemmed in, sitting in a busy restaurant, aware that their conversation was strained.

'So,' Fern said, not wanting to give Amber the chance to change the subject as they set off towards the piazzetta, 'if I haven't upset you, why the animosity? This attitude has been going on for months.'

Amber moved out of the way of a large group of people heading towards them and sighed.

'Dad walks all over you and you let him,' she said.

Fern stopped in her tracks. Whatever she was expecting Amber to say, it wasn't that. 'Okay,' she said slowly as she picked up the pace to catch up with her. 'I'm not really sure why you think that.'

Amber glanced back at her. 'Oh please, Mum. He does what he likes and you let him. Your life revolves around him.'

'Well, we're a team. He works hard and my job has always been to look after him, you, Ruby and the house.'

Amber scoffed. 'He doesn't just work hard; he plays hard too. When was the last time you had fun?'

'Don't start this again.' Anger flared inside her. They reached the main piazzetta with its far-reaching views across the island.

People were milling around and sitting outside a cafe drinking coffee. She waved her hand around. 'I'm having fun now.'

'Yeah, cos Stella's paid for us to come out here. You'd *never* have done anything like this off your own back.'

'I'd never have been able to afford to do anything like this. I'm not lucky enough to have won the Lottery.'

'I'm not talking about an expensive holiday, I mean just in general, getting dressed up and going out. Also, you could afford things if you found a better job.'

The snide remark got Fern's back up. 'There's nothing wrong with my job.'

'Seriously, it's honestly all you want to do? Work in a shop?'

Fern stopped in the middle of the piazzetta and turned on Amber. 'Why does it bother you so much?'

'I get why you got a job like that to fit around school and stuff, but me and Ruby are grown up. You don't need to be working those crappy part-time jobs any longer.'

They were in the way, with people brushing past or deviating around them, but right that minute, Fern didn't care.

'You haven't answered my question. Why does it bother you what I do?' Her eyes narrowed as she took in Amber's sleek shiny hair, fake tan and designer sunglasses. 'Do you think it's beneath me? Is that what it is? You're ashamed?'

'I'm not ashamed, Mum; it's just... I don't want to end up like you.'

Amber's words cut deep, reopening a wound Fern knew had been there a while – her worry of letting her life slip away confirmed by the sharp words of her daughter. The independent streak she'd had as a toddler and impulsive pre-schooler had only got stronger in her teen years, while the loving and cuddly side to her had disappeared, leaving behind a stranger, the daughter Fern no longer understood or connected with, unlike the more sensitive and caring Ruby whose childhood traits had been easier to understand and manage as a teen. She was also aware, without understanding why, that things had worsened in the last year or two.

Fern navigated her way through the throng of people to a bench and sat down. In front of her, steps cut down the hillside and potted vines encircled white pillars. A sweeping vista of gleaming buildings intercut the hill, nestled between narrow winding roads, pockets of trees and the green of gardens.

Amber joined her and sat silently next to her on the bench. Life continued around them; the bustle of people strolling about, shopping or finding a place to eat. A sparrow landed on the wall in front of them, perched for a moment and flew off. Laughter and chatter ebbed towards them and the smell of pizza wafted from somewhere close by.

'Mum, I'm sorry I upset you.' There was still a firmness to her voice, but her body language was warmer as she leaned closer. She put a tentative hand on Fern's arm.

'Are you really? It sounded like you took great pleasure in telling me that. And I promise, you won't end up like me.' She couldn't keep the hurt out of her voice. 'You're at university doing the course you want to do. You have ambition and prospects, the promise of a career, all while enjoying what student life offers. You didn't end up a pregnant teen like I did. *You* have nothing to worry about.'

Fern stared ahead, but the view was blurred by tears ready to spill. Amber's hand remained on her arm, which only upset Fern more, the idea that she cared enough to attempt to comfort her. She didn't dare meet her eyes, worried she'd lose it completely and burst into tears surrounded by all these people.

'You can change your life, you know,' Amber eventually said, her voice quiet and even.

Fern shook her head. 'I'm upset you think my life's that bad that I need to do something about it.'

'You really don't see it, do you?' Amber said tentatively.

'See what?'

'How he treats you.'

'Are you talking about your dad again?' Fern's eyes narrowed as she turned to look at Amber. Her head was beginning to throb; she needed something cold and non-alcoholic to drink. She hadn't liked what they'd talked about so far, but she definitely didn't like where the conversation was leading.

'Yes, it's frustrating to see.'

'This is your father you're talking about.' He may have his faults, but the way Amber was speaking about him was out of order.

'Yeah, I know. Doesn't mean he should treat you the way he does.'

Fern scoffed. 'What does that even mean? He treats me fine. You're making it sound like he abuses me or something ridiculous. I chose to be a housewife and raise you and Ruby. There's nothing wrong with that.'

Amber's jaw clenched. 'There's loads wrong with it when you do everything for him and he disrespects you. I mean, for fuck's sake, you cooked him a whole load of meals before coming out here, like he's incapable of looking after himself. It's not the 1950s.'

Fern's frown deepened. She didn't understand where this outburst was coming from. Amber had always been a daddy's girl. She doted on him and he could usually do no wrong in her eyes. Years ago, when the four of them had gone out for the day, they'd pair up: Paul and Amber, her and Ruby. It was the way it had always been. But when she thought about it, recently Amber had been decidedly frosty with him too. There had to be a reason.

'What aren't you telling me, Amber?'

Amber stood up. 'I don't know.' Her voice was filled with emotion as she shook her head. 'Just think about things. Like *really* think about them, what your and dad's relationship really is. I'm going to head back.'

Amber walked away. Fern remained sitting. She was stunned by the way Amber's words were laced with pity as much as anger. Was her underlying unhappiness that obvious? She swallowed back the bile rising in her throat. If she did some soul-searching and really thought about her life, she was scared about what she would discover.

10

STELLA

Stella felt bad leaving Fern with an obviously hung-over and disgruntled Amber, but she was looking forward to a day with Chloe. Since she'd gone to uni they hadn't had many mother-daughter days. They wandered into Capri town and hit the shops along Via Camerelle before taking the funicular down to Marina Grande and finding a restaurant on the waterfront.

Chloe had pizza, while Stella, inspired by their surroundings, tucked into sesame-crusted tuna. Colourful fishing boats bobbed on the water directly in front of the restaurant's terrace, and further along the marina, scores of tourists were disembarking from a hydrofoil at the port.

One of the Italians Chloe had met the night before messaged her with the location of their yacht, so after lunch they wandered away from the commercial port to the tourist harbour with its gleaming speedboats and luxury yachts. *The Silver Spirit* was easy to spot, its size dominating the marina. Excitement ebbed through Stella at the idea of hanging out with some young – and hopefully good-looking – Italians on a yacht as impressive as this.

Stella whistled under her breath as they walked alongside it. 'This is quite something.'

'Told you.' Chloe looked up and waved to a dark-haired Italian.

They climbed the steps to the yacht's lower deck and the Italian came over to greet them.

'This is Luca,' Chloe said to Stella.

'*Ciao*, Chloe.' Luca kissed her on each cheek. He met Stella's eyes and smiled warmly as he firmly shook her hand. 'You must be Stella. *Benvenuta*.' He looked between them both. 'Welcome aboard *The Silver Spirit*.'

Luca spoke perfect English with a gentle accent. He was tall and good-looking with strong cheekbones and a deep tan. Stella was even more certain that she wanted to spend time with them.

The polished wood of the slatted deck was warm and inviting against the shiny white yacht and just the area they'd stepped onto was huge.

Chloe glanced back at Stella and mouthed, 'OMG.'

They followed Luca across the deck to where another man was lounging on a large circular daybed. Stella had already spied another deck area on the level above and she could imagine how spacious the inside of the yacht was. No wonder Chloe's mouth was gaping open.

'This is your yacht?' Stella asked, finally finding her voice.

'My uncle's.' Luca turned to the man on the daybed, who stood and came over. 'This is my cousin, Vincenzo.'

'So it's your dad's yacht?'

Vincenzo shook her hand and smiled. 'It is.'

He was somewhere in his twenties, younger than Luca, but dressed similarly in shorts and a linen shirt, completely at ease in surroundings that Stella could barely take in.

Vincenzo turned to Chloe and kissed her on each cheek. She giggled as he led her over to the daybed and they started chatting together. It wasn't hard for Stella to see how smitten she was. Stella sighed, weighing up how much of a bad idea this was, because her heart was already betraying her head.

'My other cousin Giovanni and our friend Desi have gone ashore, so you might not meet them today.' Luca gestured to a covered seating area behind the daybed. They sat and a waitress in a crisp white short-sleeved shirt and smart black shorts brought over two glasses of champagne and placed them on the table.

'So you have people who work on the yacht too?'

He grinned. 'Of course. We have sixteen crew. Eight luxury bedrooms, dining rooms, lounges, a library, even a nightclub.'

'Wow, it's quite something.' She looked around at the shiny walnut wood interior and the incredible sight of Capri covering the hillside, the villas sparkling in the sunshine.

'As we said to Chloe and Amber last night, we're heading to Naples, then along the Amalfi Coast for a couple of days at the end of the week. You're welcome to join us.' His words hung in the air.

Stella could sense Chloe's anticipation as she listened in. She knew she was desperate for her to say yes. It felt exciting and adventurous. Probably reckless. These guys were strangers, yet it wasn't just four blokes on their own; there was a whole crew. They wouldn't be alone. She'd wanted this holiday to be an adventure of a lifetime after all...

'Do you often invite people you've only just met to sail with you?' Stella held Luca's gaze, wondering if he was going to tell her the truth or not.

'Honestly? Sometimes, yes. It's not like we don't have the space. New company is good.' He rested his arm along the back of the seat and looked intently at her. 'I know what it can seem like. We are young, we like to have fun. I think Chloe and Amber like that too, and maybe you...'

'Yeah, I do.' She lowered her voice, aware of Chloe not far away.

'But I'm also not quite as young and naive as my daughter.'

Luca raised his glass. 'I understand. You do what is right for you. But our offer stands. We like good company and new friends.'

Whatever his intentions, she was beginning to like him.

'I'll need to talk to my friend to make sure first, but can I say a tentative yes?'

'Of course. Just let us know before we depart on Friday.'

She could sense Chloe trying to contain a squeal of excitement. And, she realised, it wasn't just Chloe who was excited. A luxury yacht with young, handsome Italians was a dream. The idea of sailing with them thrilled her. Since winning the Lottery, she'd made a promise to herself to *really* start living, to say yes to opportunities, to embrace the freedom the money could bring her. To focus on the positives rather than the negatives.

After chatting more and drinking champagne, Stella swapped numbers with Luca and promised to let him know their decision as soon as possible. They said goodbye with kisses on each cheek. His stubble tickled and she got a delicious waft of a sensuous spiced aftershave.

Chloe hooked her arm in Stella's and they walked back towards the bars and restaurants along the busy Via Marina Grande. She had a pretty good idea what Fern was going to say, but somehow she needed to make sure she said yes.

* * *

Amber was already at the villa relaxing by the pool when Stella and Chloe arrived back.

'Where's your mum?' Stella dropped her bag on a chair and worked out the ache in her shoulders.

'Don't know.'

'What do you mean you don't know?'

'We didn't come back together.'

Stella frowned. It had seemed like a good idea for them to have some mother-daughter time, but the scowl on Amber's face said otherwise. She perched on the end of the sun lounger and sighed. 'What happened?'

'What I knew would happen when we were forced to spend time together.' Amber folded her arms and sighed.

Stella was sad at the distance that had grown between Amber and Fern and was as clueless as Fern about what had caused it. 'It was a chance for you to talk,' she said gently.

'Yeah, but she's so frustrating. We just talk rubbish, then when I really try to talk about important stuff, she gets all cross about it.'

'You should go easy on her.'

'I'm doing her a favour.'

Stella frowned, confused by Amber's words. She was beginning to wonder if there was more to it than just the usual friction between mothers and daughters. 'What do you mean?'

Amber looked away. 'Nothing.'

'Well, there is something because you're upset and your mum's not here. Did you just leave her somewhere?'

'I'm sure she's quite capable of finding her way back. I did, didn't I?' Her sullen look returned.

'That's not the point. What did she get cross about?'

Amber shuffled upright, dropped her sunglasses on the edge of the sun lounger and looked around. 'Where's Chloe?'

'She went inside to get changed,' Stella said. Amber's pretty face was pinched, her forehead creased. Stella thawed a little. She reached out and placed a hand on Amber's leg. 'What are you not telling me?'

Amber opened her mouth to say something but shook her head. Stella tensed, wondering if she was going to shut down completely. Then Amber met Stella's eyes.

'What do you know about my dad?'

Stella's blood ran cold. 'What do you mean?'

'You've known him, right, for as long as Mum has?'

'Uh-huh.'

'So, I'm asking you, how well do you know him? I mean, do you know what he's really like?' Her eyes were wide and imploring as if she wanted to make Stella understand what she was trying to say without having to spell it out. The trouble was, Stella knew exactly what she was getting at and could see how much she was struggling to put the truth into words. Amber held her gaze. 'You know too, don't you?'

'About what?'

'About Dad having an affair.'

Even though it was the truth, hearing the words out loud and from Amber made everything close in around Stella. The picturesque surroundings might as well have been four grey walls at that moment. Fear twisted her insides. 'How do you know?'

'I walked in on Dad and some random woman a couple of years ago. Mum was away visiting Ruby at university. I was supposed to be staying at a friend's but hadn't felt very well so came home. They'd kinda stopped by the time I appeared in the bedroom door-way, but they could hardly hide what they'd been up to.'

'Oh my goodness, Amber. I had no idea. I mean, I didn't know about that.'

'You're honestly saying you believed my dad had never cheated on my mum?'

'I don't know what I'm saying...' Her heart thumped. There were so many lies to unravel, so much that needed putting right.

'I find it so hard to talk to Mum about anything because of this stupid thing hanging over me. I want Mum to know the truth. I hate knowing this when she doesn't. I'm annoyed at myself for getting angry with her, it's just I'm cross that she doesn't see it. I know *I know*, but it's, like, majorly obvious what he's doing and although I've not caught him again – mainly cos I'm away at uni most of the time – I'm sure he's still messing around. I want to make Mum see what's going on without having to actually tell her, because Dad made me promise n—'

'What are you two whispering about?'

Chloe's voice made them both jump. She walked across the terrace towards them.

Stella leaned closer to Amber. 'Keep this to yourself for now.' She stood up and smiled at a bikini-clad Chloe. 'I'm going to go phone Fern.' She grabbed her bag and walked towards the tunnel of green that led to the villa.

'The yacht is amazing,' she heard Chloe say as she disappeared inside.

Stella's heart pounded and her head rang with Amber's words. She was also worried about Fern. Even if Amber hadn't bluntly said the truth, she'd said enough to upset her mum. She pulled her mobile from her bag and rang Fern. It went straight to answer-phone. Stella cursed, tucked her phone back in her bag and collided with Violetta.

'*Mi dispiace*,' Violetta said, gathering the pile of laundry from the tiled floor. 'I'm sorry.'

'No, it was my fault. Totally wasn't looking where I was going.' She scooped up a towel and handed it to her. 'I don't suppose you know if Fern's come back?'

Violetta nodded and gestured along the hallway. 'I think she's in her room.'

Stella headed that way, her brief relief swiftly replaced by nerves as she reached Fern's closed bedroom door. She knocked and waited. She knocked louder when there was no answer.

'Come in!' a distant voice called.

Stella pushed open the door. The room was empty, but the

French doors were flung open. Stella walked across the room and went outside. Fern was sitting on a large cushioned chair with her feet tucked beneath her. A book was open in her lap and her eyes were red-rimmed.

'Hey,' Stella said gently as she perched on the low wall next to her.

Fern stared past her to the plants shading the terrace. It was completely hidden, a private oasis in the middle of the garden. Close up, Fern's eyes looked puffy and Stella noticed a tissue scrunched in her hand.

'I've just had a chat with Amber... She sort of told me what happened.' She'd told her a lot more, but nothing she was ready to divulge to Fern right now. 'Are you okay?'

Fern sniffed. 'I'm fine.'

She looked and sounded anything but fine to Stella. 'Do you want to talk about it?'

'Not really, no.' She took a deep breath and turned to her. 'How did your day with Chloe go? Did you go to the yacht?'

'Yes, we did. It's bloody amazing. They've invited us for a cruise along the Amalfi Coast for a couple of days. They seem like pretty decent and friendly blokes.' Fern's hand tensed on the tissue. 'But we don't have to talk about it now. We don't have to decide until later in the week.'

Stella suddenly felt uncomfortable. She stood up, her movement sending a robin flying into the safety of the holm oak that shaded the terrace.

'If you want company later, come and find me. I think the girls might go out for a bit this evening...' She didn't know what else to say. Fern looked so sad. She squeezed her arm and retreated from the terrace, leaving her to her thoughts.

Paul had a lot to answer for, but he wasn't the only one.

11

FERN

Fern managed to avoid Amber for the rest of the day. Amber and Chloe went out in the evening and Stella kept Fern company at the villa. They had a simple but delicious seafood salad for dinner before watching a film dubbed into English. It passed the time and Fern was happy not to talk. She was happy not to think about anything either. She tried hard to push what Amber had said to the back of her mind, but it was seeded there now for her to worry over. Stella was probably just being kind, staying back with her rather than enjoying an evening out. Fern knew she was hardly a bundle of laughs. As she headed to bed early for a second night, she vowed to be better company from now on.

* * *

After the previous disastrous mother-daughter day – for Fern and Amber at least – there was no argument from anyone when Stella proposed they spent the day separately. While Amber and Chloe decided to head to rocky Faraglioni to swim and sunbathe, Stella suggested that she and Fern went shopping. So after a lazy morning by the pool, they did just that, exploring the boutiques on Via Camerelle and poring over designer labels. They shopped for lunch too, buying focaccia, tomatoes and a local cheese to have back at the villa. The sun-drenched streets were narrow and filled with people. The shop windows competed for attention, purple bougainvillea cascaded from balconies and little cafes with outdoor tables enticed tourists with coffee and pastries.

Later that day, they took one of the colourful open-top taxis to a restaurant on the other side of the island with a large terrace that overlooked Marina Piccola. Fern didn't think the view from the villa's pool could be beaten, but there was something about the setting that was wonderful. Maybe it was the time of day, with the sun going down to reveal the magic of twilight. The opposite cliff face was silhouetted against a pink sky that deepened to mauve and then a dusky blue by the time it merged with the sea. Villas, nestled among dark-leafed trees, glowed invitingly and the myriad of winding lanes were ablaze with warm light. Out in the calm bay, boats were lit up too, the light reflecting onto the glassy surface of the water.

A waiter brought them a bottle of white wine, poured their drinks and took their food order.

'The girls are missing out,' Fern said the moment the waiter left.

'I'm sure they've found somewhere equally as lush. Plus, I don't think they want us tagging along on a night out.' Stella raised a perfectly shaped eyebrow and sipped her wine.

'Oh I know. I have no idea why I imagined they would. It's been interesting...' Fern paused, uncertain that interesting was actually the right word. 'It's been eye-opening spending this much time with Amber.'

'Oh?'

Fern wasn't sure how much Stella had gleaned about the disastrous end to her day with Amber, but her tone was cagey. 'She's such a closed book. I really don't understand what's going on with her. I miss the closeness we had when she was younger. I don't know, she became a teenager and everything changed – I know that's to be expected, I barely talked to my parents in my teens, but it was a huge shock just how much she pulled away from me. Amber became more distant and Ruby and I became closer.'

'For identical twins they're very different, aren't they?'

'Totally. But Amber... there's this hardness about her. She looks down on me. She made such a snide comment about not wanting to turn out like me. Pathetic and a failure.'

'Oh my goodness, Fern. She doesn't think about you like that.'

'She does Stella, she told me as much yesterday.' The conversation with Amber had hurt her no end. It upset her just thinking about it now. 'You know it's not far from the truth.'

Stella opened her mouth to say something, then presumably thought better of it.

'See,' Fern said, sounding smug yet feeling devastated to know the way Amber felt about her was obvious to others too. 'She said stuff about Paul as well... disrespecting me and taking advantage.'

Stella sipped her wine and looked at her thoughtfully. 'You shouldn't let her talk to you like that.'

'No, I know.' Fern drew in a shuddery breath. 'The trouble is, a lot of what she said is how I've been feeling, but she's made me see it with such clarity.'

Stella frowned. 'What do you mean?'

Fern's heart raced and her palms were sweaty. Despite the pleasantly mild evening, she suddenly felt uncomfortably hot. 'I've felt like this for a while, that I'm just going through the motions. Life is monotonous. It's hard to explain... I've felt lost since the girls left home. I know they're back in the holidays and I have the house to look after, Paul too...'

'You shouldn't be looking after Paul. Amber's right about that.'

'Don't go there again, Stella.'

Stella looked away and picked up her glass of wine. As she stared at the view, Fern could sense the cogs whirring as if she was working out what to say.

Stella turned back. 'You need to start thinking about yourself more. Figure out what *you* want and quit worrying about everyone else.' She held up her hands before Fern had a chance to say anything. 'I know that's easy for me to say, but from the little you've said and the way Paul and Amber have been treating you... I'm worried about you, that's all. Anyway,' she continued, 'it's something all young adults go through, defying their parents and putting them down. It's normal, even if it hurts.'

Fern wasn't convinced. After all, Amber was well past her teens – it felt personal, an attack on her very being. Maybe she was being too sensitive. She let the subject drop.

The waiter returning with their starters was the perfect distraction. They focused on their food, barely saying anything beyond making 'mmm' noises as they each tucked into a Caprese salad. For such a simple dish, Fern had never tasted anything quite like it. The fresh, almost peppery basil was offset by the sweetness of the tomatoes and the smooth creaminess of the buffalo mozzarella.

'That was unbelievably good,' Stella said, the moment she finished her last mouthful.

Fern nodded and sipped her white wine. 'Everything here is better than I imagined. I thought it was going to be over-the-top glitz. I mean, there are some super dressed up, obviously wealthy people around, but the island itself is more beautiful than I thought.'

'I know, right?' Stella said with a grin. 'And it was down to pure luck.'

'Just like your Lottery win.'

Stella raised her glass but looked bashful.

Fern changed the subject and talked about what they were going to do after they'd finished their meal. *Work off all the food with a walk*, she thought as the waiter returned with their main courses.

Stella gave a gleeful chuckle as she sliced into her grilled swordfish with olives and capers. Fern's plate of linguine with squid and prawns was almost too beautiful to eat – almost.

'I'm in heaven.' Stella sighed and took another mouthful.

They focused on their food for a moment, nodding in appreciation at the deliciousness of what they were eating. The flavours were fresh, the sweet juicy tomatoes complemented by the saltiness of the mussels and prawns. The voices of other diners filled the air, along with the clink of cutlery. The aroma of grilled fish and lemon drifted on the light breeze. Since they'd arrived, the sky had darkened, making it difficult to see where the sea ended and the sky began.

'What do you think about this yacht trip?' Stella broke their silence.

'I, um... I'm not sure.' Fern wrinkled her nose. She knew how she felt about it but was conscious of not wanting to disappoint Stella.

'It's okay,' Stella said. 'You can be honest. It's not your scene, is it?'

Fern wound linguine on to her fork. 'No, not really. It would have been years ago though.'

Stella snorted. 'There'd have been no stopping you – straight on that party boat for a few boozy days. We'd have had a competition to see who'd pull the quickest.'

'When did I become so boring?'

Stella looked at her through unblinking eyes. 'You're not.'

Fern didn't believe her in the slightest. 'I am, and you know it.'

'You're not boring.' Stella placed a cool hand on her arm. 'You're sensible and have responsibilities now that you didn't have when we were in our late teens.'

'You have responsibilities too. Doesn't stop you having fun.'

'There's nothing stopping you besides yourself.'

Fern looked away, shocked at the truth of Stella's words and how much they hurt.

'I'm so sorry, I didn't mean that to sound the way it did,' Stella apologised.

'It's fine, it's the truth. We both know it. Maybe I don't want to acknowledge how much I've changed. I mean, everyone does, but I'm nothing like who I was when I was eighteen.'

They continued eating, their forks scraping against their plates.

Stella put her fork down and looked across the table. 'Why don't you go on that art retreat?'

'What are you talking about?'

'You know, the place that woman told you about on the ferry over. Take her up on her offer. I know you'd prefer that to a boozy couple of days on a yacht.'

Fern stabbed her fork into a large prawn. 'I can't do that.'

'Why on earth not?'

She shrugged. She had no good reason, other than feeling bad about being a party pooper. She was married, while Stella, Amber and Chloe were single and blatantly up for a good time. She knew the appeal that good-looking Italian blokes had on them all.

'We can always do another day trip – you don't have to miss out. I just want you to be happy and do what you want for once. Think about yourself. It's not selfish.'

'It seems wrong to go off on my own when we've all come out here together,' Fern admitted.

'Doesn't mean to say we can't do our own thing for a few days. Honestly, Fern, if it's something you want to do, then do it. This is *our time*, remember. It's what this holiday is all about. The girls can come with me.'

'Are you sure? It doesn't seem right leaving you with Amber.'

'She's a grown woman, Fern.'

'That's kinda what I'm worried about.'

'Well, maybe it's for the best, rather than you feeling like you need to watch out for her.'

'You will make sure she doesn't get up to anything silly, won't you?'

'Thought you were going to say anything I wouldn't do...'

'Oh God, I dread to think what you're going to get up to.'

'You need to relax, let your hair down. Might be harder to do on an art retreat than a multi-million-pound yacht though...' Stella winked.

Fern playfully whacked her arm. She knew which option she preferred. Laughable really when she thought back to her behaviour as a teen and how her parents despaired. That spark and self-assurance she'd once possessed had been snuffed out – through what? Marriage and motherhood? That wasn't fair. She'd allowed it to happen. Fern was suddenly annoyed with herself for losing her carefree attitude, her enthusiasm, her creativity, her confidence. The list went on and on.

'And when we're back home,' Stella said, dragging her back to the present, 'you should come out with me and the girls from work. You can't keep saying no.'

Fern made a face. 'I'm not sure Paul would particularly like me going out with a bunch of single women.'

'You shouldn't give a crap what Paul thinks.' There was venom in her voice.

Fern looked at her sharply and raised her eyebrows.

'I'm sorry,' Stella said, lowering her voice. 'He goes out with his friends loads and lots of them are single. You don't say anything to that, do you?'

'No.'

'Well then, you shouldn't worry what he thinks.'

'It's not just him. What am I going to do on a night out when you lot cop off with a bloke?'

'Honestly, Fern, we go out to enjoy ourselves, not to try to pull. I'm hardly going to meet anyone in the places we go to. We just dance and have a laugh.'

'What about that French guy you've been talking about?'

'That was different. We met him at a restaurant earlier in the evening, then again at a club later, so we got talking properly. It was a one-off thing. If you come out with us, I promise I won't dump you for a bloke.'

Fern took another mouthful of the seafood pasta. She gazed out over the twinkling bay while mulling over what Stella had said. 'I sort of feel like I don't fit in anywhere. I have friends like you who are single and enjoying that lifestyle and friends who are married but with much younger kids. The friends I made when the girls were babies are now in their fifties – I still feel as disconnected from them as I did when I was a teen mum trying to bond with a thirty-something. I don't know, I've lost who I am.'

'Maybe you've never had a chance to find out who you are and what you want from life. You went from being a teenager with hopes and dreams to a teen mum with a load of responsibility and no time to adjust to it. Having one kid young was hard enough, let alone two. You're bloody amazing, Fern. I mean that. So take this time and do something for yourself.'

Fern didn't like to admit it, because to do so was an acknowledgement of how she'd let her dreams fade and her passion for art and creativity die, but perhaps Stella was right.

12

FERN

In many ways, Fern felt ridiculous giving up the opportunity of living it up on a luxury yacht. Maybe she really was too sensible. She was beginning to see in herself what Stella and Amber saw and she wasn't sure she liked the person she'd become. Not that the qualities she possessed should be something to be ashamed of. There was nothing wrong with putting other people first, seeing to their needs, being motherly, considerate and thoughtful, but she got Stella's point about it being at her own expense. What made her sad was that she seemed to have lost part of herself over the years: her confidence and happy-go-lucky side. She used to always be willing to say yes to things. She could still have fun, but maybe she was craving something different to the kind of fun Stella was after.

In the end, she'd taken Stella's advice, knowing that spending time at an art retreat rather than on a multi-millionaire's yacht, was actually what she wanted to do. Perhaps it would be a way of coming to terms with who she was now rather than longing for the person she'd been in the past.

The following morning, she texted Edith to ask if the offer of taking her friend's place at the retreat for a couple of days was still on. She received a message back saying she'd be delighted for Fern to join her. Edith sent her further details about the retreat and after a couple of relaxing days sunning themselves around the villa pool and eating out together in Capri town, the four of them packed their bags ready for their separate adventures.

Fern was treating herself, even if it didn't seem that way to the others. And by the others she meant Amber. Although it was clear that Amber was rather pleased her mum would be somewhere else. Despite the sunshine and the beauty of their surroundings, the tension between them had rumbled on with Amber continuing to ignore Fern, and Fern didn't have the desire to question her daughter again. Goodness knew what Amber was going to get up to on a yacht full of Italians.

Quit worrying about her, Fern thought. She'd hoped that this holiday would bring them closer together, but so far, it seemed to have only driven them apart. Perhaps Stella would be able to knock some sense into her while she was away.

Fern might not have known Edith beyond one conversation on the ferry over, but she was looking forward to getting to know her and immersing herself in creativity for a couple of days. For once, she was doing something completely for herself. She told herself it wasn't selfish to take time out to focus on her own needs for a change. Taking care of everyone else had been her role for the last twenty years. This was long overdue.

Fern's palazzo trousers swished against her legs as she walked up the stone steps that led to Il Ritiro d'Arte. It was a grand entrance with stone pillars spaced out along the steps, with an occasional stone lion or owl perched on the edge. Terracotta pots alternated with the stone creatures and splashes of tangerine and coral flowers mixed with glossy bottle-green leaves. Vines curled around the pillars and the leaves of a wisteria cascaded from above – it must have looked even more incredible earlier in the spring when the flowers were out.

Edith was waiting at the top of the steps in front of the large double wooden doors. The whole place oozed a grandness with history and beauty in every direction.

Edith greeted Fern like an old friend, with a kiss on each cheek. 'When in Rome…' she said, laughing. 'Welcome to Il Ritiro d'Arte, or as I simply call it, the retreat.'

She looked like an artist, with a colourful headscarf keeping her wayward hair off her face. She was wearing loose linen trousers with a long floaty tunic over the top. All she needed was a paintbrush in her hand.

'It's incredible,' Fern said, following her inside. 'I'm not sure what I was expecting, but this… I have no words.'

'You haven't seen anything yet.' She swept her hand around the entrance hall.

Water trickled into a basin from the mouths of stone gargoyles on the far wall. The floor was tiled in a similar style to the beautiful tiles in Villa Giardino. Fern's immediate impression was of cool stone walls, a soft light filtering in from beautiful arched windows and leafy plants in large pots. Open doors led off to other parts of the villa and a stone staircase went invitingly up to the first floor.

'Matteo, the owner and our delightful host,' Edith said with a glint in her eye, 'will be back in an hour or two, otherwise he'd have been here to greet you, but I am more than happy to show you around.'

'Are you certain he doesn't mind me staying?'

'Of course not! He's the most generous man – he's been trying to refund me, but I'm having none of it; it's not his fault the room became available. We're both glad you're here for a couple of days.'

Fern followed her into a spacious living area where the patterned floor continued. A fresh breeze billowed through open patio doors and light and colour flooded in through the large windows that overlooked the Mediterranean garden.

'Matteo likes having the place filled with people. The more, the merrier is his motto – well, I don't know if it actually is, but he certainly comes across as though he loves having people to stay. It's his livelihood after all.'

Fern could only imagine what it would feel like to not only live in a place like this but to call it home. As Edith showed her around, she realised how sprawling it was, a place she imagined would feel far too big and grand for just one person. They crossed another wide hallway to reach an elegant dining room with a long marble-topped table surrounded by ten chairs, the backdrop an ancient-looking fireplace. They returned to the hallway and walked to the end and into an orangery. Light flooded through the glass roof. Velvet armchairs and a sofa defined the space, and the view through large windows to the tree-filled garden was simply magical.

'Are you inspired yet?' Edith said, motioning around them.

'I think it will be hard not to be.' The last time Fern had sketched anything was during her short-lived graphic design degree. It wasn't as if she'd never thought about pursing her love of art over the years – she'd considered doing a pottery course when the twins had started nursery but what little time she had, had been spent helping Paul build the business. But now... The sun flooded through the glass and a glorious warmth enveloped her, giving her the feeling that anything was possible.

'The first time I came here,' Edith said with a lightness to her voice, 'this place utterly stole my heart. Italy already had; I've been travelling here for years – I think I already told you about my desire to live out here, but yes, this place is wonderous.'

Edith led Fern back across the villa to the stairs and up to a long landing with doors off it.

'You're in the room I had the first time I was here. The Garden Room. It has the most stunning vista through the window from the bed... well, you'll see.'

Edith pushed open the door of the room at the end of the landing and Fern followed her in.

'Maya would have loved it.' Edith looked wistfully around and gave a resigned shrug. 'I'll leave you to it. If you want company this afternoon, you'll find me painting in either the orangery or out in the garden.'

'Thank you, Edith.' Fern smiled at her as she retreated from the room.

A wrought-iron four-poster bed took centre stage in a room that exuded history and luxury. The wooden window surround was carved with leaf and flower patterns and painted olive green, but Fern's eye was drawn past it to the view of the garden.

She kicked off her slip-on trainers and left her bag on the floor, then padded across the cool tiles to fling open the balcony doors.

The private balcony overlooked the gardens, with a glimpse of blue sea beyond the trees. The wall surrounding it was planted with herbs, their fragrance wafting on the light breeze, and flamingo-pink flowers bloomed in pots.

Fern leant her hands on the edge of the wall and soaked up the warmth and peace. For some reason, she hadn't felt as utterly relaxed back at Villa Giardino as she did now; at least, she hadn't realised she'd felt that way until coming here. It didn't make sense as she'd been with family and friends there, while here she was with strangers and she'd only met Edith so far. It felt like fate, meeting and chatting to Edith on the ferry over. It was funny how it had all worked out.

* * *

Matteo took Fern by surprise an hour later as she was walking across the large and airy entrance hall on her way outside. He strode towards her with his hand held out.

'Welcome, Fern. Edith said you'd arrived.'

Her first impression was that his hand was warm and firm. He spoke perfect English with barely an accent. Her second impression was how handsome he was, with dark brown hair and warm hazel, almost green, eyes. Stubble decorated his strong jaw. He must have been somewhere in his early forties, she reckoned, and had quintessentially Italian good looks but not in an off-putting way.

'You're Italian?' she asked, eager to fill the brief silence.

'I am. I was born in Italy, although my mother grew up in England and we spoke English and Italian at home fluently, hence the lack of a strong Italian accent.' He swept a hand towards the stairs. 'Edith assured me she'd shown you to your room. I trust you have everything you need?'

'I have, thank you. The room is gorgeous. The whole place is.'

'Thank you. We aim to please. My passion is to make guests happy and ideally never want to leave. If they feel that way, then I've done a good job. Art, creativity, food and wine is what we're all about. Our day pretty much revolves around food.' He laughed with a jolliness that Fern hadn't expected. It made her smile. 'You can choose to have breakfast and lunch in your room or wherever you wish in the villa or garden, but dinner we eat together. We like to socialise over food, chat about our day and everyone's creative plans. Talk, eat and drink.'

'That sounds wonderful.'

'You missed lunch; would you like something to eat now?'

'Oh, I'm fine, thank you. I had a big breakfast. We were fed rather well where I've been staying.'

'It seems it was fortuitous you meeting Edith.'

'I'm completely surprised by being here and can't thank Edith enough for her invite and your generosity in being okay with it.'

'Oh, the more, the merrier, I say.'

'That's what Edith said.'

He nodded and smiled warmly. 'I'll let you explore, but before dinner we must chat about how you want to spend your time here.'

Fern nodded in agreement and they said goodbye for the time being. Fern headed outside and strolled along the shaded terrace outside the living room. Matteo was as Edith had described: warm and generous, and seemingly fine with her being here in place of Edith's friend. It was also easy to see why Edith was so taken by him – he was rather handsome... Fern brushed the thought away as she continued to explore.

On the edge of Anacapri, a pretty whitewashed village on the more peaceful side of the island, the villa was perched on a hill and nestled within private gardens with glimpses of the sea between the trees. Fern could hardly believe her luck; the place felt like a dream. She was unsure how she was supposed to explore the creativity that had been buried for so long, but she was certain that this place would provide inspiration. She was nervous though, about how it would feel to do something she used to love. She felt the stirrings of creativity and the unexpected freedom felt good.

Stone steps led down to a swimming pool. The water was clear and turquoise, just one more inviting element of the tropical-looking garden. With so many beautiful hidden areas, Fern's breath was snatched away at every turn. She thought the villa Stella had rented was beautiful, but this place was even better. Despite its size and elegance, it felt lived in and loved. Everything about the place made Fern feel as if she was a movie star living someone else's life. Even on a multi-million-pound yacht, she was hard-pressed to think how Stella, Amber and Chloe's experience could top hers.

13

STELLA

A young bunch of blokes, all in their twenties or thirties, all wealthy, all decent-looking. Stella knew exactly how it looked to Fern, but she didn't care. This was a holiday to beat all holidays, but the last thing she wanted was to make Fern do something she was uncomfortable with. It seemed to have all worked out for the best. But now she was here, leaning on the edge of the yacht and gazing out at Capri without Fern, she acknowledged her anxiety about Fern going off on her own, not because she wouldn't have a lovely time, but because she seemed so fragile, like she needed looking after. Mothering. Exactly what she'd accused Fern of doing to Paul.

The yacht sparkled alongside the others in the harbour at Marina Grande. The sound of chatter and distant laughter mixed with the harsh call of seabirds. The view was magnificent across the marina to the multitude of villas, cafes, restaurants and hotels studding the hillside. Everything was bathed in sunshine, including the throng of people crowding the seafront. Somewhere far to her left, clinging to the cliff was Villa Giardino, their little slice of Capri, although they were abandoning it for a cruise along the Amalfi

Coast. That thought didn't sit easy with Stella; it was hard to comprehend the amount of money she'd paid for the three nights they wouldn't be there, but she'd badly wanted to say yes to this adventure. How good would it be, though, to actually own a property on the island with a pool to cool off in and a terrace with a view to enjoy alongside a glass of limoncello or two. The dream could be reality, she knew. But there was much she needed to get sorted back home first. She also needed to see people's reaction – and by people, she meant both of her exes, her friends and extended family – to a million-pound Lottery win before she revealed the whole truth.

'Mum, have you seen inside?' Chloe appeared on the deck, breathless with excitement.

'Not yet. I'm quite happy admiring the view.'

The two Italian brothers were still somewhere on Capri but Luca and their friend Desi had greeted them. The crew were making preparations to leave and their bags had already been taken to their rooms. While Chloe and Amber had been shown around by Desi, Stella had been distracted by the view and the feeling of awe, excitement and anticipation being on a multi-million-pound yacht evoked. They were about to head along one of the most picturesque stretches of Italian coastline. The only thing spoiling it was the tug of guilt about Fern.

Stella wedged her sunglasses into her hair and followed Chloe inside. As they walked through the yacht's interior, she took everything in, from the ridiculously soft carpet beneath her bare feet, to the walnut wood panelling and plush sofas in cream and gold fabric, piled with cushions. Everything was sparkling clean, polished to perfection and luxurious.

They took a spiral staircase down to one of the lower decks.

'You could get lost in this place,' Stella said as Chloe led her down a wide central corridor with doors off it.

Chloe stopped outside a door with a gleaming golden two engraved on it. 'All the rooms are lush, but they've given you the nicest,' she said, pushing open the door.

Stella poked her head in. Her first impression was of a first-class hotel. The bed was huge, the number of pillows and cushions stacked on it taking up half of it. It always made Stella laugh at this weird obsession to have so many cushions on the bed that you had to remove each night. As well as the walnut-panelled walls, the ceiling was a duck-egg blue, with an ornate carved pattern painted gold. *It probably is actual gold leaf*, Stella thought as she closed the door behind her and followed Chloe.

* * *

After exploring the yacht, Stella went back to her room and unpacked before heading to the deck at the stern. The other boats and yachts in the marina sparkled, bobbing gently on the turquoise water. Marina Grande was lined with colourful shuttered buildings in cream, wine red and saffron yellow. The hillside rose steeply behind, intercut with gleaming villas and luminous greenery.

They left Capri late in the afternoon. The marina blurred into a haze of colour the further away they sailed. Stella's thoughts wandered back to Fern. How she was going to get on with a bunch of strangers, Stella had no idea, but it had been her choice.

She frowned at the untruth. She hadn't really given her much choice, had she? It was either tag along with them or stay at the villa alone. The art retreat was a good compromise. She hoped Fern would see it like that. Either way, it was done. Worrying over something that was already in motion was futile.

With Giovanni, the older of the two brothers, meeting a client in Naples early the next morning, the plan was to moor up in a marina there for the night before heading back past Capri and along the

Amalfi Coast the following day. The excitement she'd felt when first stepping onto the yacht was still there, tingling through to the tips of her toes. It was the stuff of dreams: a floating luxury hotel with lounge areas, an outdoor jacuzzi, luxurious en-suite bedrooms, a bar, a chef, a crew to look after their every whim and a bunch of young, hot Italians to get to know.

She'd splashed out on her shopping spree with Fern. She was wearing her custom-made Capri sandals and a strapless lemon-print layered sundress that just reached the bottom of her calves. She'd put her hair into two plaits and popped a sun hat on. New Prada sunglasses finished the look. She looked the part, even if she still felt a fraud living a millionaire's lifestyle.

She joined the others on the lounge deck. A bottle of prosecco was chilling in a bucket of ice and everyone was sitting around the table. Not everyone, she realised; the crew were all busy, sailing the yacht, preparing drinks and dinner below deck, making sure everything was in order. It was quite something to be waited on like this.

She slid on to the seat next to Luca. He flashed her a smile. Amber was deep in conversation with Desi and Chloe was giggling with Vincenzo and Giovanni.

Luca poured her a glass of prosecco, handed it to her and knocked his glass against hers. '*Salute!*'

She smiled. 'Cheers.'

'All okay?' he asked. 'You seemed to want to be on your own?'

'I'm fine, thank you. Just a bit concerned about leaving my friend behind.'

'She is a grown woman, no?'

'She is. Still... I feel bad leaving her on Capri while I'm here.'

The yacht was slicing through the deep blue of the Tyrrhenian Sea, the Italian coastline getting slowly clearer in the late-afternoon sun. Stella imagined Capri getting smaller and smaller behind them. She needed to get a grip and enjoy the experience, just as she hoped Fern would be doing in Anacapri.

She turned back to Luca. He was sipping his prosecco, one leg casually resting on the other. He looked effortlessly cool in capri shorts and a linen short-sleeved shirt, the top few buttons undone, allowing a glimpse of his smooth, toned chest. She had absolutely made the right decision.

He caught her looking at him and grinned.

'So, tell me,' Stella said, wanting to focus on something other than her guilt, 'how you're able to be on a yacht like this – you said it belongs to your uncle?'

'*Sì*. We do this together once a year. Our downtime, is that how you call it?'

Stella nodded. 'What does your uncle do?'

'He works in fashion; my father in property.'

'And what do you do?' she asked.

'I work in property – the family business. It makes sense. My sister does too and I'm sure one day our children will as well, if it is their desire. What do you do back in England?'

'I'm a Global Operations Strategy Associate for a takeaway app.'

Luca frowned.

'You're pulling the exact face most of my friends do when I try to explain my job.'

'You like it, your job? It's a good one?'

'It pays the bills and I'm good at it, so that's a win in my eyes. You sell property?'

'Sell, yes, and invest in. Investing is how my family made money.'

Stella rested her elbow on the table and leant her chin on her hand. She looked at him intently. 'You're obviously extremely wealthy, right? I mean, I know this yacht isn't yours, but it belongs to your family. You have money.'

He nodded and gave her a cheeky grin. 'You are right. I have money.'

'Well, what advice would you give to someone who has recently come in to a lot of money?'

His smile remained, but his eyes narrowed as he focused on her fully. 'By someone, you mean you, *si*?'

'Yep.'

Stella was aware of the others, but Amber was still deep in conversation with Desi and Chloe was out of earshot, lounging on the deck with the other two, sipping her prosecco.

'How you get the money?' His frown increased.

Stella laughed. 'Not through dodgy means, I promise. I won the Lottery in the UK towards the end of last year.'

He whistled. 'And you need advice about how to spend it?'

'Not exactly spend it, but the smart thing to do with it.'

'You not get advice from who you win it from?'

'Oh yes, there's all kinds of support and financial advice, but I'm interested to hear your thoughts, being someone who has money and I assume is quite smart about it. I'd like to know what you'd do.'

'How much you win?'

'A lot.' Stella lowered her voice. 'The only people I've told about my win are here with me in Capri.' She leaned closer until she was an inch from his ear. 'And I haven't been completely truthful with them either. I've won a lot more than they realise.'

He smelt delicious. A spicy, sensual aftershave. She pulled away a little and looked into his smiling brown eyes.

'The best thing you can do is invest at least some of the money. Property, if you are smart, is always a good choice.' He pressed his hands to his chest. 'You talk to the right person.' He lowered his voice and leaned closer until his breath was hot against her neck. 'How much did you tell them you won?'

'Just over a million.'

'How much you actually win?'

Stella met his cool, brooding gaze.

'Twenty-seven point five million pounds,' she whispered.

14

FERN

Fern met Matteo in the living room early that evening. The lightest of breezes whispered through the patio doors that opened onto the terrace. Chiffon curtains fluttered and shafts of golden sunlight sent blocks of warmth across the patterned tiles.

Fern's palazzo trousers, light linen top and new Capri sandals felt appropriate for the setting. Edith had come across as relaxed yet stylish, with a creative vibe emanating from her. Fern longed to recapture some of the creative spirit she'd once possessed.

Matteo was sitting on one of four sofas that surrounded a large glass coffee table. He smiled warmly as she sat down on the end of the sofa next to him and he handed her a glass filled with a summery yellow liquid.

'Hands down, this is my guest's favourite drink.' He knocked his glass against hers.

She took a sip, the smooth, refreshing tingle of citrus hitting her tastebuds. 'Wow, what's in it?'

'Limoncello, of course, a squeeze of citrus from the lemons in the garden, vodka and soda. For me, it's the taste of summer on the island.'

She swigged another mouthful and sank back into the deep velvet sofa. 'Thank you, it's delicious. And, again, I can't thank you enough for being okay with me staying.'

'It's my pleasure, and far better than the room remaining empty. What I love about the retreat is getting to know lots of different people from all walks of life. Different backgrounds and nationalities. I like the place being full. I also feel incredibly sorry for dear Edith with her friend being poorly. I know she was torn coming here on her own. I was quite prepared to refund her, but she refused. You being here for even a short time has helped balance things out in a positive way.'

'Well, I'm glad.'

'Edith said you're on holiday with your friend?'

Fern clasped her hands around the chilled limoncello cocktail. 'Yes, with my friend, plus our daughters.'

Matteo frowned. 'But you were able to come here on your own?'

Realising what he was getting at, Fern laughed. 'My daughter's twenty-one. She certainly doesn't need me any longer and I get the feeling she's quite happy to not have me tagging along.'

'You don't look old enough to have a grown-up daughter.'

'I had her young – two of them in fact; she's a twin. So double trouble.'

Matteo smiled but didn't comment further. Part of her liked how people were surprised to discover she was a mother of two twenty-one-year-olds, yet it always reaffirmed just how young and naive she'd been.

'I like to get to know each of my guests,' Matteo said, moving the conversation on. 'Although people often come here on their own, I don't want anyone to feel alone, so I encourage us all to eat dinner together, but of course I never insist if someone prefers the time to themselves. Il Ritiro d'Arte has a communal spirit. If I get to know you a little better, then it helps me to help you achieve what you wish from your time here.' He must have seen the worried look on her face because he continued, 'Although you don't have to know what you want to do. Think of this place as a blank canvas that you can experiment with.'

'I think that's what worries me. I haven't a clue where to start.'

'Are you creative?'

'No... well, not any longer.' She drew in a deep breath. 'I was very much so when I was younger. I've sort of lost my creativity along the way.'

'But you'd like to re-engage with that side of yourself?'

'Yes, I'd love to.' She was certain of that, knowing the appeal an art retreat had over a cruise along the Amalfi Coast. Most people would think she was crazy to prefer this, but Il Ritiro d'Arte had proved to be no ordinary place, it was magical.

'Have you ever been on an art retreat?'

'No, never. I'm not sure I'd have even thought about going on one if I hadn't met Edith and things hadn't worked out the way they did.'

'We encourage all things creative, whether you want to draw, paint or write. It's a place to immerse yourself in *your* passions.'

Fern sipped her cocktail and allowed herself to relax. She acknowledged the excitement tingling through her at the idea of having the chance and time to rediscover long-lost creativity.

'Are you an artist?' she asked.

'I am, although not professionally. Art is in my blood, but over the years I've discovered that my passion is helping other people to be creative. I dabble, I teach, I enable, that's what I do. I've created places that enrich both my life and other people's. At heart, that's my true passion.'

'It's a wonderful thing.'

A breeze fluttered the curtains, bringing with it a citrus scent. A butterfly drifted in, fluttering between them and landing on the edge of the coffee table.

'As you can see,' he said, gesturing to the butterfly, 'this place is a gift, with so much beauty and nature everywhere. I want you to treat it as a home from home.'

Fern smiled. 'It's hard to imagine having a home this beautiful.'

'Well, enjoy it while you're here. Feel free to explore, sit, think and work anywhere you like. The only private spaces are the guest bedrooms; everywhere else is communal. So if you fancy sitting in the dining room to draw or in here looking out over the terrace, then please do. In the library, there are art books or novels to read, but you'll find paper, pencils, paints, everything, I hope, you could possibly need. Just help yourself. And here's a sketchbook to get you started.'

'Thank you,' she said, blown away by his generosity as she took the black A5 sketchbook from him and ran her fingers over the cover's elegant linen-effect finish.

'You're most welcome. The only set time for anything is dinner and occasionally we'll go out somewhere as a group during the day. Like tomorrow morning at ten we have a walking tour of Anacapri or to the Belvedere di Migliera, a viewpoint which I'm certain will inspire you. Apart from those things, this is your time.'

Matteo's echo of what Stella had said at dinner the other evening reaffirmed that coming here was the right decision. She rarely took time out for herself. Back home, there was always someone else to think about, things to do and worry over. Thinking purely about herself was an alien concept, but one she was very much looking forward to putting into practice.

* * *

Despite the luxury and elegance that emanated from every part of the retreat, both Edith and Matteo had stressed that dinner was a relaxed affair and that there was no need to dress up unless she wanted to. Fern kept on her colourful palazzo trousers but swapped her linen top for a black fitted one with scalloped lace sleeves.

She brushed her hair, slicked on a berry-coloured lipstick and gazed at her reflection in the en-suite mirror. She felt more relaxed than she thought possible being somewhere new and filled with strangers, but the welcome had been heartfelt and her nervousness about gate-crashing had been erased by Matteo's warmth. Her conversation with him earlier had been easier than she'd expected. Ideas had tumbled from her, a release of creativity that she'd blocked for two decades. Matteo had encouraged her, his eyes gleaming as her enthusiasm grew. She'd felt breathless with excitement as they'd parted ways. And now, even though she was only heading downstairs for dinner, that excitement had returned, making it feel as though it was a proper night out.

Fern reached the ground floor and followed the sound of voices through the villa. As she reached the living room, her phone buzzed. A message from Paul.

The chilli was lush – ta for making it. Got home late and off out for a drink so needed food. It's strange you not being here.

Was he actually missing her? With a flood of guilt, she realised that she hadn't thought about him all day or thought to tell him where she was. Not that he'd probably care, but she had an over-whelming feeling of wanting to keep the retreat to herself. She thumbed a reply.

Figured you might need a quick meal. Have a good evening xx

She tucked her phone away and went outside, past the pool and onto a terrace half hidden by foliage and surrounded by looming trees. Candlelit lanterns flickered warm light across the terrace, making shadows dance over the leaves and the happy faces of Matteo and his guests sat around the large circular table that seated ten. Fern got a thrill at being allowed to be a part of such an exclusive group.

Hellos echoed across the terrace as she joined them.

There were two empty seats and as an elderly man leaning on a walking stick joined her, she realised she wasn't the last to arrive. He was wearing an expensive-looking suit with a handkerchief tucked in the pocket.

'Good evening everyone,' he said, his twinkling eyes casting around the table before landing on Fern. 'I don't believe we've yet had the pleasure of meeting.' He held out his hand and she shook it. 'I'm Arthur.'

'Fern.'

'Delighted to meet you.' He took the glass of red wine Matteo offered and settled himself at the table.

Matteo turned to Fern. 'Red or white wine?'

'I'd love white, thank you.'

He handed her a glass and he motioned to the empty seat next to Edith. She sat down, her heart thumping. Chatter and laughter flowed across the table.

Edith leaned towards her and knocked her wine glass against Fern's. 'You are about to experience your first rather special evening at the retreat.'

15

FERN

Matteo was the ultimate host, introducing Fern to everyone, and she was made to feel welcome and not the outsider she was worried about being. Apart from a German couple in their sixties, everyone else was on their own. Of course, Edith would have had her friend with her if that had worked out. Her loss was definitely Fern's gain and she vowed to make the most of every minute.

There was an international flavour, with guests from Canada and the Netherlands as well as the UK, Germany and Italy. Fern imagined there was a lot of wealth around the table – a two-week catered retreat must have cost a fortune. Retirement – if you could afford it – would be the perfect time to come to a place like this. She felt lucky to be experiencing it now, unexpected and so very welcome.

If she thought the food she'd eaten so far on Capri was special, the combination of the setting, the company and a private chef cooking for the guests was something else entirely. The starter was simple but utterly delicious: crunchy arancini that were smooth and moreish inside. The main course of ravioli capresi gave Fern an idea about what it would be like to live somewhere like this, devouring the tastiest dishes with the freshest ingredients day in, day out. To have your own chef who cooked for you... Fern's normal life paled in comparison; it was always an effort to think about what they were going to eat each week. Freshly made pasta filled with a smooth almost sweet caciotta cheese and marjoram drizzled with a delicious tomato sauce – it didn't get much better. She could easily have ravioli as a midweek meal, but the thought took her back to their TV dinners, begrudgingly watching football or some other rubbish programme because Paul wanted to.

'It's nice for Matteo to have someone his own age around.' Edith's voice close to her ear forced her attention away from the food.

Fern wasn't sure if Edith meant anything by it or not. She didn't wink and wasn't looking at her suggestively; it seemed an honest comment. And it was true. Fern was the youngest by far and Matteo was a similar age, perhaps a little older but not by much. His dark hair was flecked with grey, which was barely noticeable and only because she'd been studying him. Hazel eyes, permanent stubble, a light tan, high cheekbones.

She stuck her fork into her ravioli and tried to focus on her food rather than wavering thoughts about a man she'd only just met...

'I suppose it's the nature of running a place like this,' Edith continued, 'surrounded by us retired old fogeys who are able to swan off to Capri for a couple of weeks. I've always thought of my retirement as my chance to immerse myself in the things I love – art, food and travel being the main ones – wine too of course.' She chuckled. 'Capri has all of those in abundance, and this place, well, it speaks for itself.'

Fern couldn't agree more. She'd never been anywhere quite like it. Just the view through the window in her bedroom was like a painting, with the contrast of olive-grey and fresh green leaves against the vibrant splashes of magenta and fiery red flowers.

'I adored having a career as a counsellor and working hard, but I knew I wanted my retirement to be more than just putting my feet up.' Edith's cheeks were rosy and a smile beamed across her face. Her relaxed hairdo was on the verge of dishevelled, but in a good way, with tendrils of white hair framing her face. Fern thought how nice it would be to reach her age and still have such vigour and passion for life. It would be a feat to get to Edith's age and know what she wanted to do with her retirement when she couldn't even figure out what she was going to do in the next twelve months.

Her cheeks felt flushed from lots of wine, unsurprising as her glass kept being topped up. By the middle of the evening, the table was littered with empty bottles. Enclosed within the private garden, it felt as if they were miles from anywhere, when in reality she knew they were on the edge of Anacapri with other grand villas clustered around.

The trickle of water from the fountain not far from the terrace was making Fern need a wee, but she didn't want to spoil the moment; she was content to sit and drink, listen to the chatter of the guests, chip in occasionally and soak up the friendly atmosphere. She was buzzing inside, having enjoyed a day filled with new people and an experience different to anything back home. She did do stuff for herself – there'd been the spa weekend with Stella, she had occasional meals out with friends, she went to work and had colleagues she got on with... She and Paul had mutual friends they went out with together too, but admittedly Paul was out a lot more than she was.

She sighed. Her life was average, boring really. Maybe Stella was right to suggest she went out with her and her friends. There was nothing wrong with going clubbing; Paul still did. It would be good to go dancing and to live a little. Exactly like she was doing now, living life to the full. Except she wasn't; she was away with the fairies thinking about all that she wanted to change in her life.

She pushed her thoughts away and shuffled upright in her chair, zoning back in on the conversation flitting back and forth across the table. Everyone was interesting and had really lived – career- and travel-wise. It made her realise how much she'd missed out on having her kids young. Not that she'd change them for the world. It was fate – well, unprotected sex – that had taken her on a journey of motherhood. Yet, on the cusp of forty, with the next couple of decades spreading out with such uncertainty, she couldn't continue to feel the way she did.

Snap out of it, she thought.

She tried again to focus on what was going on around her. Matteo caught her eye across the table and raised his glass. She returned a nod, sipped her wine and held his gaze. His hazel eyes were darker in the candlelight.

She looked away, conscious of the fluttering in her chest. She downed the rest of her wine. She'd drunk way too much. *But so what*, she thought, *it's about time I enjoyed myself.* Isn't that what Stella, Amber and Chloe would be doing right now? Drinking and partying away on a yacht somewhere off the Amalfi Coast.

The main course was cleared away and the dessert was brought out.

Edith leaned in close as a plate with a generous slice of cake was placed in front of her, along with a glass of limoncello.

'The *torta caprese*,' she said, driving her fork into the cake.

Fern sipped the limoncello. Icy cold and wonderfully refreshing after the meal, it was the perfect accompaniment to the richness of the chocolate and almond cake. Even the elasticated waist of her trousers was straining after all the food.

'I told you he feeds us well,' Edith said as if reading her mind. 'It's why I go for a walk each day – and I mean a proper pacy walk, not a stroll – just so I don't feel guilty about having pudding.'

'I don't think there's any need to feel guilty about anything here.' She was constantly watching her weight back home, while here she realised she didn't give a toss if she put on an extra pound or two. She liked Edith's idea of a daily walk, plus she was eager to have a swim in the pool. Perhaps she would early in the morning before anyone was up – if she could drag herself out of bed. She smiled; it was a novelty to have no one else to please apart from herself.

With empty glasses and only cake crumbs left on plates, the other guests began to drift away with calls of goodnight until just Fern, Edith and Matteo were left. Edith was talking about her child-hood spent in Kenya and at a boarding school in England. Fern wished she was a fraction as interesting as Edith. Her whole adult life had revolved around raising children and looking after her family. It wasn't something she should be ashamed of, yet the feeling of failure kept tugging at her.

Edith pushed back her chair and stood up. 'It's early yet for you youngsters. I need my sleep; I'm an early bird. The best light for painting.' She patted Fern lightly on the shoulder and smiled warmly – or perhaps drunkenly – at Matteo. '*Buona notte*.'

'*Buona notte*, Edith,' Matteo said as she swept away, her long shawl floating around her shoulders and nearly tripping her up as she reached the stone steps that led to the villa.

Silence descended over the courtyard. The garden was tree-filled, the edges as dense as a forest, filtering everything out. There was no traffic noise either, just one of the unexpected joys of the island. A moth fluttered around one of the candles on the table. Fern gazed upwards. Leaf-filled branches framed the night sky, an inky blue scattered with silver stars.

'It's magical, isn't it?'

Fern turned back at Matteo's deep voice. He was watching her, his hand clasped around the glass of wine he held in his lap.

'Almost as clear as in Tuscany,' he continued. 'There's less light pollution there. The sky's endless and so dark. But this spot is special.'

'I love it,' Fern said, sweeping her arm around at the surrounding green. She looked back at him. 'Do you do retreats throughout the year?'

'From April to June here. Then during the summer and autumn in Tuscany.'

'Wow, so you have a place in Tuscany as well?'

He nodded. 'I run a retreat there too.'

'Where do you spend the winter?'

'Oh, a mix of places, a few weeks here, Christmas and New Year in Tuscany. It's also when I travel or go to the UK for a bit too.'

'You have family there?'

'Yes, and friends.' He sipped his wine thoughtfully. 'Where in the UK are you from?'

'A small town outside of Bristol. Nowhere very exciting.'

'Is it where you've always wanted to live?'

'That's a good question and one I don't know how to answer. Life has run away with me. It feels like I was eighteen not that long ago, then I had children, blinked and here I am at thirty-nine, not really sure how I got here. I'm beginning to wonder where all that time went.'

'Raising a family is an honourable thing. You shouldn't be sad about it.'

'Oh, I'm not,' she said with little conviction. She met his eyes. It was as if he'd seen right through her.

'I didn't mean to say the wrong thing.'

The way he was looking at her sent a shiver down her spine.

'You didn't.' She was tempted to reach across the table and take his hand, but she stopped herself. 'The tragic thing is you're absolutely right; I shouldn't be sad, but I am.'

16

STELLA

They berthed at the Marina Molo Luise in Naples. However much Stella would have liked to have explored the city that evening, there was no need when the yacht served as a floating restaurant and bar. The TV programme *Below Deck* was a guilty pleasure, and exactly what being on the yacht reminded her of, except she was getting a taste of the life of a wealthy yacht owner.

They sat around one of the large circular tables on the deck as dusk descended and the twinkling lights of the city cut through the darkness. Mount Vesuvius was shadowed against the mauve sky, which turned to a deep purple at twilight. Laughter filled the air; the four Italians were good company with many stories to tell, ones that left Stella and the girls in awe of their lifestyle. They'd all individually made their own fortune, but they'd had a leg-up, the two brothers in particular, coming from incredibly wealthy families. Stella felt as if she was living someone else's life as a three-course meal, cooked by the yacht's chef and served by the crew, was brought out. They drank copious amounts of wine and the linguine all'astice – linguine with tender lobster meat and a tomato and white wine sauce – was one of the best things Stella had ever tasted.

The relaxed party atmosphere continued until late and they spilled out onto the comfy seating around the jacuzzi on the top deck. Wine was swapped for cocktails and Stella had to pace herself. By one in the morning, her eyes had begun to glaze over and she decided to call it a night, leaving Chloe and Amber laughing and drinking with the Italians. She stumbled her way below deck and got lost in what seemed like a luxurious maze. One of the crew showed her the way to her room and left her with a nod and a '*buona notte*'. It briefly crossed her mind that the crew couldn't go to bed until they all had. It really was like a floating and very expensive hotel.

She stood for a moment, swaying in the middle of her room as she got her bearings. The glow from outside gave her enough light to safely cross the room to the windows. The lights of Naples glittered all the way along the coast to Pompeii. Somewhere hidden by the darkness was Mount Vesuvius.

Stella closed the blinds and slipped into her silk pyjama shorts and top. All she wanted to do was fall into bed, but she managed to stagger to the en suite, have a wee, clean her teeth and remove her make-up.

The lighting in the en suite was wonderful, her make-up-free face looking surprisingly fresh for the time of night. Lightly tanned and not bad for a week away from forty. She switched off the light. She'd heard nothing from Fern and wondered how she was getting on. She thumbed a quick message.

Hope you're okay and had a good first evening. S xx

It did feel strange thinking of Fern all on her own on Capri. As if they'd abandoned her. Despite the fun she'd had tonight, they should have said no to sailing on the yacht and all stayed together at Villa Giardino. That would have been the right thing to have done. Her own advice to Fern had been to put herself first for once, but even in her drunken state, Stella acknowledged that was exactly what *she* constantly did; being here when it was the last thing Fern wanted to do simply highlighted that. The guilt was momentary. Stella reasoned that worrying about things simply but a dampener on this adventure and soon enough she'd be back with Fern.

The bed was huge and feather-soft. She threw the cushions off and stretched out on the fresh silk sheets. She was pretty certain that Chloe would head to bed alone, but Amber... She hadn't been coy about snogging Desi, and Stella had left them on the deck whispering together. Amber had flirted with them all, not seeming to care which Italian she'd end up with. Amber reminded Stella of Fern when she was younger. Perhaps that was partly the reason why Amber was trying her hardest to distance herself from her mum; she could see a ghost of herself in Fern, the life she could end up leading if she wasn't careful. Not that Fern got pregnant on purpose; she and Paul hadn't been careful enough, like herself and Gary a couple of years later. One night of passion changed both of their lives forever. She hoped that Amber was more sensible and smart when it came to spending the night with Desi. She hoped Chloe was too. They had an open relationship and Stella had laid it on thick about unprotected sex, its risks and outcomes. She reckoned she'd scared Chloe silly, but rather that than another teen pregnancy and her becoming a grandmother just as she turned forty. The idea of being a grandparent before she even felt middle-aged filled her with fear.

Maybe their girls were more worldly-wise than she and Fern had been. Or weren't idiotically irresponsible. That was how her own parents had described Stella's predicament of getting pregnant young with someone she wasn't actually in love with.

Her mind wouldn't switch off and let her sleep. Winning the Lottery had given her more to worry about than she could ever have imagined, from the decision of keeping her win private to who to tell and when to tell them. She wasn't sure why she'd kept the full truth from everyone. It had been a relief telling Luca earlier, liberating even, knowing there was now someone she could be honest with. The enormity of the win and how drastically it would change her life worried her – she hoped it would be for the better, but she was aware that money didn't necessarily make people happy. It felt simpler to keep some things to herself, to allow her the time to come to terms with it all.

It was also time to make things right with Fern. Turning forty would have been a pivotal moment in her life without a Lottery win, but the two combined... It was time Fern knew the truth about Paul. Stella couldn't continue to let her live a lie, however much she'd end up hurting Fern in the process. The fact that Amber was aware of his infidelity only accentuated the need for someone to be open and truthful with her...

Stella curled up in a foetal position, willing sleep to put a stop to her anxiety. Her head throbbed. Her eyelids felt heavy. She let them close, longing to drift off into a dreamless sleep...

Buzz buzz buzz.

She groaned, but then was struck by a pang of worry about Jacob. She reached out and fumbled for her phone on the bedside table. She squinted at the bright light in the darkness of the bedroom. There was a message, but not from Rhod.

Paul.

A different kind of worry wrapped itself around her as she clicked on the message.

You awake? Can't stop thinking about you.

She reread the message, the feeling that she'd tried hard to bury over the last few months tingling the length of her body. It suddenly felt hot in the dark, enclosed bedroom. She sent a quick reply.

Surely you meant to text Fern this?

Paul replied within seconds.

Nope. Meant for you. You know it was. I'm on my other phone.

Stella bit her lip.

I've told you before to stop messaging me.

I know you didn't really mean it. And what's the prob unless you're with her now?

If you mean your wife, no I'm not. It's late, everyone's gone to bed.

She decided not to mention that while she was on a yacht in a marina in Naples, Fern was still on Capri on her own. She hated that he'd had the audacity to message her and cursed herself for the fluttering in the pit of her stomach because he'd been thinking about her. She was certain that he was drunk; he'd probably been out at the pub with mates and just got home to an empty house. He must be alone if he was messaging her. With Fern away for two weeks, she imagined he would jump at the opportunity to bring a woman back. She wasn't jealous; she mostly wished that he would leave her alone, but there was still a tiny part of her that was glad of the attention, despite guilt twisting her insides. So much guilt. She knew she needed to deal with this and make things right with Fern. Not that it would ever be right once the truth was out. She didn't want to hurt her, but Paul hadn't just cheated with her; there were other women too. If she was in Fern's position, she'd want to know what was really going on. Maybe then Fern would have the motivation to move on and make a better life for herself, even if that meant an end to their friendship.

She glanced at her phone. He hadn't sent another message. Maybe he was actually listening for once and had realised how wrong it was to message her when she was on holiday with his wife. Her best friend.

Stella put the phone back on the bedside table and rolled over, desperately wanting to get to sleep but uncertain how she now could.

Her mobile buzzed again.

She sighed but immediately grabbed it.

Another message from Paul. She clicked on it.

In bed are you?;-) So am I. As you can see, I'm thinking about you.

She stared at the photo he'd sent. Perspiration slid between her breasts. Her heart thumped. Everything about this was so very wrong, but as her heart battered her chest and her hand slipped beneath her silky pyjama shorts, she couldn't help but acknowledge the rush of excitement, despite the wrongness of it all.

17

FERN

The sunshine streamed into the room, casting a golden-green light through the translucent leaves that framed the window. Fern yawned and stretched, thinking back to the evening before and one of the best dinners she'd ever eaten. The company had matched it too. Matteo filled her thoughts, with his smooth deep voice and booming laughter. She mulled over the late-night conversation they'd had after everyone else had gone to bed.

The fluttering in Fern's chest morphed into a tingling warmth that spread throughout her body. The more she thought about him, the more the feeling intensified, along with her guilt when her thoughts turned to Paul. She hurriedly flung the bedcover off, padded to the en suite and ran the bath. The tub was positioned so she could gaze across the bedroom to the leafy view through the balcony doors. She sank into the warm scented water and relished not just the peace but the relaxed nature of the place. There was no need to rush anything. Back home, she'd have a quick shower in the morning and plough straight into her day, whether that involved going to work or cleaning the house.

She submerged herself beneath the water, the rush of warmth

enveloping her. She re-emerged, wiping water from her face and squeezing out the excess from her hair. If she believed her wayward thoughts about Matteo would be cleansed, she was sorely mistaken. The idea of seeing him today and spending more time with him filled her with joy, she just needed to remind herself she was a guest and nothing more.

Fern got dried and dressed in a white maxi skirt with a capped-sleeved saffron-yellow blouse which was comfortable and flattering. Matteo had mentioned a walking tour of Anacapri to find places to sketch, so she put on her comfy slip-on trainers.

Before heading downstairs, she checked her phone and found a lovely long message from Ruby, plus a short one from Stella sent at silly o'clock last night. She sent quick replies to them both, saying how much she was looking forward to seeing Ruby in a few days, and reassuring Stella that she'd had a super first evening.

Breakfast was on the terrace overlooking the pool. Matteo's housekeeper, Ana, brought Fern fresh orange juice and a toasted sourdough bruschetta topped with buffalo mozzarella and tomatoes drizzled with basil pesto. She was one of the last to eat. The German couple finished their breakfast and wished her a good morning as they walked past. She spied Edith already in the garden with a paintbrush in her hand, making the most of the morning light.

Matteo was nowhere to be seen, but just as she popped the last bite of bruschetta into her mouth, she heard him. She wiped the crumbs away and downed the remainder of the orange juice. He was somewhere in the garden talking to Arthur and hidden by the lush foliage.

Fern glanced at her watch; it was nearly time to go. She headed back upstairs and tucked the sketchbook Matteo had given her in her bag.

* * *

The group split up, a few into the heart of Anacapri with Matteo, while Edith, Fern, Arthur and a couple of the others walked along the Via Migliera, a paved lane that meandered past farmhouses and vineyards. Part of her wished they'd all stayed together. She realised with dismay it was because she wanted to spend more time with Matteo, but having been invited by Edith, she felt it was right to stick with her. Perhaps that was a good thing; Matteo was a distraction. She gave herself a stern talking-to, deciding her confusing feelings were simply because she'd been swept up in the romance of the retreat and the glamour of Capri.

'I adore the idea of being able to walk in the footsteps of the Romans,' Edith said, as they walked from the sunshine into the shade of trees. 'The sense of history this island has just takes my breath away. I think that's why I love Italy and this island so much: its beauty combined with a colourful past and the most delicious food and drink. Heaven!'

Although it had been completely by chance that they'd come to Capri, Fern couldn't think of anywhere that would have topped it. Even with the tension that bristled between her and Amber, the island itself had a calming effect. Perhaps she'd been naive to think that being somewhere different would help their relationship, but at least it had given her a chance to pause and re-evaluate.

The pace was set by the slowest of the group, but even at eighty, Arthur was still surprisingly sprightly. It felt good to slow down and allow time to soak up the surroundings. Fern caught snatches of blue sea between the trees, but it was only when they reached the end of the path and it opened out that she could see the expanse of the Tyrrhenian Sea shimmering in the morning sun.

They sat in the shade beneath trees and took out their sketch-books. Fern was certain she wouldn't be able to do the view justice, but as her pencil stokes began to fill the page, she stopped caring about the end result. It felt unbelievably good to reconnect with her creative side. She loved simply sitting and noticing things that perhaps she would have missed if she hadn't taken the time to commit the surroundings to memory through her drawing: yachts crisscrossing the blue sea leaving trails of white in their wake and the Punta Carena lighthouse perched on a craggy, green-topped rock.

They sat in companionable silence. Edith smiled contentedly as she ran her pencil across the cream paper of her sketchbook. People came and went; it was a popular spot, the walk worth it for the view alone.

Fern lost track of time. She was so absorbed in her sketch, she barely noticed Arthur and the other two guests heading off. Fern was happy to remain with Edith and put the finishing touches to her sketch, but when Edith announced, 'I don't know about you, but I've worked up an appetite,' she realised how hungry she was, despite such a good breakfast.

Edith tucked her sketchbook away and slung her bag across her shoulders. Her loose patterned trousers reminded Fern of the blue and white tiles in Villa Giardino. The thought of it being empty made Fern wonder where Stella and the girls were. Somewhere out there on the endless blue sea. No doubt they were gazing at a view to rival this one.

Fern packed her sketchbook away too and followed Edith back up the path into the sunshine, which was welcome after the shade of the trees. She'd been sitting still and concentrating for longer than she realised, so it felt good to work out the ache in her shoulders as they walked.

The restaurant wasn't far away and, surrounded by vineyards and gardens, it had views to equal the one they'd just sketched. They were greeted and shown to a table beneath a pergola. The days here seemed to revolve around food – not that she minded when everything was so fresh and delicious. She would love to have the opportunity to travel and try different cuisines. Holidays over the years had revolved around the family and it had always fallen to her to look after and entertain the girls. She'd never been able to fully relax around the pool, her attention only half on her book as she'd kept an eye on Ruby and Amber. Even on the few holidays just she and Paul had had together abroad, he'd always insisted they went somewhere that served British food. It was nothing like what she was experiencing here.

Fern could have eaten everything on the menu, but knowing how well they got fed at Il Ritiro d'Arte, she opted for a seafood salad. She wasn't disappointed when it arrived: a generous plateful of octopus, large juicy prawns and mussels on a bed of rocket drizzled with olive oil and lemon.

Edith's smile widened as her plate of paccheri pasta with octopus and tomatoes was placed in front of her. 'I have many favourite restaurants on the island, but this place is a gem.' She swept her hand around at the pergola-covered terrace, where most of the tables were filled with people eating and drinking. It felt far removed from the bustle of the piazzetta and had the bonus of a sea view, a soothing palette of green and blue. Even with lots of tourists, it evoked a sense of peace.

Fern chewed a mussel and relished the salty zestiness. Italian food at home was usually a takeaway pizza or overcooked pasta. She sipped her crisp white wine and happily listened to Edith.

'What I love most about being here – apart from the obvious things,' Edith continued, 'is how much I enjoy getting to know other people, people like you, who I probably wouldn't have met otherwise.'

'And that was only by chance.'

'True. If Maya had come with me, it's unlikely we'd have had that conversation on the boat over and you wouldn't be here now.'

'Perhaps fate intervened.'

'Perhaps it did. I feel you were meant to be here.'

Fern knocked her glass of wine against Edith's. 'I do too. I was only thinking earlier how desperate I was for a holiday like this and to have time to myself. It's taken me being here to realise it. Initially, I felt guilty, not wanting to go on the yacht with the others, but I made the right decision.'

'It's not what you'd choose to do?'

Fern laughed, but it felt empty. She skewered a prawn and looked up at Edith. 'They're on a yacht with a bunch of young rich guys, something my twenty-one-year-old daughter is more than comfortable with, but I'm not.'

'But you were okay with her going?'

'God, that makes me sound like a terrible mother.'

'I didn't mean it like that. And she's an adult able to make her own decisions. Would you have even been able to stop her?'

'No, of course not. And if I'd even suggested she shouldn't go, she'd have hated me even more.'

'Oh dear, it sounds as if there's an awful lot of tension between the two of you.'

Fern popped the prawn into her mouth. In a short space of time, Edith had managed to quickly understand her and Amber's relationship.

'So I'm assuming you're married?' Edith asked as she stuck her fork into a pasta tube.

Fern nodded and said 'uh-huh' through her mouthful of the firm and succulent prawn drenched with lemon and herbs.

'I presume you didn't go on the yacht because of him?'

'It didn't seem suitable, no. I'm pretty sure he wouldn't have been thrilled with the idea.'

'But if it wasn't for him?' Edith asked slowly.

'Honestly, an art retreat has far more appeal. When I was younger, I'd have jumped at the chance of a yacht full of sexy Italians. I think I'm getting old.'

Edith nodded and chewed her mouthful of food. She kept her gaze on Fern as she sipped her wine. 'I've been where you are.'

Fern frowned. 'What do you mean?'

'Unhappy in a marriage.'

'I'm not...' She trailed off, suddenly feeling hot and flustered. She was unsure how to answer; unsure how she actually felt. Edith's words had taken her by surprise, but they seemed filled with genuine concern, unlike the upsetting conversation she'd had the other day with Amber. Fern stabbed her fork into a mussel. 'I'd rather we didn't talk about this.'

'I'm so sorry. I'm always too nosy. I apologise.'

Edith changed the subject and talked about her favourite places on Capri and mainland Italy while they finished their lunch. Afterwards, they walked back along the Via Migliera in companionable silence. Fern appreciated that Edith hadn't tried to continue the uncomfortable conversation, but the sense of unease her words had evoked remained.

18

FERN

Fern reflected on what Edith had said all the way back, a stark and undeniable truth dawning on her. It had been there for a while, buried deep inside. Amber had ignited something the other day and Stella's silence on the subject spoke volumes. Now Edith, who barely knew her, had asked a question like that.

Edith pushed open the villa's large wooden door and they stepped into the cool entrance hall. Fern's silence on the way back had obviously given Edith the impression that she wanted to be left alone, but as Edith headed for the stairs, Fern caught hold of her arm.

'You were right about me not being happy,' Fern said.

Edith turned to her. 'I was?'

She looked at her with such compassion, Fern could hardly hold back her tears.

Instead of continuing upstairs, Edith hooked her arm in Fern's. 'Come and sit with me in my favourite spot.'

Edith led Fern through the villa and outside to the furthest reaches of the garden. Shaded by feathery ferns, there was a tiny stone patio with just a wooden bench facing the trees that screened the edge of the garden. The sea was hidden from view, but the sky was a clear deep blue between the leaves. They sat together on the bench and gazed out. Fern drank everything in: the birds swooping between the branches, the trickle of water from one of the fountains hidden among the foliage; a butterfly fluttering around a flower, its cream wings translucent in the sunlight. Large stone pots filled with thyme, oregano and lemon verbena were dotted around the paving.

'This is the place I come to contemplate, to think, to make decisions,' Edith eventually said.

'You don't paint here?'

'No, it's a place for sitting and thinking. Or talking.' She gently nudged Fern's arm. 'I've asked you such personal questions, yet I haven't been completely truthful about myself.'

'Oh?'

Edith sighed. 'For someone who understands how people tick, I've not only managed to get myself into a complicated relationship, but it feels as if I'm floundering in the dark over it.'

'Why's that?'

'I told Matteo that Maya was unwell, that's why she couldn't come, but that wasn't the truth of it...' Edith breathed deeply and stared out through the trees. Sunspots and freckles decorated her wrinkled hands which were clasped in her lap. Fern waited for her to continue. 'The separate bedrooms was an expensive pretence and one I was more than happy to fork out for if it meant we were able to be together.'

An understanding of Edith's predicament slowly dawned on Fern. 'So it's your partner who wants to keep your relationship secret?'

'She had second thoughts about coming here with me in case her husband questioned her reasons... I've been in love with her for more than ten years. Perhaps she felt coming on holiday to a place I love and that I wanted to share with her was too much.' Edith sighed. 'Even if we were keeping up the pretence.' She shrugged, but there was sadness in her eyes. 'We've been friends for a long time but only together for the last four years. I wouldn't dream of asking her to leave her husband, I'm not even sure if I'd want her to. But I want to spend time with her, proper time, rather than snatched moments back home pretending to be something we're not to keep our secret, well, secret.'

'That must be hard.' Fern's heart went out to Edith.

'No good comes of falling in love with someone who's in a relationship with someone else, even if the love is returned. There's rarely a happy ever after.' She turned to face Fern. 'But what I asked you before, questioning if you were happy in your marriage or not, came from a place of understanding. I see in you the same thing I see in Maya. I know she's not happy with her husband, but she stays because it's the done thing and the scandal it would cause, not just for leaving her husband of fifty odd years but to leave him for another woman, well... she can't do it, which is fine, it's her decision and her life, but she'll spend the rest of it living a lie and not being entirely happy. Sometimes the hard questions need to be asked because they help us to move on – *if* that's what we want to do. When you said you were unhappy before, did you mean with your husband?'

Fern gazed thoughtfully across the compact terrace. The pockets of green were soothing against the taupe-grey stone and deeper rust-red of the terracotta pots.

'Partly, yes...' How could she describe how she felt? 'But I also feel trapped by responsibility and what's expected of me. It feels like I haven't done anything with my life, that the last twenty years have passed by in a flash.'

'Raising children is most definitely doing something with your life. One could argue that it's the most important thing one could do.'

'You said you haven't got children?'

'Oh, where to start with that.' She shook her head. 'I was married, but I left my husband because I fell in love with a woman.' She glanced sideways at Fern. 'I'm not suggesting you do anything as drastic as that.' Her laughter filled the sweet-scented air of the herb garden like a tinkling bell. 'I knew what I wanted from early on, I just didn't have the guts to follow my convictions. My husband was a decent man and I married him because it was what my parents expected of me. It was what it was like in those days. And, as I said, he was nice. We were friends and got on, but I knew it was a sham from the beginning.'

'Did he?'

'Perhaps not initially. He wanted children and I didn't. There was so much about our relationship that didn't work, not least because I wasn't attracted to him. I liked him, a lot, as a person, as a friend. We still talk. He remarried and is very happy. He has children and grandchildren.' Edith's voice was matter-of-fact, but Fern noticed her lips purse. 'It's as if history is repeating itself in many ways with Maya. She has a husband as I did.' She gave Fern a meaningful look. 'Except rather than being a young twenty-something and realising that she likes women and not men, she's in her seventies, has grown-up children and has been married for decades. I understand it's not the same situation at all, which is why I'm happy to go to great lengths to keep up the pretence of us being just good friends.'

She looked wistful and full of melancholy. Fern could only imagine the heartache of not being able to be with the person you loved. But at the same time she wished she had such strong feelings for someone. To be that in love, that passionate about spending time with a person... It was her turn to sigh.

'The question you need to ask yourself is, do you love your husband?'

Fern leaned back on the bench. She didn't think she'd ever been asked such a direct and personal question.

Edith must have seen the shock on her face. 'I always have known just how to put my foot in it. I was a counsellor for my whole working life, mostly dealing with addiction, but I've always been fascinated by people's relationships – married couples in particular. I have a friend back home who's a marriage counsellor and I love talking to her. Even now I'm retired, I'm still fascinated by what makes people tick.'

Fern barely knew Edith, but somehow it felt easier to be open with her than to talk to Amber or even Stella. She didn't want their judgement, or for them to weigh in with what they thought. Edith had the benefit of distance. She didn't know Paul; she didn't even know Fern beyond what she'd gleaned over the past twenty-four hours. Fern had been upset when she'd first brought the subject up at lunch, but Edith had made her really think about her situation and it was a relief to be honest with her.

'I envy you the kind of love you have for Maya. I may be married, but I don't think I've ever experienced that intense feeling for someone.'

'If you're uncertain, then no, you haven't.'

They were both quiet. Fern found it unnerving to be so open, but it was also liberating. Perhaps it was Edith's easy manner and her experience as a counsellor which made Fern want to open up. Either way, it was good to talk. In the back of her mind, these two weeks were a chance for her to get her head straight about what she wanted to do with her life now Ruby and Amber were fully-fledged adults.

'My friend asked me the other day if I was happy,' Fern said slowly, filling the quietness of the sheltered garden.

'And how did you answer?'

Fern snorted. 'By saying I wasn't unhappy.'

'Oh dear me,' Edith said, shaking her head.

'I know how that sounds.' She breathed in the fresh scent of the herbs. 'I'm not content and I'm uncertain about many things in my life, but that's more about me, I think, than my husband.'

'Hmm, I wouldn't be so sure about that. A marriage takes two people to make it work. Personally, I think happiness is of utmost importance. You sound unhappy. I assume you want to change things. How does your husband feel?'

Fern shrugged.

'You don't talk?'

'Not about stuff like that. And whenever I do try to turn the conversation around to us and our relationship, he gets cross and defensive.'

'It's hard to start those conversations that we know are going to be difficult or potentially painful.' She patted Fern's hand where it rested on the bench between them. 'I need to have one with Maya when I return home. I wish she really had been unwell. That would have been simpler to deal with. Of course, I'd have been upset that she was missing out on being here, but it wouldn't have changed our relationship. Perhaps guilt has finally caught up with her...' Edith gave a thin smile, but tears looked ready to spill. 'I wanted to share this villa with her. It holds a special place in my heart.'

'I can see why.'

'And as for you, no one deserves to go through life unhappy, Fern. I felt the same when I was married, as if life was passing me by, wishing I was with someone else.'

'I don't necessarily want to be with anyone else, I'm just uncertain about everything. And I'm definitely not gay,' Fern said, returning a weak smile.

Edith laughed. 'I didn't think you were!' She leaned in conspiratorially. 'That much is obvious from the way you look at Matteo.'

Heat rushed to Fern's cheeks.

'Don't be embarrassed. He's a handsome man – even I can see that.' She chuckled. 'I'd be surprised if you weren't attracted to him. He looks at you in the same way. And as a gay woman – and I mean nothing untoward by this – I'm not surprised that he finds you attractive too.'

Fern was lost for words. She'd been enjoying Matteo's company, but had it been that obvious? She'd had plenty to drink yesterday evening – they all had – the wine had flowed and the conversation too, both around the table and later when it had been just her and Matteo. They'd stayed up late, far later than she usually did. She'd turned into a bed-at-ten kind of person. Even on nights out, if she managed to stay out to eleven, all she could think about was getting home and going to bed. Perhaps it was the knock-on effect from having twins and barely sleeping for the first five years of their lives. It had been insanely tough and had put her off having any more children. Now she was conditioned to early starts.

Going to bed early was one of life's little pleasures and she didn't mean with Paul. She liked that he usually went to bed later than her. Many times, he'd come back from the pub tipsy and horny and she'd pretend to be asleep. He wasn't a quiet drunk. He'd slam the front door, stumble upstairs, burp in the en suite, flush the toilet, crash into bed, his hands slithering around her, dipping beneath her pyjamas. She'd ignore his advances and hope he'd leave her alone. But then the night before they left for Capri, hadn't she been upset when he'd fallen asleep before she'd got into bed? Why was that? She bit her lip. Did she want him to remember what he'd be missing while she was away and he was home alone, remind him why they were together and that once they couldn't keep their hands off each other?

'Once again, I feel I may have overstepped with my comments.' Edith's warm voice pulled Fern back to the present and the picturesque garden.

'No, you haven't. I was just thinking how things have been with my husband. If I'm feeling like this, I can only imagine he must have similar thoughts.'

'He's faithful?'

'I, er...'

'Now I really have said too much. I'm sorry.'

'You know what, don't be. You're not the first person to put the idea in my head. My daughter said something earlier in the week. Perhaps it's a question that I've feared for a long time.'

'Because you fear he is unfaithful?'

Was that the truth? She never allowed thoughts like that to have airtime, although of course they'd flashed through her mind on occasion when he worked late, stayed away overnight or came back from the pub far later than it closed, saying he'd been drinking at a mate's. He had plenty of opportunity to cheat if he wanted to.

'In many ways, I'm less fearful about him having been unfaithful than I am about the reality that I've been living a lie my whole adult life.'

19

STELLA

Stella basked in the gentle warmth of the sun as she lay on the deck of the yacht. The cushions behind her propped her up just enough to see the view without having to move a muscle. They'd left Naples that morning and were now anchored off the Amalfi Coast, where, beyond the glittering azure blue of the sea, Positano was bathed in sunshine. White, cream, honey-yellow, russet-red and coral villas studded the steep hillside, while craggy ash-grey cliffs softened by olive-green foliage soared above the picturesque town.

She felt as if she was in a bubble, the sounds around her distant, the occasional deep voice of someone speaking in Italian, the soft giggles of Chloe and Amber posing at the front of the deck for Instagram-worthy shots with Positano as the backdrop, their tans showcased in tiny bikinis.

Despite the heat on her skin, the pop of colour from the surrounding vista and the gentle movement of the yacht, nothing seemed quite real, as if she was leading someone else's life. The last twenty years had been a whirlwind: life with the kids and the complication of two failed marriages. Work had been her salvation, building her career and achieving things for herself, by herself. Not having to depend on anyone else, either her parents or a bloke, was her greatest achievement. That had all been down to hard work and juggling being a single mum with ruthless ambition. And then, with the Lottery, luck had played its part.

This could be her reality, not necessarily sailing around on a yacht, but how easy would it be to swap her life in a small town in the south-west of England for a slice of heaven on the Amalfi Coast, or anywhere else she chose to go. She knew it wasn't that straight-forward, not with Jacob at the age he was, but there was so much she could do to make their lives better. She didn't have to completely uproot them; she had the means now to buy a holiday villa somewhere hot, somewhere far from home, a place to escape to.

'I thought you might be thirsty.'

A deep voice with an Italian accent broke through her thoughts. She looked up into Luca's grinning face. He was holding a turquoise-coloured cocktail topped with a maraschino cherry and a slice of lemon.

'A little early in the day, isn't it?'

Luca pulled a face. 'Never too early.'

Her fingers brushed his as she took the glass from him. 'Thank you.'

He was the eldest of the group, somewhere in his mid-thirties, Stella reckoned. A little younger than she was. She'd got to the age where she noticed an age gap that wouldn't have bothered her just a few years ago. The last thing she wanted to do was fixate on him being younger than her, yet getting older had been playing on her mind for a while.

Luca slid onto the daybed next to her, a bottle of beer clasped in his hand.

'It is a good spot for Instagram,' he said, nodding towards the girls. 'You don't join them?'

'I'm not all that fussed about splashing myself across social media. And I'm not sure Chloe would be too happy about her mum being in the picture.' Stella raised her glass and took a sip.

'Sister maybe.'

'You're a smooth talker.'

He put his hand to his chest and pretended to look abashed. 'I speak the truth.'

'You're very kind.'

Stella was drawn to him, much like she suspected he was drawn to her. The girls had been flirting with all four of them – and a couple of the young male crew members too – but Luca reserved his attention for her. They were closest in age after all. It also must have been apparent to him after spending time with Chloe and Amber just how young they were. She'd forgotten what it was like to be that age with no responsibilities, just a desire to have fun and to be swept up in the romance of being young, free and single. She envied the way they didn't seem to worry about their actions, while she was overtly conscious of where her flirtation with Luca would lead. She sighed. She was getting strung up by overthinking rather than simply having fun. Wasn't that what she'd promised herself this holiday to Capri would be all about?

Paul had stirred things up again with his late-night drunken message. She should have put a stop to it a long time ago. Although when she thought about it, she had. It had been a one-time thing. Twice if she counted the night they'd spent together when she was seventeen. But that had been *before* he'd got together with Fern. She was kidding herself that it didn't count, not when Fern was unaware of it and not when they'd repeated that night while he was married to her best friend. And even though they hadn't slept together since, the messaging and flirtation between them had got out of control. Her life had been entwined with Paul's and Fern's for two decades. Time to sever the link. She clenched her fists. She couldn't lose

Fern; their friendship meant too much, and she knew how that sounded when she'd treated her friend the way she had.

She shifted on the daybed, suddenly uneasy about where her thoughts had drifted to. The sun was at the hottest part of the day, caressing her bare skin with its comfortable heat. They had both fallen silent, lying half propped on the cushions, their shoulders touching. Stella was only wearing a bikini with a sheer cover-up over the top and Luca was just in shorts. His smooth chest was in her eyeline, his arm resting on his tanned muscled leg. She breathed in his scent, her heart fluttering. She always had liked the chase, the flirting, the bit that came before a relationship. This was what she enjoyed and was good at, getting to know someone, chatting, the thrill of building up to the first kiss and eventually the first night together. It was once the honeymoon period was over she struggled. Perhaps she needed to remain single, although she couldn't continue messing around like a lovestruck teenager after she was forty, could she?

She turned slightly to face Luca, conscious that the movement had emphasised her cleavage. His eyes drifted downwards, then flicked up and rested on her face. He grinned. She knew exactly what she was doing.

'I can't thank you enough for inviting us with you.'

'I'm glad you said yes.'

'We'd have never done anything like this otherwise.'

'No?' He frowned. 'Even with all your new money?'

Stella wrinkled her nose.

'It is nothing to be ashamed about, being wealthy, even if many people make us feel that way.'

'Oh, I'm not ashamed, I'm just not used to it. I've done okay for myself, but I've always had to be careful. I've never been able to treat myself without worrying about it.'

'You have no husband?' His words were loaded.

Stella snorted. 'There have been two waste-of-space husbands, but not any longer. It's just me, Chloe, of course, and I have a thirteen-year-old son too.'

'So you deserve to not worry.' He looked at her with a gleam in his eyes.

'What about you?' She wanted to turn the conversation away from herself. 'No wife, girlfriend, kids?'

'I have never been married, no.' He looked away from her for a moment, gazing across the deck to where Chloe and Amber were laughing with the other three guys. 'I have a four-year-old son with an ex-girlfriend. We weren't serious, but it happened and I support them.'

'You're not in their lives?'

'She moved back to Milano to be close to her family. I spend most of my time in Roma – it's where the business is, where I work.'

'When you're not sailing along the Amalfi Coast.' She gave him a sly grin.

'Ha, *si*. That is true.' He shifted on the daybed and rested his arm along the back of the cushions behind her. 'I like my life,' he continued smoothly. 'I don't want to settle down. She knew that from the beginning, before she got pregnant. Not that I regret that happening either.'

'You see your son?'

'I'm in his life, yes.'

His fingers brushed her shoulder. She snuggled back into him, resting into the warm crook of his chest. He smelt delicious, which made her glad that she'd spritzed on the Fiori di Capri perfume she'd bought from Carthusia. The amount of money she'd spent since arriving on Capri was more than she'd ever spent on anything apart from her car and her house. But this was all luxury stuff, wonderful but unnecessary, unlike an MOT or getting the boiler fixed.

Stella stretched her legs out. She sensed Luca watching. Goodness, she loved flirting; she loved the way he was paying her attention. It briefly crossed her mind what her daughter would think, but then Chloe was still at an age where she believed the world revolved around her. Stella was pretty sure she'd either be oblivious or would choose to completely ignore it. She was living her best life too. Eighteen years old and her mum had won the Lottery, and here they were living it up on a yacht. It was quite different from her own teen years with Friday evenings out in Bristol, snogging a bloke in Ritzy's and ending the night eating chips from a kebab shop outside the Hippodrome.

'I know I'm treating Chloe with this holiday, but my worry with the money is I'm going to be doing everything for me. I don't want to be selfish. I need to think about the kids.'

'But Chloe is grown up, no?'

Stella snorted. 'As grown up as an eighteen-year-old who still relies on me doing her washing when she comes back from uni can be.'

Luca laughed, but Stella wondered if he actually understood. She imagined he'd never done his own washing in his life. They were floating on a luxury yacht with a crew of sixteen at their beck and call. It was quite the existence. No wonder he didn't want to give it up for the restrictions of family life.

'Where's your son now?' Luca asked.

'With his dad. It's a school holiday and they're coming out next week for the last couple of days to celebrate my birthday.'

'Ah, happy birthday for next week.' He snuggled closer until his hand was dangling tantalisingly close to her bikini-clad breast. 'The money will give you freedom if you don't let it worry you.' His breath tickled her ear. He was so close, so warm against her.

'It's not so much having the money that worries me, although it's a huge adjustment, and besides coming here I haven't really done much with it yet. It's more what other people will think and how they will behave, that's my concern. I've told very few people. Not even my exes know yet.'

'I am in a different situation to you. I've always had money, but I understand it could be stressful. And it's not selfish to think of yourself for once.'

'It feels like that's all I'm doing at the moment.'

His fingers connected with her skin, caressing the curve of her breast. 'Do you want to go to the jacuzzi?' Luca's deep voice was soft and sensuous in her ear. 'It'll be quieter.'

The fluttering in her chest and the warmth spreading through her intensified as they took their drinks and wandered through the inside lounge area to the top deck at the stern. The attention of a good-looking guy just wanting fun was what she craved.

They swapped the view of Positano for the glittering Tyrrhenian Sea dotted with boats and yachts anchored on the azure water. Somewhere out there was Capri and Fern. As she took Luca's hand and stepped down into the warm water of the jacuzzi, she got another wave of guilt that she'd left Fern on her own. At least from her text this morning, it sounded as if she was enjoying herself.

Luca kissing her stopped her thoughts in their tracks. She slid her arms around his waist, tugging him closer and kissing him back. The water was warm, almost as delicious as the feeling of his hands caressing her skin, gliding across her hips, her waist, up her sides, only slowing when they reached her bikini top... When they'd been lounging on the daybed she'd been thinking how wonderful that initial spark with someone was, the thrill of the first kiss and where that would lead. This was what she'd wanted; the excitement of a blossoming relationship, one that she knew wouldn't go beyond her time in Capri. He'd been honest with her – he was a player, with no desire to settle down. He was young, good-looking and rich. He probably picked up a woman in each marina. She knew the score and yet she didn't care one little bit...

He took her hand and led her from the jacuzzi towards the lower deck and the bedrooms. She knew she wasn't going to say no. She didn't want to. Right now she didn't even care if the girls found out. She was hardly ancient. God, was Fern missing out. She had given up all of this because she was married and worried about what it would look like to Paul. Well, fuck Paul. She'd make that whole mess right. But not now. Right that moment, nothing else mattered.

They didn't make it as far as the bed. Her wet bikini and his shorts landed on the soft-pile carpet. He pulled her down with him on the sofa. The blinds were open and it briefly crossed her mind as she slid on top of him that the view on to the deck towards the Amalfi Coast was utterly spectacular.

20

FERN

After her heart-to-heart with Edith, Fern wanted to phone Paul and have a long-overdue talk. Everyday life got in the way back home and whenever Fern tried to raise the subject, Paul would shut her down. Come to think of it, when was the last time he'd told her he loved her? When was the last time she'd said it to him? They definitely had long ago.

In the early days, there had been lust and possibly love; they were certainly drawn to one another. They'd laughed together and had enjoyed each other's company, even if they'd rarely been sober. And then of course things got serious pretty quickly. Paul hadn't left her in the lurch, pregnant and on her own; he'd committed himself to her and the girls. Had she loved him because of that? Over the years, had she ignored her underlying uncertainty about his faithfulness because he hadn't let her down when she'd needed him the most? Was any of that a good enough reason to stay with someone?

* * *

The rest of the guests and Matteo returned from their walking tour of Anacapri by late afternoon and as everyone had eaten out at lunchtime, no one wanted another big meal. The chef whipped up a warm salad of zucchini, avocado and squid and Fern ate hers on her balcony, soaking up the peace and watching the golden light of the sunset turn to a dusky mauve beyond the trees. She felt subdued over Paul, conscious that her underlying sadness was due to feeling unloved, undervalued too, yet she hadn't had the guts to do anything about it. On top of that, she felt pathetic for wanting to avoid Matteo because of Edith's comment about their mutual attraction. She didn't want to admit that Edith was right. She only had to look at Matteo to feel funny inside. A smile, a brush of his hand on her arm, was enough to make her feel giddy.

Coming to Capri had seemed like the perfect opportunity to get her head in order about what she wanted to do now Ruby and Amber had left home. For too long she'd put off making decisions about her future. But the more she thought about the conversations she'd had with Stella and Amber over the last few days, and now Edith, the more confused she felt.

She went to bed early, partly because her head was thick with worry, partly to avoid ending up alone with Matteo again. Confusion twisted around her as she lay on the bed, wrapped in cool sheets. Moonlight glided through the balcony doors and across the tiled floor. The window opposite the bed was open and a breeze rustled the leaves, bringing with it the comforting scent of oregano.

Paul and their life seemed like a distant dream, almost as if she was wading through someone else's memories. Over the last year, she felt as if she'd noticed things more. She'd begun to question her own happiness and the point at which she was in her life, begun to look at Paul differently. Like really look at him. Not just the way he looked but how he behaved. To her in particular. There were warning signs galore, yet she'd tried to bury her worries, not wanting to rock the boat.

* * *

Despite going to bed early, troubling thoughts had kept Fern awake. She slept in late, grabbed a quick shower and headed downstairs the next day without drying her hair. She was the last one down for breakfast. She sat at a table on the patio overlooking the pool.

'Morning.' Matteo slid onto the seat opposite her.

A touch of anxiety about being alone with him again crept through Fern. She finished chewing and brushed the crumbs from her lips. 'I was really late down this morning, sorry.'

'There's no need to apologise. There's no such thing as late here.' He looked at her conspiratorially and lowered his voice. 'I don't know if it's an age thing, but as most guests are in their, um, twilight years we'll call it, they seem to wake up pretty damn early. A lie-in on a Sunday is my idea of heaven.' They met each other's eyes and he smiled. 'But the morning light is perfect for painting. We're set up by the fountain. I'm heading there now, but there's a spot saved for you. I hope you'll join us?'

'I'd love to, thank you.'

She absently chewed her mouthful of fresh bread and jam and watched him set off down the steps until he was hidden from sight by the ferns on the far side of the pool. Edith's words from the day before about the attraction she'd seen between Fern and Matteo returned. She was a guest, and as far as she could tell, he was warm, chatty and friendly with everyone. Perhaps Edith was reading more into it than was there, but there was no denying how Fern felt around him. That frisson of excitement, the anticipation of spending time with him, the thought of being alone with him... Heat rose from the pit of her stomach, spreading across her chest.

She finished her last bite of bread, downed the remainder of her latte and followed Matteo. The murmur of voices became louder as she wound her way through the garden. She loved everything about it: all the hidden areas with flashes of crimson from oriental poppies or the fresh white of daisies; peaceful spots with benches such as the herb garden and the one Edith called the butterfly terrace filled with butterfly-loving shrubs.

Everyone was set up on the large circular terrace, their easels surrounding the central fountain. It meant they were all together, yet looking out into the garden. Fern imagined it would be easy to zone out and feel like the only one there.

Edith smiled at Fern as she approached. Matteo greeted her and gestured to the free space next to Edith.

'Are you okay?' Edith asked under her breath, her eyes wide with concern, as Fern sat next to her. 'I hope I didn't upset you yesterday.'

'You really didn't. I just needed some thinking time.'

Fern stared at the blank sheet of creamy paper on her easel. She noticed that Edith was well underway with her painting, the view of the garden already taking shape in acrylic paint.

'Don't worry,' Matteo said, joining her. 'A blank page doesn't have to be scary. Look at the scene in front of you, but don't think of it as trees, shrubs and flowers, but lines, shapes and colours. Keep it small and don't worry about it being imperfect.'

Fern laughed. 'It will certainly be that.'

'Nature in its very self isn't perfect, so embrace that.'

'How do I even start?' Since arriving at the retreat she'd begun to feel her creativity return, but she was still uncertain she had the skills to match.

'Just focus on a small part of what's in front of you.' He pointed ahead of them, drawing Fern's eye. 'What about that lemon tree in the pot with the stone wall behind it? You can chalk it out first; that way it's not quite so daunting as starting with the paint. Think of it as experimenting and having fun. You don't have to get it right – just a sense of what you can see, the colours, the shapes. And I won't watch over you, I promise. But let me know if you need some guidance.'

He left her to go and speak to Arthur, but she was still aware of his presence as she tried to focus on the paper.

Edith smiled encouragingly. 'Matteo is a wonderful artist and an even better teacher. I've learnt so much from him because he's so generous with his time. He's thoughtful and constructive. It's a shame you're not here for longer.' Edith dipped her brush into a glossy bottle-green paint. She mixed in a dash of white until it was paler, resembling the colour of the leaves of the olive tree in front of her.

Fern turned her attention to the lemon tree. The pot was a coppery colour, large and curved, contrasting with the taupe-grey of the stone wall behind. The lemons were bright against the shiny green leaves, making Fern wonder how she could translate their freshness onto her blank page.

She picked up a piece of green chalk and decided to be brave. This had been her trouble all along, not saying yes to opportunities, not having the guts to shake up her life, to leave her job and do something she was actually passionate about. Spending time sketching yesterday had filled her with joy; it was such a simple pleasure, but one she'd truly missed. It really didn't matter if her first painting was a load of rubbish; it wouldn't be anything at all unless she tried.

Lightly sweeping the chalk across the page, Fern sketched the curved outline of the pot, the slender trunk of the tree and the rough shape of the stones. The lemons and the leaves would be the hardest to get right, so maybe they should be the last thing she focused on, or perhaps she should tackle them first. She hovered her chalk over the page, unsure what to do next.

'Remember what Matteo said.' Edith gestured at Fern's sketch, then towards the lemon tree. 'You only need the sense of it – let your creativity flow. It's in there somewhere.'

Fern smiled thinly. 'Yeah, buried beneath years' worth of having no confidence.'

'That will come again in time. Channel your sadness; turn it into something positive. I believe the best artists are the ones consumed by the most heartache.'

Fern turned to Edith. 'Oh?'

Edith swept her paintbrush around, gesturing to the lush garden and the grand villa. 'Even someone who lives in a place like this can be filled with sadness.' She glanced behind her. Fern followed her gaze to where Matteo was on the other side of the fountain talking to Arthur about his painting. She leaned closer to Fern. 'He's never said much, just hinted at it. On the surface, he seems content, but we both know how well we can hide our feelings of longing, disappointment and upset.'

Fern watched Matteo for a moment longer, wondering what his story was. She looked away, conscious that she was staring. Edith caught her eye and smiled.

'We're all striving to find happiness though,' Edith said with a sadness that made Fern wonder if she was thinking about Maya, unhappy with her husband back home while she was here, happy to be in a place she loved, yet disappointed not to be sharing it with the person she loved.

Fern sighed. Why did life have to be so damn complicated?

21

STELLA

Afternoon sex with Luca had been magnificent, leaving Stella relaxed and satisfied. When they returned to the main deck to join the others, Chloe and Amber were still sunbathing with Desi and Vincenzo, seemingly oblivious to Stella and Luca having even left. Only Giovanni gave them a knowing wink as they slid back onto the daybed together.

They left Positano where they'd anchored in the bay for the best part of the day and berthed for the night further along the coast at the Marina d'Arechi. Stella's good intentions of a quieter night were thwarted by an evening out drinking and eating at a restaurant on the quay before returning tipsy to *The Silver Spirit*. She refrained from more drinks on the deck and headed to her room instead.

Luca knocked on her door ten minutes later. After pinging Fern a quick message with a couple of photos of Positano, Stella switched off her phone, not wanting to be disturbed, even by Fern, and she certainly didn't want to risk an unwanted message from Paul again. Luca proved to be a mighty fine distraction from her worries, seducing her slowly this time, enabling her to think of nothing else until sleep took over a couple of hours later.

* * *

The next day, they sailed back along the coast and anchored off the town of Amalfi to have lunch on shore before exploring its cobbled lanes and sun-drenched piazzettas. They returned to *The Silver Spirit* with the intention of having a siesta, although it was obvious from Luca's wink and the way his hands teased up her sides that he meant to do rather more.

But Stella couldn't leave it any longer to phone Fern. She'd replied to her message from the day before with a stunning photo of the art retreat's Mediterranean garden and it sounded as if she was having fun, but Stella wanted to make sure before joining Luca. She whispered that she'd meet him in her room and retreated to the empty jacuzzi deck.

Worry gripped Stella as she pressed Fern's number. She perched on the end of a sun lounger and gazed at the coastline zipping by as the phone rang. She should have called her yesterday, but then Luca had happened and all thoughts of anything else had vanished. She felt horribly guilty – a feeling that seemed to constantly follow her around when she thought about her friend.

'Hey, Stella! I've been meaning to phone you, there just hasn't been a chance.'

Relief flooded through her at how upbeat Fern sounded.

'Same here; been thinking about you loads though. The photo's gorgeous. You've been enjoying it there then?'

'Oh, I love it. I can't put into words how amazing this place is.'

The knot of tension in Stella's chest loosened a little. 'I'm so glad. So you're not regretting staying?'

'No, not at all. Don't get me wrong, I miss you guys, but it's been so good to be immersed in creativity.'

'And the people are nice?'

'Yeah, they're mostly a lot older but lovely. Edith is... I don't know, I feel like I've known her forever somehow. She's easy to talk to. And the place itself – I thought where we were staying was grand. How are you getting on?'

'It's not the same without you, but...' Stella laughed. 'This yacht, this lifestyle, is just... wow.'

'How are the Italians?'

'Great. We've all been getting on very well.' Stella bit her lip at the thought of Luca waiting for her below deck in her bed. Fern didn't need to know that. 'I'm on the jacuzzi deck at the moment.'

'There's a jacuzzi?'

'Yeah, it's quite something. We're just sailing along the coast.'

'Is it all as beautiful as Positano?'

'I'll send you more pics. It's hard to describe the colours and the drama of these incredible places overlooking the sea. Makes me not want to leave.'

They were both quiet for a moment. Stella wondered if Fern was thinking the same thing, that leaving Capri and going home to reality almost felt too much to bear.

'Where are you at the moment, anyway?' Stella asked, breaking the silence.

'In the garden. I've finished painting for the day. It's been magical to just have time to myself, you know. To not have the distractions of home. I've had time to think. It's been good for me.'

'Good, I'm glad the time to yourself is helping.'

'How's Amber?' Fern's breezy tone changed to one filled with concern.

'She's absolutely fine, Fern. You don't need to worry. She and Chloe are having the best time. Hard not to really.'

They chatted a bit longer without really saying anything. Even though Fern sounded as if she was happy, Stella was hesitant to lay it on too thick about how much of a good time she was having. After saying goodbye, she stayed sitting on the deck for a moment, watching the Amalfi Coast pass by, all vibrant greens and gleaming white villas. The Lottery win wasn't her ticket to happiness, she knew that, but it was the kick-start she needed to turn her life on its head. She needed to right her wrongs. She needed to support the people she cared for and to follow her heart if she was to have any chance of real happiness. Right now, happiness was Luca naked in her bed... But the idea of returning to her life... Changes were coming; she just needed to be brave enough to see them through.

* * *

Luca traced his fingers from Stella's bare hips upwards, pulling her close for a lingering kiss. They'd stayed in bed for so long, the sun was already setting. A pink-tinged glimmer of gold crept through the half-closed blinds. The yacht had moored up for the night, although Stella wasn't sure where. She hadn't wanted to drag herself from bed and Luca's arms.

'I'm going back to my room to take a shower.' He kissed her again. 'Maybe we can have dinner out this evening?'

'I'd like that,' she said as she watched him slip out of bed and pull on his shorts. He blew her a kiss as he left.

Stella spread out on the bed. The warmth of Luca remained on the sheet next to her. She wanted to stay within this bubble far removed from real life. She wanted to continue feeling good about herself and for life to remain simple and uncomplicated by messy relationships, both platonic and romantic. *Although there's nothing romantic about my relationship with Paul*, she thought bitterly. She was a fool for having let things get to this point.

She threw off the covers, stormed naked to the en suite and let the water pummel her body. Their villa on Capri was a dream, yet she didn't want to sail back there. She didn't want to face any sort of reality. What had her intentions been for inviting Fern on holiday?

In five days' time, they were supposed to be celebrating their fortieth birthdays together. Her best friend. Best friends didn't treat each other the way she'd treated Fern. Was the holiday a way of trying to make it up to her, to soften the blow? Could anything make up for what she'd done?

Stella got dried and put on another new maxi dress with a subtle leopard-print pattern in a flattering dusky blue and grey, strapless and soft against her skin. She spritzed on her perfume and gazed at herself in the full-length mirror. Everything about her life felt shiny and new, the possibilities of so much money and the freedom it could bring bubbling beneath the surface. Yet she felt cowardly and a fraud, because she was living a lie and had been for a long time. When they got home, she would put things right, however hard that would be.

There was a party atmosphere on the main deck. A couple of the crew were serving drinks, and nibbles had been laid out on the large circular table. Laughter sprinkled the night air, Chloe's unmistakable giggle soaring above the others. While Stella had been below deck, some serious drinking had been going on.

Desi winked as he walked past. So her and Luca's disappearance hadn't gone unnoticed. Why should she care? Chloe would roll her eyes and fake gag at the idea of her mum's extracurricular activities with a hot Italian, but she was single and deserved to have fun.

Luca spotted her, took a glass of bubbly from a tray and walked over. His stubble tickled her cheek as he kissed her. He handed her the glass. 'We have a drink here and dinner out. Just the two of us.'

Stella glanced towards Chloe and Amber.

'The girls are happy to stay,' he said, anticipating her next question.

'I think they need to eat something rather than just drink.' She realised how much of a mum she sounded. She may be acting as if she had few cares in the world and behaving as if she was the same age as her daughter, but her mothering instinct was alive and kicking.

'There will be food. I have asked the chef. You don't need to worry.'

Luca took her arm and she allowed herself to be enveloped by the evening, their last one on the yacht before they returned to Capri. *The Silver Spirit* was the largest in the marina and was lit like a beacon. It wasn't the only party boat. There were others too, with people out on the deck drinking and enjoying life to the full. Twinkling lights decorated the marina, reflecting in the gleaming white of hulls. The beat of music, the thrum of voices and drifting laughter filled the starlit night.

The drinks flowed as easily as the conversation. It had been a gamble saying yes to joining four strangers on a yacht. Stella had warmed to them all, Luca in particular, and not just because she'd slept with him. They talked, and he had treated her like an equal even before he knew that she had money. She'd never spent time with anyone who was genuinely rich. She would have liked this before she'd come into money, but now, seeing the ease of Luca's life and that – at least on the surface – he was happy, gave her hope that she could be too.

Luca slid his fingers between hers, his thumb caressing as he had a conversation across the table with Giovanni about New Year plans of all things, on a balmy evening in late May. Their conversation was fast and good-humoured, both laughing and teasing each other, often slipping out of English and back into Italian. She would miss Luca, but only because what they had right now was perfect. An actual relationship would spoil that. Having sex with him was uncomplicated and they got on well. Goodbye would only be hard because she would have to face up to reality again.

* * *

Luca had made a reservation for nine at a seafood restaurant. Stella nipped below deck to reapply her lipstick. Alcohol had taken the edge off her worries. She gave a little turn, liking what she saw. Luca's attention had buoyed her. She felt good about herself. She grabbed her purse and made her way back up.

Amber was on the lounge deck, holding onto the back of an armchair, looking worse for wear.

'Hey.' Stella caught hold of her arm. 'You okay?'

'Uh-huh. Just making my way back from the ladies'...' she slurred in a put-on funny voice.

'Just take it easy tonight, yeah.' She leaned closer and lowered her voice. 'Make sure you use protection too.'

Amber was swaying in front of her. 'You're not my mother, Stella. You can't tell me what to do.'

Stella folded her arms, taken aback at the animosity streaked through Amber's words. 'I'm reminding you to be careful, that's all. I don't want you to end up regretting anything.'

'What, like you regret Chloe and my mum regrets me and Rubes.'

'Oh wow, Amber. How can you even think that? We absolutely do not regret any of you. Your mum asked me to look out for you, so that's what I'm doing. A friendly reminder to not get knocked up won't go amiss, considering how much you've had to drink.'

Amber stabbed a finger in Stella's direction. 'My goddamn mum has no right to tell me what I can or can't do any longer.'

'Maybe not, but she's not here and I am. And no one's trying to tell you anything. I'm only suggesting you go a little slower with the drinking, with Desi...'

'Bit late for that,' she said with a smirk.

Oh to be young and foolish again, Stella thought. But then had age really mellowed her? She'd been quick enough about moving things on to another level with Luca. She was hardly one to talk, yet she was supposed to be the responsible one here. Yes, Amber and Chloe were adults, but Fern had asked her to keep an eye on Amber. Not that Stella could stop Amber from doing anything, but she'd try her best to influence her to at least think things through, even if she didn't follow that advice herself.

Stella hooked her arm in Amber's and manoeuvred her from the open lounge area into the empty library. 'It's fine you sleeping with Desi. You're old enough to make your own decisions. I'm just watching out for you, that's all. Same way I'd look out for Chloe. No need to get arsey.'

She looked at her sheepishly. 'Soz.'

'You don't need to apologise, just be careful is all I'm staying.'

'Can say the same for you and Luca. Worst kept secret on the yacht.' She hiccupped.

'Does Chloe know?'

'Course she does. Doesn't mean she gives a shit about it though.'

'What about her and Vincenzo. Have they...?'

Amber shrugged.

'You don't know or you're not going to tell me?'

'Ask her yourself.'

Stella sighed and started to walk away. Amber grabbed her arm.

'Don't tell Mum about me and Desi.'

'Why are you worried? She's not going to think badly of you for having fun.'

Amber rubbed her forehead. 'I feel bad she's missing out, because of Dad... You know.'

'I'm sure she's not thinking of it like that. Honestly, given the choice, I'm certain she'd have preferred the art retreat anyway.' Stella gently touched Amber's hand. 'Maybe when we're back on Capri, just go easy on her. Be nice. I get the impression she's trying to process a lot at the moment.'

'I feel sorry for her. Her life is shit, Stella. I want to tell her the truth about things, but Dad made me promise not to.'

'Oh, Amber, that's a shitty thing for him to have done.' Stella rubbed her forehead; a tension headache was beginning to creep across. 'It's hard to know what to do for the best.'

Amber's eyes narrowed. 'If you know my dad's been unfaithful, why have you not told Mum?'

Despite a shiver of fear, Stella's cheeks went hot. 'I think it's about time someone did.'

Amber nodded slowly. 'It would be much better if it came from you...'

Stella's nostrils flared. 'Actually Amber, it wouldn't. I think you talking truthfully to your mum about your, um, dad, would soften the blow. But you're drunk, I'm about to go out and Luca's waiting, so sleep on it and we'll talk more tomorrow. When we're sober.'

'Hung-over more like,' Amber grumbled.

Stella clasped Amber's shoulder. 'Eat some food, yeah, before you drink any more.'

'Yeah, yeah. And you go have a good night.' Amber winked.

Stella walked backwards towards the library door. 'Oh, I intend to.'

22

FERN

Fern got the distinct impression that Stella had left out a lot of what they'd been getting up to on the yacht. Fern acknowledged that there was much she hadn't told her either. It had been hard to put into words how she felt about being here, how she felt about a lot of things. She bit her lip and stared past the herbs on her balcony wall to the sun retreating beyond the shadowed tree branches.

After spending the day in the garden immersed in her painting, Fern had come up to her room to get changed for dinner. She'd stolen a moment to herself, soaking up the beauty of the evening, the sky beyond the trees flooded with ochre and dusky pink tones. She imagined painting the sunset and smiled. She'd made a start on the lemon tree but wasn't sure she liked it. Edith had pointed out that it was merely a start and was too early to judge, but Matteo had given her gentle encouragement whenever he'd come over, which she'd noticed he did often. Perhaps it was because she was the newest one there and the most inexperienced. Edith's knowing smile had suggested otherwise.

Dinner was a simple dish of linguine and prawns, which they ate on the terrace together. Perhaps because it was a relaxed

Sunday, guests drifted away early to their rooms. Fern was happy to sit and chat with Edith and Matteo, the only ones left once the empty dessert plates had been cleared away. They talked about the painting that had been accomplished that day and Edith's plans for the week. Fern gleaned that Mondays and Tuesdays at the retreat were free time for guests to do their own thing. A pang of sadness struck Fern that it was her last night and tomorrow afternoon she'd be joining the others back at their villa.

Edith suddenly stood and smiled at them in the honeyed light of the candlelit terrace. 'It's getting late and I need an early night. Catch up on my beauty sleep.' She winked. 'You youngsters should go out and enjoy yourselves. Why not take Fern to that cocktail bar you were telling us about, Matteo?'

Edith was as unsubtle as a sledgehammer. Secretly, Fern loved her for it. Edith gave them a wave and made her way to the villa. Fern watched her go. She hoped they'd stay in touch. Despite the age difference, Edith had quickly become a friend and someone who Fern felt she could talk to, someone who offered sound advice and helpfully saw things from a different perspective.

'Edith is one of my favourite guests,' Matteo said, filling the quiet of the terrace. 'I hope she eventually finds happiness.'

Fern glanced at him. 'She's told you about her friend?'

'I had it figured out when she booked the rooms, and from things she's said in the past. She was so sad when she arrived. I couldn't ignore that and I put two and two together.' He drained his glass of wine and met her eyes. 'How do you fancy going for a cocktail?'

Fern smiled. It was her last night and she wanted to make the most of every moment. She couldn't bear the thought of returning to normal life. 'I'd love to.'

* * *

Fern had yet to explore Anacapri, but what she glimpsed as they walked along a narrow tree-lined road with half-hidden white-washed villas made her love it even more than Capri town. There was an overwhelming sense of peace in the dusky evening light.

The cocktail bar was housed in a hotel. The walls and sofas were white and pillars separated the seating areas, yet it was far from stark. Candlelight flickered from within large Moroccan floor lamps, while glowing wall lights and large pieces of artwork covered the walls. The space behind the bar was filled with colourful bottles and on their way to an empty seating area, Fern glimpsed delicious-looking cocktails.

Fern sank into the padded white sofa, with Matteo next to her. His arm rested along the back of the sofa, not quite touching but close enough to make her heart pound. On their walk to the bar, they'd chatted easily, but somehow it felt very different to be out with him away from the retreat. She'd spent plenty of time alone with him over the past couple of days, so why should this be any different? She knew why. The flickering candlelight, the romantic setting and it being just the two of them... It seemed like a date. Guilt crawled through her and questions filled her head: what would Amber make of this? What would Stella say? What on earth would Paul think?

The thought that she should try to phone Paul again crossed her mind, but she didn't want to. It had been an effort the last time they'd talked and he'd left her feeling... What had she felt besides annoyance and a desire to get off the phone? Would Paul even be thinking about her, wondering what she was up to? She doubted it. Anxiety snaked through her that being out alone with Matteo was wrong. Yet she had no desire to be anywhere else.

Their cocktails arrived, one topped with lemon and a maraschino cherry, the other with an orange twist. Matteo picked them up and handed Fern her Amaretto Sour.

'What had you planned to do with your life, before you got pregnant?' Matteo's question took her by surprise. They'd briefly chatted about what Fern did back home, and she hadn't tried to hide her disappointment about her lack of career and the way her life had turned out.

'That's a very good question.' She sipped her cocktail, enjoying the smooth sweetness with a refreshing kick of lemon. 'I'm not even sure that back then I knew what I wanted to do. I don't think I thought further than the next night out. Actually, that's a lie. I had a place at university to do graphic design – art was the one thing I was decent at and put any effort into.'

'You had to give that up?'

'Yeah, I couldn't cope. I went for the first few weeks but was miserable. I tried to hide my pregnancy but I suffered with morning sickness that lasted most of the day. I struggled to make friends because I didn't want to go out and I didn't focus on the course either. There was some support, but it was an awful time. I have no idea what I would have done with my life if things had been different.'

'What's in the past is in the past. Whatever you would have done, you didn't, so perhaps you need to focus on what you'd like to do now.' He cupped his hand around his glass of Negroni and lifted it to his lips. 'What are you good at?'

'I'm good with people. I enjoy working with the general public, which isn't always easy, but I like that interaction. If people leave happy then I feel like I've done a good job.'

'You said you work in a shop?'

Fern nodded. There was no derogatory tone, just an honest question. 'Yeah, I work in a homewares store now, but I used to work in a clothes shop and when the kids were little in a supermarket.'

'And have those jobs made you happy?'

'No, but I haven't hated them – there are elements I like. I don't work because we need the money; I work so I have a focus and a reason to get out of the house. In all honesty, I'd like to run my own business, making people happy in some way, like you do. Not that I'd want to run an art retreat.' She laughed. 'But I love what you do here – looking after people and making their experience such a happy one. My mum used to work as a cleaner in a big hotel. It was hard work and nothing that I wanted to do, but I liked how she was a part of something that she could be proud of. She wanted more for me than she had and then I got pregnant. My parents most definitely believed I'd ruined my life.'

'They believed you made a mistake?' he asked gently.

'*I* knew I'd made a mistake. They were just incredibly disappointed. Our relationship has been strained ever since.'

Matteo looked unblinking at Fern for a moment, his eyes roving across her face. 'What you do in life is never a mistake or wasted even if it was unplanned,' he said seriously. 'It's what we do next that's important. The decisions we make have the potential of changing our life. You have that option. I was in a sham of a marriage for a time, neither of us realising how unhappy both of us were because we didn't talk to each other.'

This was the first time Matteo had brought this up and she was now beginning to see in him some of the sadness that Edith had alluded to. 'Did you marry with good intentions?'

'I don't know; in hindsight, perhaps not.'

Fern sipped her Amaretto Sour, allowing him time to continue.

'Before I got married, I was in love with someone else. We were young and rushed into things too quickly and had a baby.'

'You have a child?'

'She's twenty now.'

'Almost the same age as my daughters.'

Matteo nodded. 'Her mamma fell in love with someone else. We weren't married and they moved away; it was back when I was messed up about a lot of things and I threw myself into work to get over the heartache. Then I met my ex-wife and we rushed into things too quickly as well, getting married before we really knew each other, only to realise a few years later that we wanted different things from life. We weren't really in love. I think I pretended that we'd be okay because I didn't want to admit failure again. We drifted apart pretty quickly.' He suddenly laughed. 'I've been single for so long, it's hard to remember what life was like in a relationship.'

'You've not met anyone since?' She could hardly hide her surprise.

'Not anyone I've been serious about, no.'

'I feel like I've been married forever. And trapped, by the choices and commitment I made.' A coldness flooded through Fern at the thought. Was that how she really felt? 'And things that have been said recently, make me question just how faithful my husband is...'

Matteo's eyes were filled with concern. 'That's no way for a marriage to be, and if you're not happy...'

Fern waved her hand as if attempting to erase her comment. 'I said too much then. I've drunk too much.' She gestured to her nearly empty cocktail glass. After the copious amount of wine she'd had before coming out, her head was beginning to swim. 'I don't know how I feel about anything at the moment. I've just been craving "me time" for so long. I'm looking at everything from a different perspective for once.'

'As if you're an outsider looking in.'

'Exactly. And it's a funny thing; life before I had the girls feels forever ago – because it is – but in other ways, it's like I clicked my fingers and twenty years passed me by.'

His fingers connecting with Fern's bare shoulder sent a jolt through her. She was suddenly aware that over the course of the conversation they'd moved closer together. There was only the tiniest gap between his knee and her thigh. She smoothed down the leopard-print maxi skirt that Stella had lent her. She was on dangerous ground, but she felt alive. For once in her life.

She wanted to fill the silence. 'The truth of it is, all the ambition and dreams I had when I was eighteen evaporated with a pregnancy test. I remember thinking over the years, when the girls go to school, I'll go to university and do that graphic design course. Then I kept putting it off, thinking I'd do it when the girls went to secondary school. And now they're at university and I've still done nothing about it.'

'What do you think is really stopping you?' Matteo asked.

Fern shook her head. 'I don't know. Or maybe I do; I've completely lost the confidence I once had. The more time that's passed, the less I feel able to do the things I would have done when I was an outgoing eighteen-year-old. Because I was young when I had the girls, it was exhausting trying to prove to everyone that I was capable, more than capable of being a good mum. Like when they started school, I joined the PTA and threw myself into that. My life has revolved around the girls for so long, it's all I know.'

'That's not a bad thing, putting them first.'

'No, I know. I just regret losing a sense of myself over the years. I know most mums feel like that for at least a time when their kids are young, I've just never regained a hold on who I am. Or maybe because I was a young mum, I didn't have the opportunity to actually figure out who I was before becoming a mum and a wife took over.'

'I have regrets too. I think it's hard to get to our age and not have any, either about things we've done or things we didn't do.'

'What do you regret?'

'I regret not fighting for my family – not that it would necessarily have changed anything, but I regret not moving heaven and earth to have spent more time with my daughter when she was younger.'

'From the little you've said, it sounded like it was out of your hands.'

'It was to some extent, but there were things I could have done to make it easier to see her, such as moving closer.'

'But that would have disrupted your life more than your ex already had?'

He nodded. 'But to have had that connection with my daughter, it would have been worth it.' He gave her a knowing look. 'Hindsight is a wonderful thing. And the passing of time coupled with getting older gives you a different perspective on everything.'

23

FERN

Fern could have carried on talking to Matteo all night. Their lives were so completely different, yet there was a spark of something – a connection and a shared heartache woven through their different experiences. After polishing off a third cocktail each, they stumbled from the warmth of the bar into the fresh May evening. Contentment crept up on Fern as they walked through the streets of Anacapri, quiet once they had left behind the bars and cafes in the heart of the picturesque centre. An understanding dawned on her about how unhappy she was back home. A sham of a marriage; wasn't that exactly what she was in? There was no real love any longer. Even if there had been love early on, it was tied up in duty and doing the right thing. Whenever she thought of Paul, she felt confused, annoyed and frustrated. And if she felt that way about him, considering everything that Amber had hinted at, what on earth did he think about her?

Matteo had talked about not focusing on the past; it was only the future and what you did next that really mattered. Fern knew she was at a crossroads. She also knew she couldn't carry on the way she had been, feeling miserable and worthless, unsure about everything. She needed to take her future into her own hands and make decisions and changes that would be positive for her. She needed to be brave.

They'd remained quiet for most of the walk back. As they reached the retreat and Matteo closed the gate behind them, Fern wondered what he'd been thinking about. Surrounded by shadowy trees, she breathed in the sweet and heady scent of orange blossom.

'What do you love most about this place?' she asked as they wound their way along the solar-lit path towards the villa, which was half hidden from view by the holm oaks and olive trees.

'So many things, but I love it here at night. It's so peaceful when the guests are asleep and it feels as if I have the place to myself...' He grinned. 'To ourselves.'

He linked his arm in hers. She didn't pull away. A few too many cocktails had allowed her to relax and let her guard down. *Anyway*, she thought, *it's a friendly gesture*. And, considering how tipsy she felt, needed.

They started up the stone steps to the grand entrance, but in the dim light, she caught her foot on the edge of the stone and toppled into him. Matteo held her tightly as their laughter echoed into the night. He held a finger to his lips before gesturing upwards, which Fern took to mean to keep quiet and not wake the other guests.

Instead of going inside, he led her around the side of the villa and deeper into the garden. The sky was clear and moonlight slipped through the tree branches, sending a wash of silver across the paving. The only other light came from the blue LED pool lights illuminating the water.

'Fancy a swim?' Matteo asked.

'What, now?'

He peeled off his T-shirt, grinned at her and dropped it over the back of a chair. Fern's heart thudded. He definitely meant now.

He was taller and less stocky than Paul, with a smattering of dark hair on his toned chest. Fern suddenly realised that he was undoing his jeans. Heat rushed to her cheeks and she looked away. She breathed deeply and made a quick decision. Without giving it any more thought, she followed Matteo's lead and pulled off her top. She was glad that she'd worn matching underwear. She felt reckless, out of her depth, but unable to say no. Not because she'd had a bit too much to drink, but because she didn't want to. She had the sudden overwhelming feeling of not being tied down. Her inhibitions had been banished by alcohol and she felt liberated, a feeling reminiscent of her youth. It was refreshing and surprisingly welcome. She kicked off her sandals and slipped out of her skirt.

Fern gasped as she padded down the steps into the water. It was shockingly cool, even though the pool was heated. Matteo was already submerged, his grinning face watching her as the water came above her knees, then her waist until it reached just below her bra. The realisation that she was married, in a pool in her underwear with an extremely attractive Italian briefly crossed her mind, but she pushed the thought away and floated on her back, not caring if Matteo was watching. Maybe she liked the idea that he was looking.

She gazed up at the dusting of stars in the midnight blue sky. She had no idea of the time and didn't care how late it was. Long gone were the days of the girls waking her up at six, and she was on holiday after all. What would Paul make of this? Fear twisted at her insides. She wanted to bury the feeling. She flipped on to her front and swam the length of the pool, trying to clear her mind of everything.

Amber's words from the other day flashed into her head, for Fern to really think about how Paul treated her. Words that had played on her mind ever since.

'You seem in a world of your own.' Matteo swam alongside her.

Fern reached the edge of the pool. 'Just thinking about something my daughter said. Actually, I've been trying hard not to think about it because it worries me and I'm fed up of being worried and that makes me even more worried.'

Matteo laughed. 'You're making no sense at all.'

'I'm really not.' She shook her head and grinned at him. 'Bit hard to after the amount I've drunk tonight.'

They fell silent and rested their arms on the terracotta stone surrounding the pool, their legs bobbing out behind them. It was utterly peaceful even with the distant thrum of voices from somewhere beyond the trees. A moth fluttered around one of the solar lights and beyond the gentle splosh of water, there was just the rustling of insects in the undergrowth.

'It's been refreshing to do something different and share this place with someone.' Matteo's deep voice filled the silence. 'It's a long time since I've been out late in the evening here.'

'Oh?'

'My life revolves around the retreat here and in Tuscany for seven months of the year and, as I've said before, most guests are quite a bit older. Not that I begrudge that; their company is wonderful and I'm fascinated by their lives. Tonight was different though, thank you.'

Fern realised how close they were, their bare arms touching. It felt incredibly intimate being alone with him late at night. Matteo had talked earlier about how one decision could impact the rest of her life. This felt like a pivotal moment. She couldn't tear her eyes away from his gaze. She drank him in; the intensity of his eyes that looked dark in the blue glow of the pool, the shadow of stubble across his defined jaw, his full lips tantalisingly close to hers as he leaned closer.

'I'm married,' she said quietly, pushing back against the side of the pool. The intensity of the moment broke as water splashed between them.

'I'm sorry.' He slicked a hand through his wet hair and glided back on the water, increasing the distance between them. 'I got carried away.'

'No, I'm sorry. It's been such a good evening, but I... er...'

'You don't have to apologise; I know you're married.' He faltered and swam back over to her. He brushed a stray hair from her cheek. 'It's just you said you don't think he's been faithful to you...'

'That doesn't justify me making the same mistake.' *Not that kissing you would be a mistake*, her insides screamed. 'It's just that in the eyes of my parents, my family, my teachers, most of my friends, everyone really apart from Stella, they all believed I'd massively messed up my life when I got pregnant. When I married Paul, I vowed I wouldn't mess that up too – I made a commitment, for better, for worse.'

A returning knot of worry tightened in her chest. What was she doing, living out a fantasy and being swept up in the beauty of the island and the feeling of freedom? She wasn't free to flirt with a handsome man, at least not to the extent of giving him the impression there could be more.

Her feet found the bottom of the pool. It wasn't too deep, the water only coming up to her bra line. She felt suddenly sober and acutely aware that she was just in a lacy bra and knickers.

Perhaps Matteo sensed her sudden discomfort. He heaved himself out of the pool, dripping water on to the stone.

'I'll get towels.'

Rivulets of water streamed down his arms and back. His white Calvin Kleins were soaked and clung to him. She was relieved he had his back to her, but even so, a warm tingling flooded through her. And she'd been worried about what Stella, Amber and Chloe might get up to on the yacht. She was no better. No, she was worse. She was married and foolish.

24

FERN

The ease with which Fern and Matteo had chatted and flirted together evaporated the moment he'd got out of the pool. After such a pleasant evening, Fern hated how they'd ended up in an awkward situation.

She remained submerged in the water until he returned. She stepped from the warmth into the night air, the light breeze fresh against her skin. Matteo handed her a fluffy white towel. His eyes briefly flicked downwards. In just a skimpy bra and knickers, she felt more exposed than if she'd been wearing a bikini, yet a longing swept through her. She wrapped the towel around her middle.

'I'm sorry I overstepped.' His eyes focused firmly on hers. 'The last thing I wanted to do was make you uncomfortable. I've really enjoyed your company. No hard feelings?'

Fern shook her head. 'None.'

How could she be cross with him? He'd done nothing wrong; if anything, it was her fault for allowing the flirting to happen. For encouraging it. For wanting it.

They dried off, scooped up their clothes and headed inside. She followed him upstairs, the silence between them growing like a storm cloud.

Matteo paused at the top of the stairs. Their eyes met. Fern had no idea what to say to ease the tension. Moonlight streamed through the window at the end of the landing, highlighting his cheekbones and shadowing his eyes, making it difficult for Fern to see his expression.

'Sleep well.' He leaned close and kissed her on each cheek.

Her skin tingled and her heart raced.

He walked along the hallway towards his room and she sighed. She retreated to hers, banishing the reckless thought of following him. To do what? Seduce him? The idea made her stifle a laugh at the absurdity that she'd be bold enough to do something like that. Yet her insides were in turmoil at the idea of even contemplating cheating on her husband.

She closed her bedroom door firmly behind her. Breathing deeply, Fern pulled the towel tighter. Her head was filled with Matteo. The undeniable truth was she'd desperately wanted to kiss him. But she couldn't, she knew that. She had a lot of thinking to do. And decisions to make.

* * *

Perhaps Edith sensed that Fern didn't want to talk about her evening with Matteo because she didn't ask a thing the next morning. Matteo's warm smile over breakfast made Fern melt inside, a feeling that was immediately replaced by the worries she'd gone to bed with.

She picked at the tomato and mozzarella topped bruschetta. The truth of it was, she'd rather have gone to bed with Matteo. Her cheeks flushed at the thought. She glanced around, afraid someone would notice, as if her thoughts were tattooed on her. Matteo met her eyes. She grew hotter.

'It's a completely free day today,' Edith was saying. 'You could continue with your painting here or you're welcome to join me – I'm going to wander to Villa San Michele. It's utterly gorgeous. You won't be lost for inspiration there, I can assure you.'

Fern turned her attention to Edith. 'Thank you, but I'll probably stay here and do some painting. I need to speak to my friend too and find out when they'll be back on Capri, but I'll probably leave later this afternoon.'

'I'm going to be really sad to see you go.' Edith gently touched Fern's arm. 'Your company has cheered me up no end.' She leaned closer. 'And I'm not the only one whose spirits have been lifted. I'll see you before you leave.'

After breakfast, Fern retreated with her sketchbook to the bench at the far reaches of the garden. It felt too much like hard work to continue with her painting of the lemon tree. Despite Matteo's encouragement the day before, her confidence had deserted her. She wanted to be creative, but she felt like a fraud. She never had time back home. Although that wasn't technically true; she did have the time, it just wasn't a priority.

Holidays felt like an escape, but this place in particular was a fantasy, somewhere she felt protected from having to face reality. Although, so far, her time on Capri had thrown up more questions than had been answered.

She felt bad that she'd let Edith go off on her own, particularly when Villa San Michele was somewhere she wanted to explore, but she'd stayed at the villa, not because she wanted to be on her own, but because Matteo was here, that was the truth of it.

Fern breathed deeply, opened her sketchbook and stared at the blank page. What on earth was she doing? Flirting with the idea that something could happen between her and Matteo? She sketched the outline of a rose and stared at the tentative graphite marks on the paper. *There's nothing wrong with fantasising,* she thought. Did she really believe that Paul never fantasised about other people? Was she certain that he'd never acted on those fantasies?

Tears blurred the pencil strokes. She was torturing herself, thinking about Matteo in a way she'd never thought of another man – beyond lusting after famous people and having a giggle with friends. This felt different. This was different. These were feelings for someone she'd got to know over the past few days, someone she was drawn to, someone who crept into her thoughts from the moment she woke to the moment she fell asleep.

Fern angrily swiped her eyes and grabbed her phone from the bench. She pressed Stella's number.

'Hey,' Stella's familiar voice said. 'I was literally about to phone you.'

'Are you on your way back?'

'Um, no, not yet... Are you okay? You sound weird.'

Fern breathed deeply and focused on the leaves of the rose bush in front of her, shivering in the light breeze. 'I'm fine. I just wanted to figure out what time I should leave and go back to the villa.'

'Yeah, about that. It's kinda why I needed to talk to you... Please say no if this isn't okay... I know it's a lot to ask. God, I feel so bad asking you this...'

'You haven't asked me anything yet.'

There was a slight pause. A cream-winged butterfly landed on the edge of a large terracotta pot.

'The guys are going back to Positano for a party. They've invited us.' The nervousness in Stella's voice was obvious. 'Which will add another night, meaning we wouldn't get back to Capri until later tomorrow. I said I wasn't sure; I wanted to check with you first.'

The butterfly fluttered away, swirling high into the sunshine. Stella was giving her the chance to stay longer, to enjoy the freedom she'd found here, to spread her wings... 'It's fine. Go if you all fancy it.'

'Really?' There was now disbelief in her voice.

'I'm positive.'

'You can always go back to the villa if you prefer – I can let Violetta know.'

'That's kind, but no, I'm fine. I have sketches to finish.'

'Not naked ones I hope?' Stella joked.

An image of Matteo emerging from the pool last night with water beading his toned torso flitted into Fern's head. 'I've just been sketching scenery. There's been no life drawing.'

'I take it you're having fun then?'

Fern gazed up at the perfect blue sky and sighed. 'It's been eye-opening.'

'Okay,' Stella said slowly. 'In a good way?'

'I hope so.'

'You want to talk about it?'

'Not really.' She had so much she needed to get her own head around first before she could even begin to explain it to Stella.

'Are you absolutely sure it's okay?'

'Yes. It's only another day. Not long at all. I'll see you tomorrow.'

Fern didn't want to carry on the conversation and risk Stella probing her about why she was happy to stay. They said goodbye and the peace returned to the garden.

Anticipation rushed through her at the thought of another day and night here. Would staying for longer be a mistake? Probably, but she knew she was relieved that she didn't have to leave yet and that she had the opportunity to explore... What? Her creativity? Or was she really thinking about Matteo, and the way he made her feel? Perhaps it was more about sifting through her emotions about Paul.

She closed her sketchbook and wound her way back through the garden to the villa. Her heart battered against her chest. Hushed voices filtered from somewhere close by, but it didn't seem as if anyone else was about. Perhaps most people had followed Edith's example and had gone out to find inspiration.

It was cool and quiet inside as she made her way along the tiled hallway. The German couple were sitting together in the orangery, the wife's legs curled beneath her on the sofa as she gazed out through the large windows. Arthur was in the lounge, sitting on a sofa that faced the garden, so he didn't notice her slip past.

Matteo's study door was open. On her first day, he'd explained how he always left it open, an invitation to the guests to come and chat to him, to talk through their ideas. Fern hovered in the doorway. One corner of the room housed bookshelves and two armchairs. A fireplace with an ornate marble surround was filled with dried flowers. Matteo was sitting at a desk facing patio doors that led to a small terrace with an easel set up. A stack of books and paper were piled on the floor next to the desk. The room was lived in and filled with creativity.

She knocked gently.

Matteo spun round on his chair, a smile lighting up his face as his gaze fell on her.

'Sorry, I didn't mean to disturb you.'

'That's okay, I was just finishing up. How can I help?'

Fern's palms felt sweaty and she was conscious of how much her heart was pounding. 'I, um... I just wondered if it would be okay if I stayed another night?'

Matteo frowned. 'Really? I thought your daughter and friends were back today?'

'They were supposed to be, but there's been a change of plan. It's not a problem if it's not okay. You've been so generous and I don't want to outstay my welcome.'

'Of course I'm happy for you to stay, but I was just about to come and find you to say goodbye.'

It was Fern's turn to frown. 'Oh?'

'I'm about to go to Tuscany. A whirlwind visit. The beginning of the week is a chance for the guests to explore the island or focus on their art in their own time. Plus it means I have some free time too and they're well looked after by Ana.'

'Yes, Edith said.'

He stood and walked over to her. 'I just wish we didn't have to say goodbye quite yet. Unless...' He seemed flustered, his cheeks reddening as he looked seriously at her. 'How would you like to come to Tuscany with me?'

25

STELLA

Stella was puzzled by Fern's quick agreement at them extending their time on the yacht. The conversation had been surprisingly easy, but Fern's tone had left her on edge. She seemed happy to stay at the retreat for another night, but there was something about how she'd sounded that Stella couldn't quite pinpoint. Even with Fern's blessing, it didn't stop Stella from feeling guilty once again.

Was she being ridiculously selfish? Probably. Did she want to spend another night with Luca? Hell, yes. The girls wanted to stay as well; it wasn't just her decision. Clutching her mobile, Stella made her way to the main deck to deliver the good news.

Rather than heading for Capri, they sailed for Positano. As Stella slipped off her dress and settled herself on the sun lounger in her bikini, she told herself there was no point in worrying about Fern. It was done and they'd see her tomorrow.

The yacht sliced through the sea, the breeze offsetting the lush warmth. It was only the end of May but they'd been blessed with glorious sunny days, so Stella was determined to top up her tan while she had the chance.

The girls were lounging on the daybed with Desi and Vincenzo, all lithe, tanned limbs. She watched Chloe now, flirting with Vincenzo. From what Amber had said and from what she'd gleaned from Chloe herself, that was all it was, just flirting. Amber's behaviour on the other hand was a reflection of her and Fern when they were young.

Positano got closer, its sweeping hillside covered in colourful villas slowly coming into focus. They'd seen it from afar but Stella was keen to explore and she was looking forward to a night away from the yacht. The promise of an exclusive party at a hillside villa only confirmed her thought that she was living the dream.

* * *

They took a tender from the yacht to the shore. As they strolled across the beach, Stella sensed people watching and she suddenly felt the millionaire she actually was. She was dressed like one too, in a Fendi white silk skirt with a simple spaghetti strap top that she'd bought in Capri. She'd been living in her Capri sandals, the most practical but beautiful things she'd ever owned. It truly felt as if she was living someone else's life, walking in the footsteps of the rich and famous.

The girls stopped on the beach for an Instagram photo, posing with the backdrop of pastel-coloured buildings decorating the steep hillside. Luca hooked his arm in Stella's and took a selfie of them grinning together. She felt on top of the world as they left the beach and got two taxis up through the narrow, winding streets, past tiny shops and cafes clustering at the edge of the road and beneath washing hanging from balconies.

The taxis stopped in front of a gated entrance and Stella glimpsed the cream and salmon-pink walls of a villa and the lush gardens that surrounded it. Luca and Vincenzo paid the drivers and the taxis sped off. Stella, Amber and Chloe followed the Italians through the gates into the villa's grounds, which were perched high up with a bird's-eye view over Positano.

They were welcomed with open arms by their host and his wife, friends of Luca's, both somewhere in their late thirties with dark hair, deep tans, designer sunglasses and gold jewellery. They were loud and all-encompassing, and Stella and the girls were swept up into the party atmosphere. The Italian conversation was fast and musical, and laughter filled the air.

With the yacht anchored off the coast, their overnight bags had been sent on ahead to the villa. Stella didn't question that she and Luca had been given a room together. She noted that Amber was sharing with Desi too, but Chloe had a room of her own. There was no assumption from Vincenzo; she respected him for that. She respected Chloe too; she'd done something right raising her, or perhaps Chloe was fearful of turning out like her mum. She was impressed by her restraint though, not jumping into bed with someone at the first opportunity, although Stella certainly had no regrets about taking things further with Luca.

Stella drank too much and laughed a lot. She was left giddy from the experience – an exclusive party with only a handful of guests, all of them obviously wealthy, the multi-millionaire host happy to welcome them to his home. Luca introduced her to people in a way that made it obvious that they were together. It didn't bother her in the slightest that he'd probably have someone else on his arm when she returned home, while he continued to live it up in the Med. She was living the dream too and was more than happy to lap up the attention and enjoy the experience while forgetting about everything else.

The villa achieved the sort of outside living that she craved back home, but Nailsea was hardly the place to attempt a Mediterranean lifestyle. Huge stone pots were filled with flowers and glossy cheese plants, and tiled floors and intricately painted ceilings gave a sense of colour and history. It was the vista though that stole the show for Stella. Perched on top of the cliff was a pool with an uninterrupted view over the beach to the hillside scattered with villas. Stone walls enclosed hidden terraces with lounge chairs beneath the shade of trees. Flowers bloomed in pots and the cracks of stone walls. With an abundance of colour and beauty in every direction, it truly was a little slice of paradise.

As the night wore on and darkness descended, lights threaded the hillside of Positano. Stella was heady with wine. Luca was speaking Italian to a friend, but he slipped his arm around her waist. Wasn't finding a hot Italian and having a fling what she'd dreamed about? Fern must have known this would happen, which was partly why she'd opted for the art retreat.

Fern.

Guilt twisted through her yet again. Stella had told Fern that it was *her* time to do what *she* wanted, but Stella was sad that her friend didn't have the passion or excitement in her life that she could have...

Her phone pinged. She looked at the message and her heart sank.

I miss you.

Paul.

Even here, in the most beautiful place, during an evening filled with happiness, her past mistakes still followed her, reminding her of all the wrong she'd done.

She slipped away from Luca and found a quiet shadowed spot far from the flickering light and everyone on the terrace. Should she reply to Paul or ignore him? Telling him that he needed to stop contacting her seemed to have done no good. He was persistent, and considering the time, probably drunk. Did it mean because he was contacting her he wasn't cheating on Fern with someone else while she was away? She hoped so, but it was a hollow hope because she knew him too well. She was certain he wasn't sending Fern late-night texts.

Warm hands slid around her waist, making her jump.

'Sorry,' Luca whispered, nuzzling her neck.

Stella switched off her phone and clasped it to her chest. She wanted to empty her mind; she wanted the reminders of home, her past and her mistakes to stop, even for a short time. Surely that wasn't too much to ask?

Luca led her to a love seat surrounded by foliage in a corner beyond the pool. She curled her legs beneath her on the cushioned seat and he put his arm around her. Stella rested against his shoulder. The party had begun to quieten down. A few guests had left, chauffeured back to their villas along the Amalfi Coast. Half a dozen or so people remained, sipping cocktails on the terrace above the pool. Chloe and Amber had disappeared and so had Vincenzo and Desi. Giovanni was still there, chatting to a glamorous woman in a glittery black dress.

'You are very, erm... thoughtful tonight,' Luca said, tracing his fingers along her bare arm and sending tingles through her.

He'd noticed; she liked that.

'Have you ever regretted something you've done?' she said.

Luca snorted. 'Of course. I make many mistakes, but always at the time I think they were the right thing to do. It is the only way to look at things. Or you are forever too hard on yourself.' He caressed her arm and slid his fingers between hers. 'What do you regret?'

Stella breathed in the sweet scent of roses and gazed at the black-blue sky decorated with stars. From where they were sitting,

Positano was almost hidden, only a faint glow suggested there was anything beyond the pool.

'I regret sleeping with my best friend's husband.'

If Luca was shocked, he didn't show it.

'Your friend who is here on Capri?'

'Yep.' Saying it out loud sounded even worse than it had in her head. She was a terrible person. 'I've been in love with him since I was eighteen. At least, I thought I was in love. I'm pretty certain it was only teenage lust – I was too young to understand my feelings, but at the time they felt all-consuming. We slept together once a long time ago, a drunken thing at a party – we didn't even spend the night together. My friend Fern knew nothing about it – she still doesn't – and to be honest my memories are pretty hazy. He fancied Fern though and they became an item, then she got pregnant and he married her. He may have done the decent thing at the time, but in reality he's a dick. I know it because in a moment of stupidity I had fling with him just under a year ago...'

'Does your friend know her husband is a shit?' Luca held her gaze.

'I'm not sure. She's not heard it from me. I haven't yet had the guts to tell her.' Stella gave a hollow laugh. 'I've always been drawn to the wrong type of bloke.'

'Huh. The wrong type. Is that what I am?' he said playfully.

'Are you?'

'You tell me.'

'You're not the right type, that's for sure. Inviting us on your party boat to sail along the coast for a couple of days. We'd have been naive as hell to not know your true intentions.'

He gave a knowing nod. 'And yet, here you are.'

Stella grinned, appreciating his frankness. 'Here I am. To be fair to you, I was kinda hoping for this outcome.'

'*Certo.*' He held his hands up. '*Lo so.*'

'What does that mean?'

'I say of course, I know.' He shrugged. 'And that you like me.'

'You were that confident, huh?' *Of course he was*, she thought.

His hand slid down her side until it rested on her hip. And she'd been certain in her confidence that they'd end up together. A few hedonistic days before reality took over again. Yet her reality was going to be very different, she knew that. Her secret would soon be a secret no more. She would deal with the fallout and move on with her life. Whatever happened, she was going to make the best of what life dealt her.

'You still love him, this man of yours?'

'Oh, he's not mine and never will be. And no, I don't love him any longer. I've lusted after him over the years. I was jealous for a long time that Fern got to be with him. After my second marriage ended, I was in a really bad place. Fern was there for me, but Paul was too. He was a good friend. He's friends with my ex-husband too, but sided with me when things got messy – he was an unofficial mediator and helped us to get through our divorce on speaking terms.'

Stella paused, thinking back over the series of events that had led her to make a monumental mistake. 'And then, last year, I bumped into him on a night out – Fern wasn't with me – and one thing led to another. I also know it wasn't the first time he'd cheated on his wife. Paul talks to my ex and I've found things out. I've made huge mistakes, but I can't forgive Paul for the way he's treated Fern. I think I was just in love with the idea of what could have been, if we'd got together properly a long time ago, before he got serious with Fern.'

'Do you think your friend would have stayed with him if they had no kids?'

'No.' Stella snorted. 'No chance. She was trapped by pregnancy, shame and the pressure of doing the right thing and the fear of being alone. The truth is, she'd be better off without him. I know that; I'm sure her daughters do too, and perhaps on some level she knows it. I just need to have the guts to own up to my mistakes, however hard that will be.'

'Why are you telling me this, Stella?' He paused his caress, but as he shuffled to look at her, his sly grin gave away the fact that he was teasing her.

'Because when you take us back to Capri, I'm never going to see you again. Plus it's helpful to talk my shit through with someone far removed from the situation, who doesn't actually know me. I feel as if I can talk to you honestly without judgement.'

'That's true.'

'Which bit?'

'All of it, although you're welcome to let me know if you're ever back in Italy. I like you. I like your spirit, your independence. I like that you are okay with this being some fun.'

'And nothing else.' She cupped her free hand around his stubbled jaw and drew him closer. She liked him too and would miss him, but... it was a holiday fling, nothing more.

She kissed him. Sliding her leg between his, she manoeuvred herself closer. His tongue flicked against hers and his hand ducked beneath her top, smoothing across her bare skin to her lacy bra.

'You deal in property, right?' she asked between kisses.

He nodded. His hand remained beneath her top, caressing, making it difficult for her to put her thoughts into words. He left kisses on her neck, travelling along her collarbone to the top of her breasts.

'Perhaps you can give me some advice about buying on Capri.'

'You want a place for yourself?' His voice was muffled against her skin.

'It's a thought. You suggested investing. I'm not sure about uprooting myself completely; I don't think my son would thank me for that when he's happy at school with his friends, but a second home. Or two' – she smiled – 'might be a smart move.'

'I will be happy to help you find the perfect place.' He took her hand and pulled her from the depths of the love seat. He grinned as he started to lead her towards the villa. 'But not tonight. *Stasera è per amore.*'

26

FERN

Fern had already started packing earlier that morning. She took a final look around The Garden Room, a wave of sadness hitting her as she closed the door. She'd only been on Capri for a little over a week and at the retreat for just three nights, but she felt its magical pull. She paused outside Edith's room, slipped a note under the door and headed downstairs to find Matteo.

It was inconceivable to Fern to be wealthy enough to charter a helicopter to fly from Capri to Siena to stay at his property in Tuscany for just twenty-four hours. His life was so far removed from her own that taking a helicopter as if he were catching a train blew her mind. His wealth was evident, yet even now, sitting next to him as they flew over the sprawling city of Naples, it didn't feel as if he was trying to flaunt it.

Was it completely reckless to be travelling on her own with a man she'd only met a few days ago? Maybe, but she trusted him and was undeniably drawn to him. The acknowledgement that she'd never felt this way about anyone wasn't lost on her. Stella, Amber and Chloe were oblivious to what she was doing. They were somewhere off the coast and she was getting further and further away from them. Matteo's housekeeper knew she'd gone with him, and Fern's note for Edith explained where she was. She'd see her before she returned to Villa Giardino. She had much to thank Edith for.

What would Paul think? Fern clenched her fists. Why was she worrying? This was her time. Did she really believe he was thinking about her, wondering how she was doing, if she was enjoying herself? She doubted it very much. Going with Matteo to his villa in Tuscany was no different to Stella and the girls getting on a yacht with four Italian men Amber and Chloe had met.

Except it was different. Instead of meeting on a drunken night out, Fern had had the chance to get to know Matteo and to form the beginning of a friendship. She craved his company and thought about him far more than was healthy for someone who was married. She fought back the thought that she was cheating emotionally. Matteo was becoming a friend, that was all. Yet it felt more than that, and she couldn't bury the feeling that she was on dangerous territory. If she'd been worried about leading him on the other night, what did saying yes to going to Tuscany with him suggest?

* * *

Tuscany was more beautiful than Fern had imagined. She'd been in awe of the view as they flew across the country, but the taxi journey from Siena through rolling countryside was even more impressive, the road often lined by Tuscan stone villas and cypress trees, the green fresh against the warm, earthy gold and apricot tones of the ancient stone buildings.

Fern gazed out in silence. Matteo was sitting next to her in the back of the taxi, yet he allowed her to quietly soak up the view of villages filled with stone villas and monasteries, the differing greens of vineyards and olive groves revealing themselves as they raced down hills.

The driver turned off the main road onto a narrower one, leaving behind any hint of civilisation. A golden shimmer threaded itself across the countryside, bathing the green hills, pockets of woodland and vineyards in light.

They crested a hill and, through the front windscreen, Fern spied a series of typically Tuscan stone buildings set within expansive walled grounds.

'There it is,' Matteo said with a smile. 'Il Ritiro Toscano. Home.'

Fern was lost for words as the taxi turned onto a dirt track that ran alongside one of the walls. They pulled up in a parking area outside an arched entrance.

Matteo paid and thanked the driver. Fern got out of the taxi into the peace of the late afternoon. Matteo joined her and the taxi churned up dust as it sped off.

Fern stared in awe at the graceful lines of the buildings. The stonework was a myriad of earthy colours, warm and inviting, with arched windows and a muted red tiled roof flecked with lichen.

'It's utterly stunning,' she finally said as she followed Matteo through the archway. Various stone buildings – living quarters, towers and stables – clustered a large area of grass within the sprawling walls.

'It dates back to the early sixteenth century and was once a monastery. It's been in my father's family for a long time. My great-grandparents restored it from ruins; my grandparents added to it and turned it into a successful hotel; I've since developed it into a retreat. It's a place people can escape from the stresses and trials of life.'

They went through the double wooden doors of the largest building and into a stone entrance hall. Wooden beams crossed the curved ceiling, and carved pillars dominated the space. They were greeted by a couple in their fifties who Matteo introduced as the husband-and-wife team who kept things ticking over whether he was there or not. Fern found the idea of owning somewhere large enough to need its own staff quite incredible, and Stefano and Teresa headed up a team that not only looked after the building and its guests when the retreat was open, but the wider estate with its vineyards, olive groves and woodland.

Stefano took their overnight bags to their rooms and Fern followed Matteo as they explored the inside of what must have once been a sombre and serious place for monks to worship. Matteo talked about the restoration, and as they moved from room to room, Fern began to get an understanding of how much love and attention his family had put into the place.

Art covered the walls, much of it in keeping with the sixteenth-century monastic buildings, but there were lots of modern pieces too, some painted by Matteo himself. The history of the building had been preserved, with exposed stone and wooden beams, large floor tiles and stone fireplaces with centuries' worth of engrained soot. Apart from the colourful art, the materials and decor were natural. As they walked, Fern took in the little details: the iron door handles that she imagined countless hands had touched over the last five hundred years; the cosy throws in muted colours on beds and sofas; and a wall of windows in the dining room looking out onto a central courtyard and beyond to a distant tree-clad hill.

Regardless of Matteo having a team of people to look after his properties, there was a loneliness that surrounded him. He'd briefly talked about his family on his father's side restoring the Tuscan retreat, but he'd swiftly moved the conversation on, which made Fern wonder if he had as strained a relationship with his parents as she did with hers. Whereas the retreat in Anacapri was an oasis in the midst of enclosed Mediterranean gardens, the Tuscan retreat was sprawling and open. Its beauty came from the stone walls contrasting with the verdant meadows and the silvery grey-green of ancient olive trees. It wasn't hard for Fern to imagine spending her time here. She had the distinct feeling that one day wouldn't be enough.

* * *

The sunset cast a mauve wash across the horizon and, with dusk, the stars twinkled in the clear night sky. A table had been laid on a terrace sheltered on two sides by the stone walls of the building and a pergola entwined with clematis and vines filtered out the fresh May breeze.

The smell of the Tuscan stew that Teresa had cooked for them made Fern's mouth water. She'd been living on fish, seafood, pasta and pizza, but a hearty stew with beans and tomatoes with fresh, oven-baked bread to soak up the juice was perfect for the setting. Matteo dished spoonfuls of the steaming stew into two bowls and they tucked in greedily, eating in silence, the only sound the music drifting from the villa and their spoons hitting the sides as steam escaped into the night.

A breeze rustled the leaves. It was cooler here than on Capri and Fern shivered. Matteo reached for a dove-grey throw and handed it to her.

'Thank you.' She smiled and wrapped it around her shoulders.

'I like sitting out here in winter, snuggled under a blanket with the outdoor heater on. And then we have the fires lit inside, which I love. The place is cool in summer and cosy in winter.'

'I'm surprised you'd ever want to leave – even with the other villa on Capri.' She dipped a chunk of bread into the juice at the bottom of her bowl and popped it into her mouth.

'It can feel claustrophobic on Capri, particularly in the summer with hordes of tourists, which is why I come back here. This place is home. It's where I lived from the age of seven till eighteen. It was the place I always came back to when my grandparents were alive.'

'You grew up here with them?' It was quite a place to have grown up, so far removed from the 1950s semi she'd lived in with her parents and brother.

'From the age of seven, yes. Before then, I lived with my family in Florence. My parents were art collectors and had numerous galleries in London and Italy, the main ones in Rome and Florence. My mamma was a renowned artist. I got my passion for art from them, although my talent isn't a patch on my mamma's.'

Even in the subtle light, she could see tears glistening at the corners of his eyes. She wanted to reach across the table and hold him.

'What happened, Matteo?'

Her voice sounded tentative in the stillness of the evening. Drawn to the light and unable to escape, a moth batted against the glass lamp. The sky was inky black and, beyond the retreat, the dark was endless, only broken by the moon half hidden by a patch of cloud. The stars speckled the sky as if silver glitter had been thrown across it. Somewhere in the distance, an owl hooted. One of the horses in the stables nickered in reply.

Perhaps Matteo didn't want to talk about the past. It was obvious to Fern that there was hidden heartache.

He rested his elbows on the table and clasped his hands. 'My parents died in a car crash when I was seven.'

He said it so matter-of-factly that Fern didn't know how to respond, so she waited, certain that emotions were fighting within him despite his assured tone.

'They'd been celebrating their wedding anniversary in Rome when a car sideswiped them.' He drew in a long breath. 'My sister and I were with our grandparents at home in Florence. Everything changed in a few seconds.'

'I am so sorry.'

'It was a long time ago; most of my life has been without them, yet their influence continues to weave itself around me. I only have a few true memories of them, everything else is gleaned from photographs and what my grandparents and sister told me.'

'I didn't realise you have a sister.'

'She's ten years older, that's why I've relied so much on her memories of our parents. She was nearly an adult when the accident happened, and while I came here to live with our grandparents, she went off to university in London and only came back in the summer. The age gap was too big for us to have ever been close, and when I needed her, she left. Not that I blame her. Getting on with her life was the only way she knew how to cope. Our parents would have been proud of her for moving forward and making a success of herself.'

'Where is she now?'

'In Paris with her family – her husband and my niece and nephew. She studied fashion design in London and worked as a model for a while. She caught the attention of a property developer at a London show and she's been with him ever since. He's quite a bit older, so my grandparents had concerns that she was with him because she craved a father figure in her life, but they've stood the test of time.'

'Do you see them often?'

'I see them more than I used to. Gianna wasn't around much while I was growing up. It was too hard for her to be in Italy and all the memories it held without our parents. As well as the art galleries, our parents had property in Rome and Florence. Gianna didn't want our Florence apartment, so I inherited it, while she sold the Rome apartment. We weren't left wanting for anything financially and our grandparents, with this place' – he swept his hands around them – 'were wealthy too.'

'So was the villa on Capri theirs as well?'

Matteo shook his head. 'No, I bought it after I sold the Florence apartment. It had been rented out when I was growing up, but I had no intention of ever living there again. Just the thought of it and the memories it held filled me with sadness. I didn't want to be reminded about that time. I went on holiday with a girlfriend to Capri and spotted the villa. It was run-down, the garden overgrown. The whole place needed renovating but there was something about it. I put in an offer before we left the island. The relationship fizzled out, and I moved to Capri not long after. I wanted somewhere that was mine, somewhere that didn't constantly remind me of the past.'

'Like this place?'

'This place is filled with happy memories though – I have to hold on to the thought that I was lucky to have wonderful grandparents. I wasn't sad here. I loved it far more than I loved living in a city. Don't get me wrong, Florence is wonderful, but I found peace and happiness here after my whole world collapsed.'

27

FERN

Matteo talked a little longer about his life growing up in Tuscany with his grandparents. He shared how the combination of heart-breaking loss at such a young age and experiencing life as an only child, with his sister away, had made him grow up far too fast, missing out on a carefree childhood.

They finished off the Tuscan stew and sipped glasses of a full-bodied local red wine, while Fern shared her vastly different experience of growing up with her parents and a brother in England. Although she was nearer in age to her brother than Matteo was to his sister, they'd never been close. Their lives were different yet neither of them seemed truly happy.

Fern rested back in her chair. Matteo looked at ease next to her as he gazed out across the retreat's shadowed grounds. Fern knew that Stefano and Teresa lived on the estate, yet it felt as though she and Matteo were the only people for miles. There was a peace that she'd never experienced before. Surrounded by countryside and without light pollution, there was something magical about being far from people and the stresses of a city. Even on holiday, especially when the kids were young, she'd never experienced anything remotely like this. When she and Paul went away, they always had to be close to civilisation and near a pub that had Sky Sports. Given the chance, she knew they'd both choose different things, and not just on holiday, but in life too. There was very little they had in common besides the girls and a handful of mutual friends.

'You're quiet,' Matteo said, his voice deep and soft. The classical music that had been playing from somewhere inside had stopped, accentuating the silence of the night.

'I can't get over how peaceful it is. I don't think I've been anywhere quite like it.'

'It takes some getting used to if you only know city living. In Florence, we lived in a big apartment in a large historic building. We were surrounded by the history and beauty of Firenze, but there was all the noise of other people and traffic. I played out on our balcony but wanted open space like we have here, like I enjoyed during holidays with my grandparents. I didn't appreciate that we had a view of the Duomo from nearly every window.'

'Wow, that's incredible. But then there's lots that children don't appreciate. I can understand how being able to run around somewhere like this has far more of an appeal to a seven-year-old than being confined to a balcony.' Fern finished the last sip of her wine and placed the glass on the table. 'Growing up, I never experienced anywhere that had this feeling of freedom.'

'What do you mean?'

'We lived in a semi-detached house in the town I still live in with a tiny garden overlooked by the surrounding houses. One lot of grandparents lived in the same town, the other lot in the suburbs of Bristol. The only freedom we ever had was playing out in the street with other kids. I didn't know any different, but once I had the girls, I wanted more for them. We have a bigger house than my parents did; we're not as overlooked. We have a big garden too, but there's not much difference and I'm certainly no happier than they were.'

'You want more from life?'

Fern shrugged. 'Who doesn't?'

Matteo looked thoughtful but nodded.

'Walk with me.' He took her hand. It was firm, warm and comforting. She didn't pull away.

Although the retreat was large, it felt safe, enclosed within the ancient stone walls. They walked together across the spongy grass, leaving behind the floodlit old monastery. Ahead, the sky seemed endless, with swirls of stars and wisps of clouds.

Fern was far from home, in a place where anything felt possible. She wished anything was. The happiness she'd experienced since being on Capri needed capturing and injecting into her life back home. But it wasn't just because of the island... She glanced at Matteo beside her; he looked so content as they strolled across the magical place he called home. It would be a wrench to leave all this behind tomorrow, to have to say goodbye to him.

They reached an infinity pool that jutted out through a gap in the wall and looked over the valley. Shrouded by darkness, the view of the Tuscan countryside was hidden, apart from the glowing walls of a villa perched on a distant hill, the trees surrounding it dark silhouettes against the moonlit sky.

Matteo stopped on the wooden decking to the side of the pool. 'This is my favourite spot in the whole world. It makes me think of my parents – my grandparents too – imagining them looking down on me from up there.' He let go of her hand and gestured out into the night. 'I haven't talked to anyone about my family for a long time. At least not to someone who doesn't know our history.'

Fern swallowed the lump in her throat. How difficult must it be for him to open up, yet she sensed his relief at unburdening a past filled with sadness. She took hold of his hand. 'I'm glad you did.'

He turned away from the starlit sky back to her. 'I had an incredibly happy time living here. There was heartache because I missed my parents; I missed my sister, but I was lucky with what I gained. I also realise I was luckier than most, having a lifestyle like this as a child and an adult.'

They gazed at each other. Matteo reached for her face, his palm smooth against her cheek. Then his hands found her waist and gently tugged her to him. Time slowed and her senses came alive. His hands were warm through the material of her top and he smelt delicious. The stillness of the night was only broken by the tu-whit and tu-whoo call of tawny owls. His eyes lingered and Fern allowed hers to do the same, drinking in his shadowed eyes that she knew were hazel flecked with green, his strong jawline dark with stubble, the tousled hair she wanted to run her hands through.

He broke their trance, leaning in just enough for their lips to touch. She found herself kissing him back. His arms encircled her, while she slid her hands across his broad shoulders. Their kiss deepened. She was intoxicated. And yet, mixed with the tingling sensation flooding through her was a chill of dismay that what they were doing was so very wrong. What she was doing...

She pulled away. 'I can't. I'm so sorry.'

This was the second time she'd refused him, yet this time she'd tasted his lips, had felt his hands on her skin. She ached for him and knew how close she was to being unable to stop. Because she didn't want to stop. She wanted to keep kissing him; she wanted to smooth her hands across his bare chest and she wanted him to do the same to her. She wanted him to lead her back to the villa, to his room, to pull her down on the bed, to feel his weight on top of her, to feel loved...

'No, I'm sorry.' Matteo's voice was startlingly loud. His hands rested on her chest, just at the top of the curve of her breasts, as if he was attempting to push her away but couldn't.

She reached up and took his face in her hands. 'Don't be. I didn't mean to lead you on.'

He rested his forehead against hers. 'You didn't. I invited you here knowing full well that nothing could happen, and I didn't mean it to. Honestly, I just wanted to show you this place. I... I enjoy your company... I *love* your company.'

If Fern's heart could have melted, it would have done. His words were harder to deal with than the kiss. She felt the same. She treasured spending time with him and the thought of not seeing him again threatened to overwhelm her.

'Honestly, the last few days have been just magical,' she said, her voice cracking. She had to look away otherwise she knew she would cry. She wanted to put words to how she was feeling, but she was unsure how. 'The truth is, I've been unhappy for a long time...'

'With your husband?' Matteo said slowly.

'Yes, but not just because of him. It's my own doing. My unhappiness comes from my inability to accept what I've feared is really going on. It feels like such a huge decision to make after twenty years together – to walk away. I'm not sure what's stopping me – fear, I guess, or worry that I won't cope. I think I've been scared of ripping up my life and going it alone, although the irony is, I constantly feel alone.' A familiar feeling of upset washed over her, manifesting itself as a lump in her throat. The idea of breaking free was as scary as staying. 'I've been pretending for a long time that it's better to keep our family together, but it's making me miserable.'

'You need to learn to live again. You deserve happiness; we all do.' He gazed off into the moon-bathed distance. 'If he doesn't care for you or treat you right, why stay?' He turned back.

'Because it's all I've ever known.'

A breeze drifted across the decking. Fern shivered.

'It's fresh tonight,' Matteo said. 'Let's go inside.'

The moment was broken.

Matteo didn't take her hand, accentuating her sense of loneli-ness as they walked back towards the pooling light of the terrace beneath the pergola.

They cleared the table in a couple of trips to the large kitchen with its curved ceiling and flagstone floor. It didn't take them long to stack the dishwasher. At the retreat in Capri, staff looked after them, Matteo included, but here he mucked in. It was his home after all, even if it was a place fit for a king. Stefano and Teresa ran the place, but he wasn't waited on. She liked that. She also liked that he didn't try to push her further about Paul. Nor did he ques-tion her decision to not take things further after their kiss, or try to talk her into doing something she knew she shouldn't. Not because Paul deserved her faithfulness, but because she'd taken a vow and the last twenty years needed to stand for something. She needed to be the one to hold her head high. She needed to be the better person, because deep down she knew her husband wasn't.

It had been a long day that had started off in Anacapri with her thinking she was returning to the villa to see Stella and the girls. The last thing she'd imagined she'd be doing was ending it alone with Matteo at his Tuscan home.

They left the kitchen and wandered through the sprawling main building of the old monastery to her room. They stopped outside. They'd talked a lot, but there were still things Fern wanted to say to him, but couldn't.

His hands glided down her bare arms. He leaned closer and kissed her gently on each cheek, perhaps lingering a heartbeat longer than a friend would... She wished she could take hold of him and kiss him properly.

'*Buona notte*, Fern.'

'*Buona notte*.' She tore her eyes away from his, retreated into her room and closed the door.

All the dark thoughts that plagued her back home had been

replaced by the worry of doing the right thing, even if it meant misery. Not that she felt miserable right this minute, just confused. She was feeling a lot of things, emotions that had been quashed for years.

She turned on the bedside lamp. The curtains were drawn across the large oval window. The muted, earthy colours had a soothing effect, from the chalky-coloured flagstones and the saffron-yellow bedspread to the natural stone walls and the dark wooden beams. Candles and cushions littered the two steps that led up to the fireplace, the focal point of the room. She imagined how cosy it would be in the depths of winter with a fire crackling in the hearth. She sighed and shivered again. The temperature had dropped and she longed to get into the tempting warmth of the bed. She washed, changed quickly and slipped beneath the heavy covers.

Sleep evaded her. Fern spread out, playing the day over and over. The room was dark, with only a sliver of moonlight creeping through a gap in the curtains. The thick stone walls kept the place remarkably cool, so she was grateful for the warm bedspread. Her mind wandered to other ways of keeping warm. Matteo was just along the hall, alone in his bed. She couldn't get him out of her head, thinking of what they could be doing right now... Nothing good would come of tormenting herself about what might have been if things were different.

28

FERN

Fern's sleep was filled with erotic dreams about Matteo. It was an unsettled night and she woke late. Sunshine slid through the gap in the curtains. Dust motes swirled in the golden light. Her limbs were tangled in the bedsheets and her skin was beaded with sweat. She threw off the covers and went to the en suite for a shower. She emerged feeling refreshed, if tired.

Being in Tuscany with Matteo had opened her eyes to the possibility of a different future, one filled with hope, freedom and happiness. Matteo had ignited something. The strength of her feelings scared her. She'd been stuck in a rut and trapped by expectation and the pressure she'd put on herself to be a dutiful wife, a perfect mother, to keep everything together, when, in reality, their 'happy' family had been falling apart. She'd turned a blind eye to what was really going on, both around her and inside her heart.

Staying at Il Ritiro d'Arte had reminded her of who she'd once been and showed her who she had become. It had given her time to think about who she *wanted* to be. She'd made new friends and had talked to people who didn't know her, who weren't frightened to ask the difficult questions. It had been the reality check she'd needed.

Anxiety attacked her stomach as she dressed in a mid-length skirt and blouse and went to find Matteo. He hadn't been fazed when she'd stopped their kiss. She'd loved that. She was also touched by the way he'd opened up to her too.

Over breakfast, he was as warm and open as he'd been on Capri. Then, with business to attend to, he met with the staff that looked after the retreat, and she explored. While the views on Capri had been dramatic and a glamour permeated the place, the Tuscan retreat was nestled in tranquil countryside. Vineyards studded the landscape, and cypress trees and the stone walls of an ancient fortress topped the rolling hills. It was hands down the most beautiful place she'd ever visited.

Right then, gazing out at the calming green, Fern made a promise to herself that she wasn't going to continue feeling lost and pathetic.

* * *

They stayed for lunch, a simple but delicious spread of fresh crusty bread, sun-dried tomatoes, salami, vine tomatoes and a couple of local cheeses. The whirlwind twenty-four hours had – unsurprisingly – flown by and all too soon they were heading back along the picturesque Tuscan road towards Siena and the heliport.

It was quite the life he lived, with a luxury villa on Capri and a sprawling sixteenth-century monastery-turned-retreat in Tuscany. Despite opening up to each other, much had been left unsaid, particularly when it came to their feelings. Matteo was constantly surrounded by guests, friends and staff, yet a loneliness enveloped him, a feeling that Fern connected with. She had a husband, two daughters, plenty of friends and work colleagues, yet so much of the time she felt completely on her own.

They were both subdued and lost in their own thoughts when

they eventually reached Anacapri. Fern was left feeling emotionally
wrung out. They were welcomed back by Ana and Arthur who
drew them in to the orangery to talk to Matteo about his painting.
Fern made her excuses and went to her room to finish packing
properly. Stella had messaged her to say they were already back on
Capri. Fern couldn't put off leaving any longer.

Edith wasn't at the retreat; Fern was rather relieved because she
thought she might burst into tears if she'd started asking questions
about Tuscany.

Matteo booked a taxi to take her to the piazzetta. She met him
downstairs in the entrance hall. Her heart thumped and her palms
sweated as she gazed up at him.

'Tell Edith goodbye, but I'll come back and say goodbye properly before I leave Capri.'

'Good, I'm glad we'll see you again.'

His eyes traced her face and he took her hand in his. She swallowed back the lump that had formed in her throat. All she wanted
to do was fling her arms around him and never let go.

'Thank you for everything.' She reached up, kissed him on each
cheek and left.

Villa Giardino was shadowed, but music and chatter drifted from
somewhere outside. Dusk had descended. The moon shone
brightly, casting a silver glimmer across the dimly lit grounds. Fern
considered retreating to her room. She didn't want to face anyone,
didn't want to try and put into words the impact the last few days
had had on her or share anything about it. She stopped for a
moment. The garden reminded her of Matteo's retreat, with its
winding path, looming trees and the sweet scent of flowers. She
gazed up at the sky speckled with stars. It was easy to imagine she

was back there, but she wasn't and she'd have to see the others at some point. She'd already received a message from Stella wondering where she was.

Fern sighed, hefted her rucksack higher on her back and followed the path that meandered around the side of the villa through the garden thick with foliage and flowers. She loved the enclosed garden at Il Ritiro d'Arte with its hidden patios and over-sized pots spilling with flowers and herbs, but the terrace at Villa Giardino with its glowing pool and sweeping view of Capri twinkling with lights still took her breath away. It was the epitome of glamour, yet she longed for the peace of Anacapri and the retreat within its private oasis.

Stella, Amber and Chloe were sitting at the table, facing the view, chatting and laughing together. She wondered if their few days on the yacht had had as profound an impact...

'Fern! You're back!'

The peace was shattered by Stella. They scraped their chairs back as Fern walked over.

'We were expecting you to be here before us.' Stella pulled her into a hug.

Fern dropped her rucksack on the ground and joined them at the table. Chloe smiled warmly and Fern met Amber's eyes. She smiled, but there was a coolness which reminded Fern that she was back to reality.

'You're just in time for dinner,' Stella said. 'Or have you already eaten?'

'I did, but much earlier. I've room for more.'

Lunch on the terrace in Tuscany had only been a few hours ago, but somehow it seemed like a lifetime.

Violetta brought out a large dish of pasta puttanesca and there was a copious amount of wine. Fern relaxed and listened to the conversation fly between Stella, Chloe and Amber. Chloe showed

Fern their Instagram photos as they described the breath-taking beauty of the Amalfi Coast, the dinners they'd had onboard and the party they'd been to in Positano. Fern got the sense that they glossed over some of the details and weren't telling her the full story. She noticed Amber go red at the mention of Desi, and Luca featured a fair bit whenever Stella was talking.

As the evening wore on, a drunken happiness enveloped them. Fern was content to let them dominate the conversation and they were more than happy to share their time aboard a multi-million-pound yacht. It was beyond anything any of them had ever experienced. Much like Fern's time in Anacapri and then Tuscany... Her own cheeks reddened from more than just the wine.

* * *

After the pasta and three bottles of wine had been polished off, Fern escaped to her room to unpack. Despite the tiredness washing over her, it felt too early to go to bed, particularly when they were all back together after days apart. She returned to the pool terrace. Chloe and Amber were whispering together, their smiling faces tanned in the warm light of the terrace lamps.

Stella wandered over, hooked her arm in Fern's and steered her away from the girls.

'Why are you quiet?' Stella asked.

'I'm not.'

'You are, unusually so.'

Fern drew in a long shuddery breath.

'What's up?'

Fern shrugged.

'Are you regretting missing out on our yacht trip filled with sun, sea and—'

'I can imagine what your days were filled with. And no.'

'Did something happen?'

Did something happen? Fern thought. Nothing and everything had happened. Matteo consumed her from the moment she woke, his smiling face beaming into her thoughts, his hazel eyes twinkling mischievously. Everything had been heightened, from the slightest brush of his hand against her skin, to their long chats into the evening where her mind would wander to what it would be like to kiss him. How was it possible for so much to change in just a few days?

'What's going on, Fern?'

'Nothing.' Her tone was sharper than she meant, but she was worried that Stella would see through her, that she'd cheated on Paul emotionally if not physically... apart from the kiss which she'd cut short. Flustered, she breathed deeply.

She'd never been tempted by someone else. Not in twenty-one years. More than half her life. Yet something had awoken inside her, something more than the feelings of lust she'd had as a free spirit in her teens when she'd believed she was in love with Paul. Did she avoid going out with single friends, Stella in particular, because she feared that she'd be tempted to stray? And on the occasions she did go out, if a guy danced behind her and slid his hands around her waist, the tingle of excitement she'd felt when young and single had been replaced by confusion and worry. She was married with kids, her life far removed from what it once was. And here with Matteo... They'd talked and bared their souls. A look, a touch meant more to Fern than she'd thought possible. How could she begin to convey the way she felt to Stella? Stella who still behaved like they had as teenagers, who'd gone on the yacht to have a good time, and by a good time, Fern knew exactly what she meant.

'Well,' Stella said, sighing, 'if you want to talk, I'm here.' She patted Fern on the arm as if she was about to leave her to her thoughts, but faltered. 'Do you know, despite my protestations, I honestly had this romantic notion that I'd come out here and find love. Silly, I know. Maybe it's because I desperately want to meet the love of my life before anyone knows I have money. And I haven't yet met the one.'

Fern glanced at her. 'What about the guys on the yacht?'

'Oh, I had the time of my life with Luca, but it was nothing more than a bit of fun. Exactly as I expected and exactly the reason you weren't keen to go. We both knew that was all it was going to be, a few days of enjoying each other.' She raised an eyebrow. 'Now I'm back here and he's sailed off into the sunset to carry on with his life.'

'And you're really okay with that?' Fern frowned.

'Yes, absolutely. Do you know, if there's one thing this holiday has taught me it's that I'm okay on my own. I never want to compromise on a relationship again and end up tied to someone for the sake of it, all because I don't want to grow old alone.'

Fern snorted. 'Is that a dig at me?'

'God, no. I didn't mean it that way.'

Except there was something in her tone that suggested she did; Fern assumed she just didn't have the guts to tell her.

29

STELLA

'A package has arrived for Fern,' Violetta said. 'I left it in the hall.'

'Thanks, I'll take it to her room.'

Stella wandered through the villa, noticing how it seemed even more peaceful than usual. Chloe was still in bed and Amber had taken Fern out for breakfast in Capri. That in itself didn't bode well. Stella sighed. Someone had to come clean to Fern; perhaps it was better it came from Amber.

She reached the entrance hall and spotted a large flat parcel leaning against the wall. It was beautifully wrapped in brown craft paper with green and white striped string tying it together. Stella took it to Fern's room. Unlike her own room, Fern's was tidy, with everything put away and no clothes left scattered across the bed. All the make-up on the dressing table was neatly laid out, organised like Fern's house was. Everything had its place; home was somewhere she was in control. On the outside, Fern seemed perfectly happy. Stella had lost count of how many times Fern had said that Paul and the girls were her life, but it was becoming more and more evident just how unhappy she really was.

Stella was about to put the package down when an envelope

caught her eye. It wasn't stuck down. She faltered, momentarily torn between doing the right thing and a desire to find out who it was from. She slipped the envelope from beneath the string and held it in her hands. Fern wouldn't have a clue if she opened it. She glanced behind her at the empty room and, without another thought, pulled out a postcard with a painting of a tropical garden on the front. Turning it over, she read it, then read it slowly two more times.

> Dear Fern,
>   You left your painting here; I thought you might like to have it. You have talent.
>   I miss our late-night chats so much.
>   I miss you.
>   Yours, Matteo x

Stella read it for a fourth and final time before sliding it back in the envelope and tucking it beneath the string. She left the package on the end of the bed. There was an awful lot Fern hadn't told her about her few days on the art retreat. And from that note alone, Stella wasn't surprised. It accounted for her reticence and why she seemed so distracted.

Good for her, Stella thought. It was about time Fern finally lived a little.

* * *

Stella was sitting in the living room reading when Fern and Amber returned a couple of hours later. She was certain that Amber wouldn't have been able to keep her secret any longer, but from the relaxed chatter coming from the entrance hall, they seemed quite happy. Was she cowardly wishing for Amber to break the news about Paul's infidelity? Not that it would soften the blow in the slightest when the whole truth came out.

Amber paused in the doorway of the living room. 'Where's Chloe?' she asked.

Stella put her book down. 'Still in bed as far as I know. Go wake her up, otherwise she's going to miss lunch as well as breakfast.'

Amber disappeared in the direction of the stairs and Fern wandered into the living room.

'Everything okay?' Stella asked.

Fern sat on the opposite end of the sofa. 'Yes, surprisingly it is. We just had a really rather lovely breakfast and chatted about Amber's course and what she'd like to do once she graduates. Admittedly, this is the first time she's been friendly with me the whole time we've been here, but I'll chalk that down as a win. What have you been up to?'

'Oh, just chilling.'

'Good book?'

'Uh-huh. A parcel arrived for you.'

'Oh, really?' Fern frowned.

If the only way to get Fern to confide in her was to initially piss her off, then so be it. Stella couldn't hold her tongue. 'Who's Matteo?'

Fern looked at her sharply.

'I wasn't sure who the package was for, so I read the note,' Stella lied. 'Sorry.'

'He's the owner of the art retreat.'

'Uh-huh.' Stella watched Fern carefully. She knew the look, the flush of embarrassment because there was something there, because whoever this Matteo was, Fern really liked him. 'What's going on with him?'

'Nothing.' She was too quick to answer. The redness of her cheeks deepened.

'These late-night chats, that's all it was, talking?'

'Of course! I'm married.'

'I know you are.' It was Stella's turn to feel embarrassed. She'd witnessed it for too many years, Fern plodding through life being the dutiful wife and a perfect mother, keeping the house clean and tidy while muddling along, working jobs her heart wasn't really in. The spirited friend she remembered, who used to throw all caution to the wind, who drank too much, snogged strangers, was passionate and funny, naughty and courageous, that Fern would have done more than just chat.

'Why would you even insinuate that I'd do something like that?'

Her embarrassment had seemingly turned to rage. Stella glanced towards the hallway, concerned Fern's rising voice would filter through the villa.

'I really didn't mean to upset you.'

'It was a thoughtless thing to say.' Fern scrambled to her feet, stalked across the living room and went out through the patio doors.

Stella sat quietly for a moment, contemplating what she should do. It was an impossible situation. Fern was bound to get hurt, the one person who didn't deserve to and the person most likely to. Whatever this Matteo meant to her, it was obvious that he'd ignited something. Stella believed that Fern hadn't cheated, but she sensed her anger was there because she'd at least thought about it.

She made a decision and went upstairs to find Amber. Chloe's door was still closed. She leaned in close but couldn't hear anything. She wandered along the landing and knocked on Amber's door.

'Come in!'

Amber was sitting on her bed, a stack of pillows wedged behind her. Her room was probably the best one, overlooking the pool with its own private sun-flooded balcony.

Amber glanced up. 'If you're looking for Chloe, she's getting a shower.'

'I came to talk to you.'

Amber frowned but put her phone down.

Stella perched on the edge of the bed.

'Why didn't you talk to her this morning? When we spoke on the yacht we thought it would be better coming from you.'

Amber folded her arms. 'It's just Dad—'

'Screw your dad and what he made you promise. He's the one in the wrong.'

'*You* need to tell her.' Amber shook her head. 'I can't do this. I can't break Mum's heart; she hates me enough as it is.'

'Your mum does not hate you.'

'That's what you think. I've given her every reason to.'

'Only because your dad put you in a terrible position.'

Amber swiped angrily at her eyes. 'I should never have agreed to not say anything. The longer it's gone on, the harder it is to tell the truth. I just wish Mum would open her eyes and see what's staring her in the face.'

'I think she's beginning to...' Stella gazed towards the balcony and wondered where Fern had gone.

Amber sniffed. 'Well, with Dad and Ruby coming out tomorrow, it might all kick off. Will be about time too.'

Stella's attention snapped back to Amber. 'What do you mean your dad's coming out?'

Amber avoided her gaze. 'I messaged him when we were on the yacht that if he didn't fess up to Mum, then I would. I was drunk and angry.' She shrugged. 'It was after you gave me that bollocking about using protection and going easy on Mum. Think I freaked him out a bit. He told me yesterday he'd managed to book a ticket.'

The walls were closing in. Panic pulsed through Stella. One way or another, the truth was going to come out before they left Capri.

'Does your mum know he's coming?'

Amber shrugged. 'He asked me not to tell her. Don't know if Ruby has.'

'Oh for fuck's sake, Amber. I know you're trying to do what you think's best for her, but your dad showing up is not going to help things at all.'

Stella stormed from the room. She leant on the banister at the top of the stairs. The blue and white tiled floor below blurred though her tears, the pattern shifting, making her head woozy. She felt nauseous, that all too familiar feeling of everything closing in overwhelming.

She fumbled for her phone and scrolled through until she reached Paul's name. It rang and rang, then went to answerphone. She didn't leave a message. She tried him again but on his other phone, the one Fern didn't know about. It was switched off. She swore and pressed end call.

The banister was firm and smooth beneath her fingers. Her knuckles were white, her breathing ragged. She tried to take long deep breaths to slow her thudding heart as she thought things through. She'd made one mistake and it was about to ripple through everyone's lives. There really was only one option. She should have done this a long time ago. She took the stairs two at a time and headed outside.

The day was still and humid. The pool glistened beneath the midday sun, and the green of the garden was welcome with shady spots. Stella found Fern at the furthest reaches of the grounds, standing by the stone wall that ran the length of the property, separating it from the soaring island view. Red and white wallflowers grew from the gaps in the stone.

Stella joined Fern and tried to steady her breathing. 'Do you like him, this Matteo?' she asked quietly.

Neither of them looked at each other, their focus on the view over Capri.

'We got on well. He's a nice guy.' Her voice was clipped.

'But do you like him like him?'

Fern turned to her. 'What if I do? What difference would it make? It's not like I would ever cheat on Paul.'

A coldness swept through Stella at the truth of Fern's words; her faithful friend, a loyal wife and mother. Everything Stella wasn't. Fern was right to hold her head high and be angry with her for suggesting she'd do something with a man she'd met on holiday. But she sensed how conflicted Fern was. She could imagine the sorts of thoughts tumbling around her head. The right thing to do might not always be the right thing. Good advice for herself too. Long-held secrets needed to come out, but it was the impact on other people she feared the most. The impact on her friend.

'I don't doubt you, Fern, but I know you're not happy with Paul. And for good reason.'

'What does that even mean?'

'He's not worth it.'

Fern spun round, her lips pursed, eyes flashing with anger. 'My marriage isn't worth it? Is that what you're honestly saying?'

'Well... I'm sorry... but, yes.'

'Why? Why do you think that?'

'I think you know why, deep down. You know what Paul's like... You know he's not faithful.' Her heart shattered as the words tumbled out.

Fern turned away, her shoulders hunched as she leaned on the wall. 'How do you know?' Her voice was faint and she looked smaller and more vulnerable than Stella had ever seen her before.

'Because I do.' She gingerly placed her hand on Fern's arm.

Fern shrugged her off.

'Amber knows too. I'm so sorry, Fern. She caught Paul with

another woman. She's wanted to tell you, but he made her promise not to...'

'He did what?' There was an iciness to Fern's voice that sent a shiver through Stella. It was as if the warmth of the sun had vanished, the birdsong had been muted, the colour drained from the flowers, trees, sea and sky. There was just her and Fern left standing, emotions and lies bound tight around them.

Somehow Stella managed to find her voice. 'There's something else I need to tell you.'

30

FERN

Fern didn't have a clue where she was going, she just needed to get away. The sense of peace and happiness she'd discovered during her time at the retreat in Anacapri and then in Tuscany had dispersed like smoke on the wind with Stella's words. She stormed away from the villa, her feet pounding the narrow twisting road. Tears streaked her face and blurred her vision, making the green trees merge with the grey stone of the walls.

How had everything come crashing down so suddenly? At least it felt like that, even if she knew it had been building to this. But Stella's confession... A sob caught in her throat. She'd left the villa without anything: no phone, no money or any idea of where she was headed. *To hell with it*, she thought. She wasn't going to go back. She couldn't face Amber and she certainly didn't want to see Stella.

She reached Capri town and people flooded the streets, hemming her in. She wanted to escape somewhere peaceful, away from everyone. She forced herself forward. The glamour around her in the shop windows, the flowers spilling from balconies and the good-looking couples sitting outside cafes sipping espressos jarred with the anger churning inside. She was glad her sunglasses hid her puffy eyes.

She had no money to get the funicular or one of the brightly coloured open-top taxis, so she took the path Matteo had told her about, known only to the locals, that led between beautiful gardens and villas all the way down to Marina Grande before she found her way to the steep path that led back up to Anacapri. There was only one place she wanted to go. She had a vague idea of how to get there on foot, even if it was a trek.

The start of the Scala Fenicia was unassuming, just narrow steps next to a stone wall right on the edge of the road. Fern started up them but immediately had to squeeze past a couple coming the other way. She pushed onwards past villas and olive trees, her pace fast considering the climb. She was relieved when the path led beneath the leafy canopy of the wooded hillside. The shade was welcome, although in the humidity, it didn't help to cool her down. Only snatches of blue sky could be seen through the branches and the sea was hidden by the screen of trees. She didn't want to stop. She knew if she did, her energy would desert her and she was finding it a hard enough struggle as it was to put one foot in front of the other, her thighs protesting with the effort. Her mouth was dry and she envied the people she passed heading down the hill to the fresher air of the marina, but there was no way she was turning back.

By the time she emerged from the trees back into the sunshine, sweat trickled down the sides of her face, her calves ached and her sandals were rubbing her toes. She'd power-walked up hundreds of steps, anger and frustration surging with the effort. She paused to catch her breath, barely taking in the sweeping view down to the marina. The day was becoming increasingly muggy, with iron-grey clouds beginning to cluster over the hillside opposite.

Fern continued her climb. The narrow walkway beyond the

ancient doorway that had once separated the two parts of the island was rammed with people taking selfies, soaking up the view and standing chatting together. She brushed past them, not caring if she was asking politely or not. She was hot, flustered and desperate to be somewhere cool and calm, away from the bustle of so many people. Mostly, she wanted to get away from her thoughts. Walking had helped to work off some of her anger, yet it had given her a huge amount of time to think and relive not just her conversation with Stella, but conversations with Paul over the past few years. And Amber. It broke her heart that she'd been a part of his lies. Fern wiped away fresh tears with the back of her hand.

The last bit of the walk was a slog, along an incredibly steep and winding path before she crossed the cliffside road and puffed her way past Villa San Michele – the place she never got to explore with Edith.

More tears welled when she reached the gates of Il Ritiro d'Arte. She pushed them open and was enveloped into the soothing calm of the garden. The sun was extinguished by a cloud, the sudden dullness matching her mood. Even now, with her mind in turmoil as she walked the path between lemon trees and glossy green bushes, it still felt like somewhere she could block out real life. A place to escape to. Wasn't that exactly what she'd done?

Hushed voices travelled across the garden, whoever was talking obscured by the undergrowth. She caught a few words in German. She wondered if Edith was here or out somewhere in Anacapri with her sketchbook.

Fern headed towards the villa and up the wide steps to the grand entrance. She faltered outside the doors. She couldn't just wander in; she wasn't a guest any longer. She thumped the large knocker and waited.

She was expecting the housekeeper, Ana, but as the door swung open, her heart skipped at the shadowy form of Matteo.

'Fern?'

Yet more tears welled at the sight of him and the comforting familiarity of his voice.

'What are you doing here?'

'I'm so sorry, I didn't know where else to go.'

He moved closer and wrapped her in his arms. She sobbed against him, dampening his linen shirt. How many times had she longed for him to hold her over the past few days? And the one time he had, the one time she'd allowed herself to give in to her feelings and they'd kissed for the briefest of moments, she'd stopped him. But she hadn't wanted it to be like this – hurt and upset by an awful truth that had finally come out.

'Hey,' he said, gently wiping away her tears with his thumbs. 'What's the matter?'

She sighed and thought, *How to even begin*.

Matteo took her hand and led her through the villa. It was the middle of the afternoon and quiet. Fern imagined the guests were still out exploring or tucked away somewhere painting. They reached the empty orangery and he closed the door behind them.

Despite being surrounded by glass on three sides with the view into the garden, the usually bright and sunny room was as dull and grey as outside. The storm clouds that had been clustering as Fern had walked across the island now covered the sky.

Matteo switched on the lamps on the tables at either end of the sofa, sat down and patted the space next to him.

'Talk to me, Fern. What's happened?'

'I told you I had suspicions that my husband had been unfaithful...' She sat down, took a deep breath and looked him in the eye. 'Well, Stella just confirmed it.'

Matteo's eyes narrowed. 'How does she know?'

'Because she's just one of the people he's been unfaithful with.'

Saying it out loud to Matteo made it all the more real. More so than even Stella, just a couple of hours earlier, standing on the villa terrace admitting something that had shocked Fern to her core. How had she not known? How had she been so blind to the feelings that Stella had carried for Paul all these years. The feelings her best friend had for her husband. Life was beyond cruel. The one person she had always turned to had betrayed her.

'I've slept with Paul.' Stella's words had wrapped around her heart, twisting and squeezing until she felt barely able to breathe. It was as if time had slowed and she'd noticed every detail: the tears glistening in Stella's fearful eyes; the beads of sweat on her top lip; and the way she clasped the stone wall, knuckles tensed white. Once she'd started talking, it was as though a floodgate had opened, the whole sordid tale tumbling out, from Stella and Paul's drunken antics at a party before Fern and Paul had even got together to another drunken decision almost two decades later when loneliness had driven Stella into Paul's arms.

Matteo was watching her, waiting for her to continue speaking. She realised she'd been lost in her thoughts, playing over the conversation with Stella. She steeled herself; she'd come here for a reason. Matteo was sitting with her, ready to listen, his face full of concern.

'About a year ago, my best friend slept with my husband.' She said it matter-of-factly, as if she was talking about someone else. 'She assured me it only happened the once since we were married, but she's not the only person he's been messing about with. He has, um, a second, secret phone and he gives the number to women he's sleeping with, Stella included. That's the short version.'

Matteo's jaw clenched as he shook his head. '*Che bastardo.*'

'I couldn't agree with you more.' She swiped away a tear from her cheek. 'I've been such an idiot.'

'You can't think like that, Fern.' He shuffled closer, concern written in his furrowed brow. 'There's nothing wrong with putting effort into making a marriage work.'

'I'm an idiot for ignoring all the signs and for not listening to the niggling voice inside about him. I've gone on for years, being played for a fool.'

Large drops of rain splattering on the glass made them both jump. Ominous dark clouds had turned the bright afternoon to a premature dusk. It felt safe cocooned within the glass walls of the orangery as the rain lashed down, splashing off leaves and thundering on to the path outside.

She turned back to Matteo. 'I've felt guilty for so long for not being happy with my lot. For not being satisfied by a lovely home, a husband, healthy happy kids.'

'You shouldn't feel you have to be satisfied by any of that. Certainly not by a cheating husband. And now your children are grown up, you need to think beyond them and focus on yourself. You're doing them no favours if you're unhappy. If they care for you and love you, then they won't want to see you like this.' He reached for her hand and clasped it. 'I get it, though, that guilt. Sometimes I feel guilty for thinking how different my life would have been if it wasn't for the accident. The idea of not having grown up at the Tuscan retreat fills me with sadness, but then I realise what that means and the guilt is terrible, because, of course, if I could go back in time and change my parents' fate, I would in a heartbeat.'

They fell silent, their hands entwined together, the drumming rain somehow comforting.

'I'm angry about all the lies,' Fern eventually said. 'I don't care about Paul. He obviously hasn't cared about me for a very long time. This is the push I needed to change my life for the better. To leave. My get-out-of-jail-free card.'

'If that's truly how you feel, then it's the right thing to do.'

She held his gaze and drank him in, wishing they'd met under different circumstances. Just looking at him now left her conflicted about how she felt and what was right. She breathed in the citrusy scent of the orangery, which was as comforting as Matteo's presence, quiet and dependable.

Exhaustion washed over her. So many emotions were whirling. It wasn't just anger, sadness and heartache she was battling with; there was excitement too, possibility, hope. A mishmash of feelings that left her unable to think straight.

'Can I please stay here tonight?' Her hand tensed in his. 'I can't face going back and seeing everyone.'

'Of course, the room's still yours.'

They met each other's eyes. She knew what he was thinking, because she was wishing it too, that the passion bubbling beneath the surface could be acted on. She adored him for not pushing her into doing something she might regret; she adored him for understanding and supporting her, for offering his friendship without the expectation of anything more.

* * *

After spilling her heart to Matteo, Fern retreated to her room and slept. It was dark when she woke. The rain had stopped and it felt fresher, the air curling in through the open window, bringing with it the scent of vegetation and damp soil. Fern regretted leaving the villa without anything, not even a cardigan. She wondered what Amber was thinking and then felt awful for not talking to her before storming out.

She switched on the lamp on the bedside table and forced herself off the bed. A fresh breeze made the petunias sway in the window box outside. She shivered and forced the window closed. Was she foolish to have run away instead of facing up to things back at the villa? Would they be worried about her? She drew in a deep breath; she needed to think about herself for once.

A knock made her jump. She padded across the room and opened the door. She was expecting it to be Matteo but found Edith holding a tray instead.

'I've been talking to Matteo.' She gave Fern a knowing look. 'We thought you might be hungry. I said I'd bring it up to you.'

Fern had a hard job containing her tears at their kindness. 'Thank you,' she said, stepping back to let her in.

Edith set the tray on the table next to the armchair and handed Fern a bowl. 'Risotto with prawns flavoured with lemon from the garden. We had it for dinner this evening. Matteo didn't want to disturb you.'

Fern had lost track of time. She gratefully cupped the bowl in her hands and sat in the armchair while Edith perched on the bed.

'So, Matteo got you up to speed with everything that's happened?' Fern took a spoonful of the risotto.

'He did. I hope you don't mind?'

Fern shook her head and savoured the fragrant, citrusy rice. She was relieved to not have to retell the whole story. Once was enough. What on earth did Matteo think of her? It was hardly fair to have burdened him with her heartache and sorrow. It was hard to believe they'd known each other for less than a week and yet she'd retreated here, finding comfort in two strangers. *No, not strangers,* she thought. *Two new friends.*

She looked up from the risotto to Edith. 'What would you do in my situation? If you'd just found out that your husband was a lying, cheating bastard.'

Edith folded her hands in her lap and sighed. 'Now, there's a question. What would I do...? I'm not sure I'm the best person to ask, considering I have many regrets and have made many mistakes when it comes to affairs of the heart. So, I can only advise you from my unqualified viewpoint. I know this much: when I go home this time, I need to be true to myself. I'm having an affair with a married woman who's made it clear that she's not going to leave her husband and she's also ashamed of what we are. It can never be public; we can never be truly happy.'

Fern put down the bowl and went over and sat beside her. 'Oh Edith, I'm so sorry.'

'Oh don't be, dear Fern.' She patted her hand. 'If anything, coming here once again by myself has made me realise I'm happy on my own. Don't get me wrong, I love company. I've adored spending time with you and Matteo and all the other guests, but I can't continue to live a lie. And I think it's the same for you. You weren't happy with your husband even before you found out the truth. Now you know, without a doubt, what he's really like. You deserve so much more. You deserve to be happy and if that means striking out on your own, however hard and scary that may be, in the long run won't that be the best thing?'

Fern nodded, unable to speak for fear of bursting into tears.

'Have you spoken to your husband?'

Fern shook her head. 'I can't, not yet. Right now I'd be happy if I never saw or spoke to him again. I'm so angry. I'm angry with both of them, but Paul...' She clenched a handful of the bedspread, imagining for a second that it was Paul's neck she was squeezing.

'I admire your restraint.'

Fern frowned. 'What do you mean?'

'By not screaming down the phone at your husband. I'm not sure I'd be able to hold my tongue. But also your restraint with Matteo.'

She met Edith's eyes.

'The chemistry between you is electric. You'd have to be blind not to notice it. And however much Matteo would like there to be more between the two of you, your behaviour has been honourable...'

'It really hasn't...'

Edith held up her hand. 'How you've behaved and the restraint you've shown is admirable,' she said firmly. 'It makes me think that Matteo will only love you all the more for it.'

31

STELLA

A couple of hours after Fern had stormed out, Amber had found Stella sobbing in her room and had comforted her before the whole truth had spilled out and Amber's concern had morphed into anger. Stella couldn't face retelling the sordid story again, but she knew she had to, so she called Chloe and made them both sit down in the living room. It felt as if she was talking about someone else as she matter-of-factly revealed her messy past, admitting to a one-night stand with Paul and the knowledge that he'd been unfaithful with other women more times than even Amber knew.

Chloe remained quiet and ashen-faced. When Stella finished talking, she didn't say a word, just shook her head and rushed from the room. Amber's earlier rage had evaporated and she stayed, looking confused and subdued. They sat in silence, the stormy weather raging outside. The wind rattled the windows and drops of water pattered on to the paving. Stella shivered and pulled her cardigan tighter.

'You have every right to be angry with me.' Stella eventually found her voice. 'God knows Fern is.'

Amber huffed but didn't say anything. She was frowning, her

arms folded across her chest, a scowl on her lips. To Stella, she looked as if she was still trying to process what had happened. It was a lot to take in, she knew.

'You do realise you've destroyed your friendship,' Amber said coldly.

Stella tried to keep her voice steady. 'I'm well aware of what I've done. But I couldn't not tell her. She deserves to know the truth. You know that as much as I do.'

Amber sniffed. Her face looked pained, as if she was trying to hold back tears. 'After catching him that one time, I... I didn't think it was the first time. I assumed there were more women. I didn't think you'd be one of them. He's treated Mum like shit. You have too.'

'I know. *I know*. There's no excuse. I convinced myself that it wasn't really cheating because I'd already slept with him before he was even with your mum, but somehow that just makes it worse, as if I've been hiding this big dark secret from her for all these years.'

'You have.'

Stella held out her hands, attempting to placate Amber whose face was a storm cloud of emotion. 'I can't change what's happened, but if there's anything I can do to help Fern get through this, I will.'

Amber suddenly stood, knocking a candleholder off the coffee table in her haste. 'You've done enough, don't you think?'

'It doesn't mean I don't care or that I don't want to attempt to put things right.'

'I don't want to discuss this any longer. It's my parents you're talking about. My dad you've...' She breathed in deeply and bit her lip. 'I'm going to my room.'

'You need to phone your dad and persuade him not to come out here tomorrow.'

'No. I don't have to do anything. This is your problem.'

Stella watched Amber stalk away. Moments later, a door

upstairs slammed. She slumped on the edge of the nearest sofa. She'd messed up on an epic scale. She'd pissed off her own daughter and Fern's daughter. And poor Fern. She couldn't blame her for fleeing, probably into the arms of the Italian she so obviously fancied. Stella berated herself, knowing full well that would be the last thing Fern would be thinking about and even if she had, Stella understood she was in no position to judge. She'd left the villa because she'd wanted to escape from *her*. *She* was the cause of her heartache. Actually, no, not just her, Paul too. He'd made vows and had broken them countless times. He didn't deserve to get off scot-free.

She grabbed her mobile from the coffee table and called Paul's number. Still no answer. She rang his private number. It went straight to answerphone. She threw the phone on the sofa.

Maybe she should get a taxi and go to the retreat, apologise again and try to talk to Fern. It was a stupid idea, she knew. Fern had left for a reason and needed the time to process everything. The least she could do was give her that.

With Fern gone, Paul not answering and the girls in their rooms, there was nothing else Stella could do. She briefly considered calling Luca. She sighed. They'd said goodbye on Capri's marina with a kiss. They'd swapped numbers and befriended each other on Facebook. They were going to keep in touch and he was going to help her find a villa on the island, but she was uncertain if there'd be any more to it than that. The last thing she was going to do was call him with her tearful story of what a total and utter bitch she'd been. Instead, she went to bed early, with a miserable evening spent on her own before her.

* * *

Stella woke to a watery sun straining through the windows. The sky was pale blue and streaked by high white clouds. Her head felt like she'd done ten rounds with Tyson Fury, but it wasn't a hangover.

The day might be fine, she thought as she showered and dressed in a daze, *but a storm is brewing.*

Breakfast was a sombre affair, with neither Amber nor Chloe wanting to talk. If Violetta sensed that anything was wrong, she didn't ask.

'Enough of this,' Stella eventually said, once they had drunk their lattes and had eaten fresh bread with strawberry jam. 'You're pissed with me, I get it, but it's not helping anyone.' She scraped back her chair and paced across the terrace and back again as she tried to formulate her thoughts. She looked at a sullen Amber. 'I tried phoning your dad yesterday evening, but he's not answering. He and your sister will be arriving this afternoon.' She turned to Chloe, whose scowl had remained from the night before. 'Jacob and Rhod will be arriving too. And Fern's missing and upset and doesn't know that Paul's even going to be here. Not to mention we're supposed to be celebrating our birthdays tomorrow. So, you know, fun times.' She folded her arms and glared at them. 'You can be as angry at me as you like, but we need to make sure Fern's okay. Do you agree with me or not?'

They both nodded. Stella was relieved that they seemed to understand the gravity of the situation and didn't make a snide remark, which she knew she deserved.

'So,' she said. 'Fern is our priority.'

'We don't even know if she's okay,' Amber said with a wobble. 'She left her phone here.'

'I think it's about time we went and found her. And by we, I mean you. I know where the retreat is; let's get you a taxi.'

32

FERN

It was a relief to be back at the retreat spending time with Matteo again, particularly after the events of the last twenty-four hours, but Fern was dreading having to say another goodbye. She was dreading heading home on the weekend too, back to Paul and her disastrous life.

Edith was a comfort. Her unexpected friendship was much-needed and Fern hoped it would continue once they returned to the UK. She wasn't in the mood for socialising with the other guests; she didn't want to relive her heartache by telling the story to anyone else. She also knew that she couldn't hide out here forever. Ruby would be arriving in a couple of hours and she was, at least, longing to see her. Ruby had messaged her yesterday morning full of excitement about her flying visit to Capri. Fern had to go back and face up to things. Anyway, she was still wearing clothes from the day before and felt a fool for running away.

It was time to say goodbye to Matteo and Edith, and perhaps this time, with only three more nights on the island, it would be the final one. Not that she wanted it to be. A huge array of emotions surged through her as she closed the bedroom door behind her and walked along the tiled landing to the stone staircase.

Tuscany drifted into her mind. It had been twenty-four hours spent in a bubble of happiness. It was crazy to have even contemplated being able to hold on to that sort of contentment. Life didn't work like that. Perhaps she'd thought so when she was a young, naive teen who believed she was invincible and the world was hers for the taking but not any more.

Matteo was walking towards the staircase. 'I was just coming to find you. You have a visitor.' He gestured behind him and stepped back.

Fern walked down the last few steps, her eyes landing on the familiar figure standing awkwardly in the large entrance hall.

'Amber?'

'Hey, Mum. Thought I should come and find you. Make sure you're okay.'

Her eyes were red and blotchy, her usually tanned and perfectly made-up face paler and natural. Her worried look made Fern's heart melt. It wasn't just herself who had been put through the wringer.

Matteo gently put a hand on Fern's shoulder. 'Go and talk in my study; you won't be disturbed there.'

Fern led Amber to the study just off the hallway. It was Paul and Stella who had done wrong, yet Fern felt ashamed for Amber having to track her down, for finding her here with Matteo. Not that she was 'with' him in that sense, she was just worried about how it looked. She was also upset that Amber had been put through all of this because her father was a cheat and had drawn her into his lies to protect himself.

Fern closed the door and they sat in the armchairs by the corner bookshelf. She was acutely aware of how much disruption she'd brought into Matteo's life and his peaceful retreat, unloading her woes on him as if she'd known him for years rather than days.

'I'm so sorry, Mum.' Amber broke the silence.

'What are you apologising for?'

'For being so shitty to you. I had no idea about Stella and, um...' She broke off and clenched her jaw.

'But you knew he'd cheated on me?'

Amber nodded. 'Yeah.'

'It's me who should be sorry. I should have seen through everything; the way you were behaving. I get the animosity you had towards me was probably frustration that I couldn't see what was going on. Or chose not to see it. I think I've known but I couldn't accept the obvious. I didn't want to feel like I'd wasted my life with someone who doesn't give a shit about me.'

Amber reached across the short gap and clasped Fern's knee. 'Mum, you haven't wasted your life. I'm not a waste, am I? Or Ruby.'

'Apart from raising you two, which I'm immensely proud of and wouldn't change for the world, I've done nothing with my life. You've said as much.'

'I was out of order.'

'But it's the truth. I have no career, no real passions. I've been drifting since you and Ruby left home. I've been so unhappy but not brave enough to do anything about it. And then there's your dad...'

'Who has treated you like shit. But now you know and can do something about it. I'm so sorry for keeping it secret. I should have said something ages ago. I was totally torn about what was the right thing to do.'

'Your dad put you in an impossible position. He should *never* have done that. He's the only one to blame... well, not the only one.' Fern's eyes blurred with tears. She realised she was more hurt at Stella's betrayal than at Paul's.

'Hey, don't cry, Mum.' Amber perched on the edge of Fern's armchair and put her arms around her. 'It'll be okay. He may be my dad, but I hate what he's done to you and our family. And I'm sorry I've been so horrible to you.'

'Well, if any good is to come out of all of this, it's bringing us closer together. I'm thankful for that.' Fern held her close and sobbed into her shoulder, relishing the comfort of having her daughter in her arms after the strained relationship of the last couple of years. More than anything, Fern would never forgive Paul for forcing their daughter to be a part of his lies and putting that amount of unhealthy pressure on her.

She released her and plucked a tissue from a box on the desk to wipe away her tears.

Amber smiled weakly. 'I've only seen a bit of it, but this place is lush.'

'It is. I'm going to miss it.' She met Amber's eyes and saw a warmth and understanding that had been absent for so long. She acknowledged her own fluttering heart. Leaving would swap one sadness for another. She was in a tangled mess of emotions; in many ways she was so sure about what she needed to do, yet there was much uncertainty about her future and her own happiness. Dealing with the fallout with Paul would be relatively simple compared to what would come after that.

Amber stood, took Fern's hand and pulled her to her feet. 'Are you going to come back with me to the villa?'

'Yep, I can't hide away here forever. We're supposed to be celebrating our birthdays tomorrow.' She laughed bitterly. 'Got to face the music sometime.'

'About that. I kinda put my foot in it with Dad on the yacht the other night. I was drunk and angry and texted him to say that I was going to tell you the truth, then totally chickened out of it. He said he'd managed to book a ticket and was coming out here with Ruby. I'm so sorry.'

A chill flooded through Fern along with even less of a desire to return to the villa. 'So he doesn't know that I know everything? About him and Stella too?'

'No, he doesn't know that; he panicked because he thought *I* was going to tell you. He asked me not to. Stella's been trying to get hold of him to stop him flying out.'

'I bet she has.' Fern glanced at her watch and took a deep breath. 'Right, we'd better get back then.'

The prospect of coming face to face with her best friend and husband, the two people in her life she'd trusted the most, and the two people who had betrayed her the most, was inevitable. There was no point in putting it off any longer.

* * *

Fern said goodbye to Matteo and Edith but promised them, and herself, that she'd come back and say a proper goodbye before leaving the island for good. The confusing emotions that had been churning her insides returned on the taxi ride back.

Enclosed within its lush gardens, the villa at least had a calming effect on Fern. The peace reminded her of the retreat and then of Tuscany, and yet again a wave of sadness washed across her.

Amber went ahead and pushed open the large wooden front door. Fern took a deep breath and stepped inside.

'We're back!' Amber called, her voice echoing around the entrance hall.

Fern had planned to slip in and go straight to her room for a shower, but perhaps Amber announcing their arrival would get the inevitable out of the way. Although how she and Stella were supposed to move on from this, she had no idea.

Footsteps tapped across the tiled floor and Stella appeared in the living room doorway with puffy eyes and frown lines. Fern's immediate reaction was to hug her, but she stopped herself. This was all Stella's doing. *No*, not just hers, Paul's too, but Stella was the one standing in front of her.

'Hey,' Stella said quietly.

Chloe appeared behind her mum, brushed past her and flung her arms around Fern. 'Glad you're back.' She released her, gave a weak smile and beckoned to Amber as she headed towards the stairs.

It was no surprise that Chloe was emotional; they'd all grown up together. Fern was like an auntie to Chloe, the same as Stella was to Amber and Ruby. She could only imagine how conflicted Chloe must feel about her mum having slept with Fern's husband. It wasn't as if Chloe didn't know Paul either; they'd all spent so much time together over the years: birthday parties, days out, barbecues in each other's gardens, holidays, sleepovers... the list was endless, which made everything all the more heart-breaking and difficult to comprehend.

Amber kissed Fern on the cheek and followed Chloe upstairs.

Fern and Stella eyed each other across the hallway. There was nothing for it now.

'I hear Paul will be turning up shortly.'

Stella's tanned cheeks reddened. She shook her head. 'I've tried calling him but there's been no answer.'

'Funny that.'

'Has he contacted you?' Her voice was filled with fear.

'I have no idea, but I doubt it. I've only spoken to him once since we've been here and that was because he wanted something. But maybe this is the best thing. Him being here as well will get *every-thing* out in the open. He can't hide the truth any longer.'

Stella took a tentative step forward. 'I am so sorry, Fern. If I could turn back time and do things differently, I would.' Her cheeks clenched as if she was trying to control her emotions. 'Are you okay?'

'I'm fine.' Fern folded her arms. She knew she was trying to convince herself that it was true.

'I'm glad you found comfort with Matteo.'

Rage swept through Fern. 'Don't you dare.'

'What?' Stella held her hands up.

'Insinuate the way he comforted me.' Fern shook her head. 'It's so far from the truth and my reason for going there. I needed to escape *you*. And yes, it was a comfort to *talk* to Matteo *and* Edith, people who aren't involved in this... this... mess. Because that's what it is. A total mess, Stella. How could you?'

Stella looked at her sheepishly. 'I'm sorry, I didn't mean to suggest that something had happened between you and Matteo, I just hoped it had.'

'Would that have made you feel less guilty, if I'd slept with him? And you know full well why I didn't.' She glared at her. 'I'm not like you.'

'No, you're not. Do you know how much I've envied you, since we first met? I envied how popular you were, how effortlessly pretty you are, with your rosebud lips and flawless skin. And I envied you for capturing Paul's heart.'

'You mean ensnaring, don't you? Isn't that what you think I did with Paul by getting pregnant?'

'No. God, Fern, no. I know it was an accident. You wanted to go to university and escape your parents, escape everything. I knew you weren't really in love with Paul.'

'But you were?'

Stella shook her head. 'I don't know. Maybe, maybe not. I envied you, that's the honest truth. I still do. You're the loveliest person I know. Me and Paul had that one-night drunken thing, then he got serious with you. I kinda expected you two to eventually fizzle out and then who knows... When you got pregnant... I don't know, it changed everything really.'

'It mainly changed everything for me. I was stuck living with my parents while you escaped to university, met new people and managed to get a degree before your "accident" happened. But by then you were in a far better position than I was.'

'You didn't have to marry Paul,' she said matter-of-factly.

'Oh really? You don't think so? What options did I have besides staying at home with parents who were hugely disappointed in me? Paul did the right thing, although I'm pretty certain he thought about walking away. We had pressure from both sets of parents. We'd been stupid and were skint. What else do you think we could have done? And I fancied Paul. Back then, I probably even believed it was true love. I focused on us as a family and made the best of a bad situation. I would never have chosen to have kids that young. It was hard bloody work and I was grateful to Paul for stepping up and shouldering some of the responsibility. And maybe that's why I've turned a blind eye to things, because he could have walked away, but he didn't. However he may have behaved since, he did stick by me.'

'You don't owe him anything, not any longer.'

Fern knew that was true, but it wasn't as straightforward as simply starting afresh. She shivered in the cool of the hallway. With the girls upstairs, the villa was quiet. She wondered where Violetta was, hoping that she wasn't overhearing this conversation. She was probably in the kitchen preparing food for when everyone arrived. Worry gripped her again. Stella was watching, waiting for her to say something.

'Does Rhod know about you and Paul?' she finally asked.

'I don't know.'

'Did you have sex with Paul when you were with Rhod or Gary?'

'No. I was single when it happened and it was the one time. I promise.'

'Apart from the time before Paul and I got together. So twice.' Fern took a deep breath and steadied herself. Oddly enough, she felt quite calm. Anger, hurt and frustration simmered beneath the surface, but she needed to hold it together, for Jacob's sake at least. And Ruby's. She had no idea if Ruby knew any of this, if Amber had ever talked to her, or if she'd questioned the reason why her dad had decided to join them all in Capri for the last few days.

With the imminent arrival of their families, the sprawling, elegant villa suddenly seemed claustrophobic. Soon there would be four more people to add to the mix, and more tension. Fern made a decision to be the better person and approach the situation with calmness. There would be plenty of time to talk to Paul away from everyone else, but she was not going to cause a scene.

She looked coldly at Stella. 'Is there enough space for everyone? Because he's not sleeping with me.' She faltered, but was unable to refrain from having one final dig. 'Although, of course, there's always your bed, isn't there.'

She walked away to ready herself for the arrival of Rhod, Jacob, Ruby and her goddamn husband.

33

STELLA

How the hell Fern kept her cool and welcomed everyone as if nothing had happened, Stella had no idea. She cringed as Paul stepped into the entrance hall with a big grin, focused his attention on Fern and said, 'Surprise!'

There was a flurry of activity and little time to think as everyone welcomed each other. Jacob gave Stella an uncharacteristic hug.

'You missed me, huh?' she said, ruffling his hair. He needed a haircut. She also thought he'd grown since she'd last seen him and at thirteen, he was already as tall as her.

'Hey,' Rhod said, kissing her cheek. 'Nice place.' He raised an eyebrow.

She ushered them further into the villa, while attempting to keep her attention on Fern and her family. Paul was doing all the talking – *overcompensating*, she thought, *thinking he might be in the shit*. Little did he know.

'I just thought it, uh, might be nice all of us being together for once,' he was saying in reply to why he was here. He put his arms around Amber's and Ruby's shoulders.

Amber's face was telling. She looked seriously uncomfortable compared to Ruby, who gazed in wonder at their surroundings.

'You actually managed to take time off work, did you?' Fern's voice was curt and full of disbelief.

'The advantage of being the boss.' His deep voice filled the hallway.

Stella led them through the villa and onto the sun-flooded pool terrace, relieved to have Jacob's excited chatter accompanying them.

Violetta had already laid the table for a late lunch, which provided the perfect distraction from the underlying tension. After the view was admired and the pool terrace explored, they all sat down to tuck into the mezze-style fare of fresh bread, olives, cheeses, salami and salads.

Stella's appetite had deserted her, leaving a churning stomach. She picked at her plate of food, feeling unusually hot and uncomfortable despite the gentle warmth and light breeze. She noticed Fern barely ate either. Jacob made up for it as he piled bread, salami and cheese on to his plate. No salad, she noticed.

Rhod, Ruby and Paul were happy enough to talk about their journey. Fortunately, not being particularly attentive, Rhod and Paul didn't think to ask how their time on Capri had been. For once, Stella was grateful that the men in her life, apart from Jacob, were idiots.

Ruby was upbeat, chatty and won over by the villa and its grounds, so she happily steered the conversation. Stella was glad that Ruby had made it out to Capri even for a fleeting visit. She worked hard and had a caring nature, not just because of the career in nursing she'd chosen, but her temperament too. Stella was also grateful that Fern would have both girls to lean on in the coming days, weeks and months.

She gripped the edges of the chair and tried to calm herself. It was awful to think of her friend's life disintegrating around her and she knew that was how Fern was feeling, even if she was putting on a brave face.

She nibbled a bit of bread and chewed a salty black olive. Most of the food had been polished off, and after being introduced by Amber, Violetta began clearing away.

Stella noticed Amber whisper something to Ruby and Chloe. Not long after, the three of them disappeared into the villa. Fern caught Stella's eyes and gave her a steely look and a subtle nod before grabbing an empty bowl and following after Violetta.

Jacob and his dad were talking about football of all things, but she guessed there was no escaping that with her football-mad son, even on Capri. Now was her chance.

She scraped back her chair, stood up and looked across the table at Paul who was nursing a beer. 'Can I have a word.'

Perhaps he sensed that her tone was a command rather than a question because, with a frown, he set down his beer and followed her. She reached the edge of the terrace where the pool curved and the view of the hillside down to Marina Grande and the shimmering sea was uninterrupted. Stella stopped and turned to Paul.

'Fern knows,' she whispered. 'About us.'

He looked at her as if she'd gone mad, frowned, then laughed. 'You're pulling my leg, right? She's said nothing. Behaving perfectly normally.'

She took his arm and led him away from the terrace and the possibility of the prying ears and eyes of her son and ex-husband. They went into the pool room and she unlinked her arm from his.

'You have shit for brains, you know that?'

He glowered and folded his arms.

'You only thought Fern was behaving normally because you don't notice your wife any longer. You haven't for a long time. Not only do you not pay her attention, but you can't see what's going on in front of you and how fucking miserable she is. Of course everything on the surface seems okay, because while you're off shagging whoever it is you're shagging, Fern's at home keeping things together as she's always done.'

He rubbed his forehead with the palm of his hand. '*If* she knows, why's she so calm?'

'Oh, Fern's seething; she's just holding it together until she gets you on your own.'

'How the fuck did she find out, Stell?'

'I told her.'

'You did what?' He slammed his fist against the wooden side of the pool room. She flinched but held his gaze. He was so close, she could smell his familiar woody aftershave, see the spittle on his lip and the brown flecks in his otherwise blue eyes. Stella wondered what she'd ever seen in him.

'She needed to know the truth,' she said calmly. 'She deserved to know.'

'Amber didn't tell her anything?'

'Amber had every intention of telling her and tried to, but she found it too hard to break her mum's heart and her promise to you.' Stella held his gaze. 'You should never have made her lie for you. She's gone through hell covering your arse. She's been angry and frustrated at Fern for not seeing what she thought should be obvious. Were you really meaning to come out here to ensure Amber kept her mouth shut? How on earth did you think you were going to do that? Manipulate her like you do Fern? Emotionally blackmail her?'

'Don't you dare speak to me like that.' His voice was ominous, his hand still rammed against the wall, his breath hot on her face.

'I can and I will,' she said with a steeliness that she hoped wouldn't betray how much she was shaking inside.

'She's going to hate you for what you've done.'

His words were like a punch to the gut, but she knew them to be true. 'Maybe so, but it was the right thing to do, to own up and tell her. It's her choice now what she does with that information. She knows the truth.'

'I thought we had a good thing. Why the hell spoil everything?'

Stella studied the face of the man who was as familiar as her own reflection. For so long, her feelings about Paul had been such a jumble, a weird mix of lust, hate, perhaps love, sometimes disgust, at what they'd done behind Fern's back. She'd get a message from him and her heart would flip, but whether from excitement or fear, she wasn't sure. The other night on the yacht when he'd sent explicit messages and pictures she'd given in to her darker feelings for him, the lust that had remained since she was a teen. Looking at him now, she knew how the thought of that made her feel, how much she hated herself for betraying the trust of her friend, how much she didn't want to be anywhere near him in that way ever again. It really was over.

Stella slipped out from beneath his arm. She could sense the anger simmering off him. She was glad Jacob and his dad were just outside. Her marriage may have failed but Rhod was a good dad and she knew he'd be there for her if she ever needed him.

'When we get back home,' she said, once she'd moved far enough away to the pool room door, 'I don't want you contacting me again. You understand.'

'You'll come back for more. I know you too well.'

'No you don't, and I won't. You need to concentrate on your wife and stop disrespecting her.' She faltered for a moment, taking in his clenched jaw, stocky shoulders and buff arms. He left her feeling cold. 'Good luck when Fern gets hold of you.'

Rage soared through her as she escaped. She darted round the side of the pool room, not wanting to face Jacob or Rhod. She needed a moment on her own.

Paul was everything that was wrong about the men she

normally ended up with: self-centred, laddish, still behaving as if they were twenty instead of in their forties with kids, wives and responsibilities. Not all men were like that or behaved in the way Paul did; she had plenty of friends who'd married decent guys. Maybe she was drawn to men who she knew, one way or another, would eventually break her heart if she let them get too close. With Paul, she'd been part of the problem, having a fling with him, knowing full well he was married to the one person she truly cared about, the one person in her life who was like family. She was closer to Fern than she was to her own parents and she'd let her down in the worst possible way.

As she went the quiet way around the villa to her room, she vowed to somehow make it up to Fern. She couldn't change what she'd done, but Fern had to come out of this mess stronger and happier for it. Stella knew that Fern would be better off without Paul, she just needed her to believe it.

34

FERN

Throughout lunch, Fern felt as if she was having an out-of-body experience; she was physically there sitting with friends and family, yet it was all such a blur that it was as if she was looking down on herself. She could barely eat, let alone speak, she was so worried that all her hurt and anger would come spilling out. She didn't want that, not in front of everyone. She wanted to get Paul on his own.

Once lunch was over, as planned, Amber and Chloe took Ruby off, and Fern left as well to give Stella a chance to talk to Paul. It had been Stella's idea to talk to him first – she'd practically begged Fern to let her. Why Fern had been okay about giving her the opportunity, she had no idea. Was it that she was grateful Stella would be the one to face him first, or was she just relieved to put off the inevitable for a little longer?

Fern went to her room and waited, certain that Paul would come and find her. Twenty minutes of nervous pacing later and footsteps on the tiled hallway made her heart thump. Ruby flew through the door with Amber on her heels.

'Mum, are you okay?'

Fern pressed her hand to her chest. 'I thought you were your dad. I'm fine. Well, I'm not fine, but I will be.'

Ruby threw her arms around her and hugged her tight. 'Amber and Chloe just told me everything.' Her voice was muffled in the crook of Fern's neck.

'You really didn't know?'

Ruby pulled away and wiped her eyes with the sleeve of her top. 'No, nothing.' She glanced at Amber. 'I still can't believe you kept it secret all this time.'

'I think Amber was protecting us both.' Fern smiled weakly and offered her hand. Amber took it and squeezed it.

'What are you going to do, Mum?' Ruby asked.

'I don't know,' she said honestly. 'But I need to talk to him first. Give him a chance to explain himself. How are you holding up?'

'I'm not the one who's been cheated on.'

'No, but you came out here to have a break and enjoy yourself. It's not quite what you expected. For any of us.'

She looked at Amber. Her face was drawn and worry pinched her brows. Fern drew them both to her and held them close, for the first time in a long time, she reflected. Probably since they were kids. She breathed deeply and looked between them.

'Right, it's no good us all moping about. We have three days left, let's please try to enjoy ourselves. Ruby, there's a pool out there with your name on it, and you have to get Violetta to make you a Limoncello Mojito. Go on, Amber, show Ruby around.'

Neither of them looked convinced by her upbeat reassurance, but with faces filled with worry and pity, they kissed her cheek and left.

* * *

Fern stayed in her room for another hour, long enough to realise that Paul had decided to avoid her. She felt strangely calm as she went to look for him. Violetta had made up the bedroom attached to the pool room and that was where she found him. *So, he retreated here instead of facing me*, she thought.

She stood quietly in the open doorway, her face in shadow while the early-evening sun warmed her back. Paul was unpacking, putting away the couple of pairs of shorts and T-shirts he'd brought with him.

He met her eyes and faltered. He placed the clothes on the bed and walked over to her.

'I was just coming to find you.'

Bullshit, she thought, but instead said, 'So, is it true?'

He looked at her and shrugged.

'About Stella?' She stepped out of the sun and into the room. 'About the other woman Amber found you with?'

'Yes,' he said bluntly.

Even though it was the truth she'd been dreading, she felt numb. 'Have there been more?'

His jaw clenched. 'Yeah.'

Fern shook her head. 'That's all you can say? No apology? No explanation? No regret?'

'Hey.' He moved closer, his arms outstretched as if to pacify her. 'I've been stupid, but I can stop.'

'Don't kid yourself, Paul. How long have you been unfaithful for? Since the beginning?'

He stared at her, his lips pursed.

'If you can't even talk to me about it, how on earth do you think we can move forward?' She held his gaze. 'You know what, I don't want to talk about it. I just wanted to hear the truth from you.'

Maybe she was too calm, too reserved, too much a shell of her former self. Teenage Fern would have laid into him. Somewhere over the years, she'd lost her drive, her passion, her gumption, while Paul remained as cocky as he'd been when they'd first met. He was a coward, hiding behind a wall of silence. The truth was out, but he showed zero evidence of remorse. Fern left him to his moody silence.

What was left of the day passed by in a blur. Jacob and the girls were content to swim in the pool. Paul and Rhod left the villa and went into Capri; Fern was sure Paul would tell his version of events, probably while they were holed up in a bar somewhere, drinking until late and steering clear of her. Rhod probably knew already. All of Paul's friends probably did. She imagined she'd been a laughing stock for years. But not any more. *Not* any more.

* * *

The day of Stella's fortieth birthday dawned, and, Fern thought bitterly, the day that was supposed to be a party and celebration for them both. Amber and Ruby had rallied around Fern the evening before, while Stella had spent the evening with Chloe and Jacob. Fern had no idea what time Paul and Rhod had returned to the villa and didn't care.

Fern was in no mood for celebrating and she suspected it was the same for Stella, but they went through the motions with cocktails around the pool and a light lunch before the evening celebrations when caterers had been booked to serve a five-course meal. The bracelet she'd bought as a present for Stella to symbolise their friendship remained in her room, unopened.

It should have been the perfect end to two perfect weeks. Fern had been desperate for a break from the monotony back home, but in the relatively short time she'd been away, her life had been torn to shreds. Secrets had been revealed, heartache shared and new friendships forged. Fern had secrets of her own. Those feelings she'd tried to bury when she was around Matteo were fighting to be set free. She felt as tightly wound as a coil, ready to explode, and she didn't think she was the only one feeling that way. Tension simmered throughout the day and into the evening.

The distraction of food as the waiters brought out each course was much-needed. The food was exquisite, but Fern hardly tasted it; she ate because everyone else was eating, but her head was elsewhere, fighting the barrage of thoughts and emotions that constantly battered her. Even the creamy tiramisu seemed tasteless.

The conversation around the table was stop-start and mainly centred on Ruby, Amber, Chloe and Jacob and how they were getting on at school and university. Safe subjects that focused the chatter on something positive.

Fern felt relief when the last course was cleared away and champagne was brought to the table. The evening would soon be over. And then Violetta appeared on the terrace, holding a cake blazing with forty candles.

They all stood and a painfully half-hearted rendition of 'Happy Birthday' filled the air. Stella's cheeks were red, Fern assumed from the embarrassment of them going through the motions of putting on a show to keep up appearances. Normally she'd have lapped up being the centre of attention.

Violetta placed the chocolate cake in front of Stella and, with help from Jacob, she blew out the candles. Smoke pirouetted into the night. The lanterns edging the pool flickered in a sudden breeze. Fern shivered.

'To Mum,' Chloe said, raising her glass. 'And Fern.'

'To Stella and Fern,' everyone echoed.

The words tasted bitter to Fern.

They sat back down, but Stella remained standing, clutching her glass. A hush fell around the table.

'I'm not going to make a speech, but I just wanted to say, to my friends and family, thank you. Thank you for everything.' The emotion threading through her words was obvious, to Fern at least. Stella looked pointedly around the table, her focus falling on Chloe, Jacob and resting on Fern. 'To friends.'

Fern looked away. A lump caught in her throat as she downed her glass of champagne. She scraped back her chair, dropped her napkin on the table and walked across the terrace to the villa doors. She felt everyone's eyes on her, Paul's and Stella's in particular.

Locking herself in the downstairs bathroom, she leant on the sink, breathing hard, all the upset and anger she'd been battling to contain rising to the surface. Fern wanted to rage at Paul, but she felt detached whenever she looked at him. She should have told him where to go yesterday, demanded that he stay some-where else so she didn't have to see his smug, remorseless face. Yet she was conscious of how that would have impacted the girls. What upset her the most was how his lies had affected them, particularly Amber, that he'd upset them as much as he had her. Perhaps more so. There was no longer any love between them, but he was the girls' dad and him disappointing them was a hard thing to deal with when they *did* love him. She loathed him for that.

Had there ever been love? Initially, it was just lust. But lust had turned to duty. Finding herself pregnant had forced her to grow up fast. Her whole future changed by two red lines. She'd wanted to stay with him because she'd been scared stupid of ending up alone, a pregnant teenager living with her parents, her life ruined. But if fate hadn't intervened would they really have lasted? She was hard-pressed to think what would have kept them together. Not love. Their teenage lust had diminished pretty quickly, long before they were knee-deep in dirty nappies. The girls had kept them together. That and her fear of being on her own. She'd put up with stuff because she didn't want to rock the boat, because their life was comfortable, because they muddled along and now this is where she had ended up.

Fern wiped away her tears and left the bathroom. She went back outside but slipped quietly into the shadows away from the pool. She needed fresh air to focus her thoughts before re-joining everyone.

There'd been plenty of times over the years when she'd wondered why Paul was with her. Fern's easy-going, fun-loving side had been replaced by the stress and responsibility of young motherhood. His responsibility had been different. He'd worked hard to provide for them, but when she thought about it, his life hadn't really changed. Yes, he'd become a dad at nineteen, but his building apprenticeship had continued, while her dream of graphic design at university had been short-lived. While she was bottle-feeding twins and doing the million other things that needed doing on a daily basis, he was making friends at work and socialising at the pub in the evening.

Fern gazed across the pool terrace to the faces of her friends and family lit by the glowing lanterns and candlelight. It should have been a joyous occasion, a celebration for her and Stella. Her best friend. She should be hearing laughter and chatter drifting across the pool, but instead the evening had been subdued and an awkwardness pulsated around the terrace.

Paul had his back to her, a beer clasped in his hand. His social life had continued while hers had stalled. Back then, after having given birth to twins, sex or any sort of intimacy had been the last thing on her mind. Had she really believed that he didn't get up to anything on nights out with his mates? That he didn't pull girls who were free and single, girls who weren't bleary-eyed, greasy-haired and covered in baby sick? Had she been so naive to think that he'd remained faithful all this time? Or was it simply denial? Ignoring those worries had protected her sanity.

There had been moments of happiness in their marriage, and it wasn't that her life was without affection, yet it often felt as if they were going through the motions of what was expected. More recently, she'd had mixed feelings about being intimate with him; part of her longed for him to desire her, yet despite his good looks, he also left her feeling cold. She often longed for sex, but not with him. Time away had opened her eyes, a combination of Amber's harsh words during that first week and the physical and emotional reaction she had to Matteo. It wasn't as if she was able to control the way she felt about him or the effect he had on her, but then, as Edith had pointed out, she'd shown restraint. There was nothing to feel guilty about. Something had changed though; something she wanted to hold on to with all her might.

Fern left the shadow of the pool house and wandered across the terrace past the soothing blue glow of the pool, her thoughts shuffling and taking shape, beginning to slot together like a puzzle. She knew what she needed to do. Since Paul's unexpected arrival, the knot of anger and upset buried inside had intensified. A future without him was scary and unknown, but over the past day or so, whenever she thought about forging her own path, it felt as if the knot loosened – just a touch, but enough to make her realise that she might well be better off on her own.

She took one last look at the glittering hillside, a deep breath of orange-blossom filled air, and walked back across the terrace. If anyone paid her any attention, she didn't notice. Her focus was on Paul and only Paul.

She stopped next to his chair. 'I need to talk to you.'

She didn't look at anyone else and she didn't wait for a reply. She paced to the villa and into the living room. With everyone outside, it was quiet and far enough away for their conversation to not be overheard.

Her heart thumped, but she felt calm and more sure of herself

than she had in a very long time, as if an emotional clarity had
cleared her mind of any uncertainty.

Paul was frowning as he entered the room. 'I don't think this is
the—'

'I want a divorce.' She held his gaze and stood her ground.

'Fern, hey, hey,' he said soothingly as if trying to placate her like
she was an overexcited dog. He closed the gap between them and
caught hold of her hand. 'You don't really mean that.' His pale-blue
eyes bored into her. He was achingly familiar and had been part of
her world for more than half of her life now, yet the way he was
looking at her made her skin crawl. To have so little respect for her,
yet still have the audacity to question why she would want to leave
him, only made her more determined.

'Actually, Paul, I do.' She yanked her hand from his. 'I've never
been more certain about anything. Deep down, I've known all
along that you're a complete and utter cheating bastard; I know for
certain now.'

'I've made mistakes.' He held up his hands. 'But I can change.'

She scoffed and shook her head. 'Oh my God, Paul. You can't.
You know you can't. *I* know you can't. And I don't want you to,
because I don't want to be with you any longer. What I don't get is
why you would even want to stay with me?'

'We have a good thing—'

'No.' She physically backed away from him. '*You* had a good
thing. You stayed with me because I turned a blind eye and you had
a cushy life. I looked after you, I looked after the girls, looked after
our home, while you worked and then enjoyed yourself. For arse's
sake, I cooked and froze bloody meals for you because I felt guilty
that you'd have to look after yourself while I was here.'

'Don't forget, you have a damn good life too.' His tone had
changed, a hardness creeping into it. 'You really think you're going

to cope on your own? What are you going to do for a job? For money?'

'You're a piece of work.' Fern shook her head. 'I've been coping on my own pretty much the whole time we've been together. And if you don't think we're a partnership when it comes to the business, then you're stupid as well as a liar and a cheat. Yes, you've always worked hard, but don't forget, I single-handedly raised the girls and supported you building that business in the early days. Who did the bookkeeping, huh? Who answered the calls and booked jobs while dealing with toddler tantrums or tried to squeeze everything in between school hours while also keeping the house clean and tidy, cooking and bloody looking after you? You've had it so good. And I've been an idiot for putting up with it for so long.' Her heart raced and sweat dribbled down the side of her face. Gone was the cool calmness she'd entered the room with. She took a deep breath and held his gaze. 'When we get back home, I'm filing for divorce.'

'I'll believe that when it happens,' he said. 'You'll be lost without me.'

He walked away. Fern didn't attempt to go after him. His callousness and disregard for how much he'd hurt her made her all the more determined to go through with everything she'd said. She'd prove him wrong; she was certain of it.

35

FERN

The birthday celebrations fizzled out not long after Fern had confronted Paul. While he disappeared into his room with a couple of beers – no doubt to wallow in self-pity – Fern returned to the terrace. Stella and Rhod were lounging by the pool chatting. The girls were still at the table playing cards with Jacob and drinking prosecco. Jacob was swigging Coke and demolishing his third slice of birthday cake.

Instead of feeling buoyed by standing up to Paul, Fern was at a loss. The anger that had made her confront him had deflated and she was left feeling emotionally vulnerable and at a crossroads.

She only told Ruby and Amber where she was going. She didn't want to wait until they were about to leave to go and say goodbye to Matteo, so she'd messaged him to ask if she could pop by that evening. His reply had been swift.

Yes, of course x

Fern didn't care that it was dark, she felt safe walking the winding road edged by the stone walls of villa gardens to the piazzetta. The taxi journey didn't take long, through the honey-lit streets and up the steep mountain road with its hairpin bends to Anacapri. The walk to Il Ritiro d'Arte was familiar, the peace soothing and needed after the evening she'd had. She slipped inside the retreat's grounds and made her way up the grand stone steps to the entrance.

Matteo was waiting and greeted her with a welcoming smile as he ushered her into the villa.

'I'm sorry it's so late,' she said, stepping inside the entrance hall. 'I just couldn't leave without saying goodbye to you. Edith too.'

'That's okay; a few of us are still outside finishing off a bottle of wine.'

There was a distance between them. Fern was uncertain whether to greet him with a kiss on each cheek. She sensed his reservation too.

'Edith's already gone upstairs to bed,' he continued, 'but if you go up now you should catch her before she sleeps. Come and find me afterwards.'

Fern took the stairs two at a time. The villa was grand but homely, particularly at night with lamps pooling warm light. She reached Edith's room, knocked gently and waited.

The door swung open. Edith was wearing oversized striped pyjamas, her white curly hair loose without the usual scarf keeping it off her face.

'Fern!'

'I know it's late, but I had to come and say goodbye; I didn't think there'd be time otherwise.'

'Come in, come in,' Edith said, stepping back.

'I won't stay; Matteo said you were going to bed. I just wanted to say goodbye and thank you for being such good company and a true friend. It feels like we've known each other a lot longer than two weeks.'

Edith grasped her hands. 'Oh Fern, I feel the same. What for me started as a holiday full of sadness has turned into a blessing. If Maya hadn't refused to come with me, I would probably never have met you and you certainly wouldn't have stayed here. It seems to me it was written in our stars that we'd meet each other, and' – she squeezed Fern's hands tighter – 'that you'd meet Matteo.'

Tears welled in Fern's eyes as she nodded.

'We have each other's numbers. We'll keep in touch.' Edith leaned in and kissed Fern on each cheek. 'Now, go and say a proper goodbye to that gorgeous man downstairs.'

There was so much more Fern wanted to tell Edith, but it would have to wait. She knew that however much she would miss Edith's company, it was Matteo who had drawn her back. She went downstairs and headed through the villa to find him.

Voices drifted in from outside. Candlelight flickered through the living-room windows from the terrace where she'd enjoyed that first meal with everyone. It was only a few days ago, yet so much had changed in that time.

Matteo met her by the French doors. He had obviously been looking out for her.

'It's a gorgeous night,' he said, leading her away from the villa and into the shadowed garden.

It really was, clear and starlit, with the moonlight outlining the leaves against the dark sky. He took her hand and clasped her fingers. The gesture reminded her of that night in Tuscany.

Kept company by the fluttering moths, they followed the winding path lit by solar lamps. They reached the edge of the garden, where a gap between two cypress trees framed the view past another villa to the opposite hillside, which was twinkling in the darkness. Somewhere over there was Villa Giardino and her family. A fractured family, but one that would begin to heal through separation. Instead of feeling sad about her marriage ending, she felt hopeful and was looking forward to the future. Whatever the challenges, it would be *her* future.

She turned to Matteo. 'I think I just changed my life.'

'You did?' He stood back and looked at her, a glimmer of a smile lighting his handsome face.

'I told my soon-to-be ex-husband what I thought about him. He doesn't deserve me; I realise that now.'

'No, he doesn't.' He swept a strand of hair from her face, his touch light but sensual.

She gazed up into his eyes.

'I don't know what this is,' she said, motioning between them, 'but I'd like to stay in touch, if you'd like to as well?'

He took both of her hands in his. 'I would love that. And maybe you can come out here again. Or to Tuscany.'

Choked for words, Fern nodded.

Matteo put his arms around her and held her close. She slid her arms around his waist and rested her head against the top of his chest, soothed by the beat of his heart, the warmth of him and the strength of his embrace. Whatever happened next, at least she'd made lifelong friends in Edith and Matteo. But right then, apart from being there with him, nothing else mattered.

36

FERN

The sky was a frosted grey, the narrow streets of Capri quieter now they weren't packed with tourists. Seven months had gone by since Fern had been on the island, and it was starkly different to the fine days of late spring. The one thing that remained the same was the company of Stella puffing up the hill next to her, their icy breath streaming into the chilly December air.

The holiday to Capri and the truth that had come out had been a catalyst. An Italian dream had turned into a nightmare but had paved the way for her to find happiness.

Fern had stayed true to her word and started divorce proceedings the week after they'd returned. It had been a sombre journey home. Fern had been sadder than she believed possible. Her heart was torn and she wished for more time, and it wasn't because she'd been sad to leave the island. Matteo had remained imprinted on her thoughts. They'd held each other for an age in the garden of his retreat. He'd kissed her gently, lingering long enough to send a feeling of longing flooding through her. And then they'd said goodbye and she'd left before ending up a sobbing mess in his arms. She'd cleared her head with a walk through Anacapri, soaking up the beauty of the trees and villas, while the sound of laughter, a beep of a scooter and the waft of citronella candles had accompanied her. She'd caught a taxi back to the villa with her mind made up about her future.

Matteo had messaged her the day she got home and then their messages had become more frequent until they were messaging each other every day. By the time Paul had moved out at the end of the summer, Fern and Matteo were chatting on the phone at least twice a week.

Paul didn't fight the divorce, although Fern knew that he was shocked that she'd actually gone through with it. It was scary heading into the unknown and forging a new life for herself. Amber and Ruby were behind her 100 per cent. Paul had a lot of work to do to repair the damage to his relationship with the girls. However hard it was for everyone, Fern was relieved that Amber and Ruby were adults. Whether it had been a mistake to have wasted precious time staying with him for so long, she'd done her best for the girls – she didn't regret that one bit.

They reached the piazzetta at the top of the hill and were rewarded with the sweeping view over the island, the winter sun casting watery light over the hillside.

'There, that wasn't so bad,' Fern said with a grin.

Stella's cheeks glowed. 'Hmm,' she huffed. 'We're going to get a taxi to Anacapri. No arguments.'

Fern didn't argue. Even with their luggage being taken on ahead, she had no intention of hiking the steep path all the way there. Although the island was quieter, at dusk and close to Christmas, there was magic in the air with Capri lit by thousands of twinkling lights.

It didn't take long to reach Anacapri. They paid the driver and stepped back out into the chilly winter day.

Fern turned to Stella. 'You don't have to be on your own;
Matteo's offered you a room at the retreat.'

'I know.' Stella placed a gloved hand on Fern's arm. 'I'll be fine
at the B&B. It is a luxury one after all. I want you to have quality
time with him. You deserve this. My God, you've been waiting for
this for months.'

That was true, but now the moment was almost upon her, her
nerves were building. Despite messaging each other every day and
talking on the phone countless times, Fern had not actually seen
Matteo since leaving Capri in a whirlwind of heartache and
emotion. Since then her life had been turned on its head and she'd
gone from unhappily married to divorced and free. Her return to
Capri was poignant because it was where her life had changed and
where she'd made the decision about her future. It was where Stella
had broken her heart as much as Paul had, and where Matteo had
given her hope about her future. She had no idea how she'd feel
seeing him again and more importantly – and worryingly – how he
would feel about seeing her.

Fern's worries evaporated when Matteo greeted her with the
warmth that she'd been longing for. He wrapped her in his strong
arms and they enjoyed a deep lingering kiss in the hallway. Il Ritiro
d'Arte was empty of guests and staff, but Matteo had invited her.
Despite its size, it somehow managed to feel warm and cosy.

Matteo led her through to the living room where a fire crackled
in the large stone fireplace. The darkness outside was offset by the
glowing wall lights and the twinkling Christmas tree. They snuggled together on the sofa with mugs of hot chocolate clasped in
their hands and smiles on their faces. Fern felt as comfortable with
him as the last time she'd seen him, their connection all the

stronger from months of getting to know one another. They sipped their drinks and chatted with the same ease they'd had over the phone, the conversation eventually getting round to the topic of her divorce being finalised.

'Have you figured out what you're going to do next?' Matteo put his empty mug on the coffee table and took her hand. 'You were talking about a change of direction with work.'

Fern gazed into his smiling eyes. 'I can't tell you how much I long to hand in my notice. Not that I don't like the people I work with, I do, they're the only reason I've stayed so long. Well, that and not having the nerve to find something else, but I'm desperate for a change and to do something different. Something I'm passionate about.'

'Any idea what that might be?'

'I enjoy looking after people, but I don't ever want to be taken advantage of again.'

'You won't, Fern.' He squeezed her hand tighter. 'You know you won't.'

'When we've sold the house, and there'll be money from the business too, I'm thinking of moving somewhere where I can get a lot more room for my money. Somewhere with countryside and space. Perhaps Wales. I'm not certain yet. What I am thinking about is having a place big enough for the girls to stay and for me to also open a B&B. Something small, just a couple of rooms. Boutique style.'

They chatted a little longer about Fern's hopes and dreams. She was inspired by Matteo and what he'd created both here and at his Tuscan retreat. She knew whatever she did wouldn't be on such a grand scale, but all she wanted was to finally do something for herself, something that would make her happy.

* * *

As the evening wore on, Matteo went to prepare food, while Fern went to her room to unpack and shower. She liked that he hadn't assumed they were going to spend the night together, even if Fern had every intention of doing so. There was nothing stopping them any longer. They'd done little more than tease so far, that first lingering kiss in the hallway and kisses and cuddles on the sofa. Her heart ached for him. No, not just her heart, her whole body. Those feelings that Fern had tried so hard to bury when she was last on Capri were unleashed.

She spritzed on the perfume she'd bought in Capri in the spring, dried her hair and put on tights and a dress. She slicked on mascara and a wine-coloured lipstick to match her dress and padded downstairs to find Matteo.

The coffee table was laid out with an array of tapas dishes and a pan of chestnuts was ready to be roasted.

They sat together on the velvet sofa directly in front of the fireplace. Matteo poured the wine, the ruby liquid glistening in the cut glasses. Flickering firelight danced across them and the wood spat and crackled. The smell of woodsmoke reminded Fern of her great-grandparents' house in Wales with its open fires – a rare happy childhood memory.

'*Salute.*' Matteo tapped his glass against hers. 'Honestly, I can't believe you're here. I've been dreaming of this for so long.'

The anticipation of what the night would hold left Fern feeling dizzy. 'I have too,' she said.

All of her senses were alive from the taste of the spiced mulled wine, the warmth of the crackling fire and the deliciousness of her perfume mingling with his cologne.

Matteo took the wine glass from her and slid his arms around her waist, tugging her close. He kissed her and she responded, but unlike that first gentle kiss in the hall, this one was urgent and passionate. She dipped her fingers beneath his jumper to find hot firm skin. A jolt of excitement ran through her. His hands smoothed beneath her dress, caressing up her thighs.

I shouldn't have worn so much, she thought as he reached the top of her tights and began to wriggle them off her. She breathed deeply as his warm breath met her cool skin. He discarded the tights. She met his smiling eyes and reminded herself again that they were alone and she was free. She pulled off his jumper and started undoing his shirt buttons. Her fingers fumbled, unable to work properly through nerves or anticipation. Or both. Matteo laughed and helped her, undoing the last two and dropping the shirt on top of her crumpled tights. He pulled her dress up and over her head and kissed her deeply.

Everything was more sensual and romantic than she'd ever experienced before. The longing that she'd had for Matteo had only grown over the months apart. There'd been times when she felt foolish for thinking anything could come of it, but the more they'd talked, the more apparent it had become that they both wanted more.

This is the stuff of dreams, Fern thought as Matteo gently pulled her down onto the soft rug, their bare skin warmed by the crackling fire and each other. Fern lay back, the heat and heaviness of Matteo on top of her all-consuming. She wrapped her legs around him, drawing him even closer, finally able to act out the fantasy that had played over and over in her head from almost the moment she'd met him.

37

STELLA

Stella didn't disturb Fern by messaging her. They'd spent the last forty-eight hours apart, although she had a pretty good idea what Fern had been doing and couldn't be happier for her. Stella had embraced the time on her own. She'd always believed that she was someone who needed to be surrounded by people. Having spent much of the last twenty years as a single mum, she'd filled the time when the kids were with their dads with friends, socialising and dating, and when Chloe and Jacob were with her, she had a good network of mum friends. Recently, however, she'd realised that she was beginning to like her own company.

When it came to love, she'd made bad choices. Of course, she didn't regret having Chloe and Jacob, but she regretted rushing into things with their dads. And she sure as hell regretted the mistakes she'd made with Paul. She was proud of Fern for standing up to him and for going through with the divorce. She knew Paul had doubted that Fern would have the guts. He'd have been happy to continue getting looked after while having fun behind her back. And Paul was out of Stella's life for good. He hadn't tried contacting her since they'd got back to the UK and she didn't miss him in the slightest.

Fern still had much to sort out and even though Stella knew how anxious she was about striking out on her own, she was ready for a new start. Their friendship had been damaged, perhaps irreparably, but Stella was doing everything in her power to piece it back together again. In many ways, they were tied to each other like family, their kids as close as cousins, if not siblings. Fern was reserved with Stella, but they did talk and Stella was blown away by Fern's ability to move forward.

Stella had had every intention on her fortieth birthday to announce to everyone the real truth about her Lottery win, but the series of events with Fern and Paul had put an end to that. It certainly wasn't the right time to flaunt the fact that she was a multi-millionaire. What it had given her was more time, to think things through, to look into properties and investing, to talk to a financial advisor and the advisors at the National Lottery. She started to make plans for her, Chloe's and Jacob's futures. Their happiness and security were of the upmost importance. Her happiness too, although it seemed more and more unlikely that she was going to ever find that with a bloke. The last thing she wanted was a relationship. No, from now on she was focusing on herself, her kids and her friends.

It had been Stella's idea for them to come back to Capri together, although Fern had refused her offer of paying for her flight. Stella knew that Fern was working hard on being financially independent. She got the sense that Fern didn't want to rely on anyone but herself, although her head and heart were consumed by Matteo. Not only did Stella understand that Fern needed a push to see him again, she believed it would be a cathartic experience for them both, plus it was part of her plan to begin to make amends for all the wrong she'd done.

* * *

Stella thumped the large knocker on the impressively grand front door of Il Ritiro d'Arte. She hadn't been here before, but even in the depths of winter, the place was majestic.

The door opened and she got her first look at Matteo. Fern had kept her time at the retreat pretty much to herself and the only photos she'd taken were of the villa and the garden. Matteo wasn't on Facebook – Stella had tried looking him up, of course she had. But standing in front of him now, she was struck by his immediate warmth and welcoming smile. He had perfect white teeth, a shadow of stubble, good bone structure, beautiful smiling eyes and dark, slightly curly hair. No wonder he'd stolen Fern's heart. A laddish, cocky, stocky ex-husband – although he could certainly be described as good-looking – wasn't a patch on the Italian in front of her.

'You must be Stella.' He held out his hand and she shook it.

She stepped inside and he closed the door on the cold December day.

'It's nice to finally meet you,' he said.

'You too.'

She had no idea what he knew about the situation between her and Fern, but if he held any animosity, he didn't show it. From everything she'd gleaned from Fern, he was one hell of a decent guy.

'I'm a little early,' she said, glancing around at the tiled entrance hall with its sweeping staircase. 'But I was hoping to steal Fern away for a couple of hours.'

'Of course, she's just grabbing her bag. You must come back and have dinner with us later. We'd both like that.'

'I'd like that too, thank you.' She didn't feel as if she deserved his kindness, but she could tell his openness was heartfelt. He understood that Fern being here with Stella was the start of repairing their friendship and he was willing to make things as easy as possible. Fern had finally found someone worthy of her love.

Footsteps sounded on the stairs. Stella and Matteo turned as Fern walked down dressed for a Capri winter in chocolate-brown boots, skinny jeans and a dove-grey jumper, her bag slung across her shoulder and a coat over her arm.

Stella had never seen her look so happy. Just the way she caught Matteo's eye and the smile she gave him spoke volumes.

Matteo leaned in for a kiss. Stella turned away, pushed open the front door and waited outside.

Moments later, the door thudded closed and Fern joined her. There was a twinkle in her eye and, Stella realised, an essence of the Fern she used to know, except this version was far more content. A happiness emanated from her that had been absent for years.

'If you can drag yourself away from Matteo,' Stella said with a smile, 'I want to show you somewhere.'

They walked together into the heart of Anacapri. The place was much quieter than earlier in the year, with many of the boutiques closed and far fewer people wandering the streets. It was as if the colour had drained from the place, the vibrant greens, the potent pink flowers, yet a quiet beauty remained, along with the mesmerising view to the cool blue sea.

Stella knew Fern well enough to know she'd talk about Matteo in her own good time. She wasn't going to press her for details. She was satisfied enough by their smiles to know they'd been more than happy to see each other again. Although Stella had sworn herself off men, for the time being at least, she was immensely glad to see Fern looking so happy and deservedly so.

It wasn't far to the villa. Stella caught Fern's frown as she pushed open the gated entrance to a front garden filled with lemon trees. The green leaves and fresh yellow were bold against the white of the villa walls, a surprising sight in the depths of winter. They reached the front door and Stella pulled a bunch of keys from her bag.

'I picked these up yesterday,' she said.

Fern looked at her, wide-eyed with disbelief. 'You bought it?'

'Yep, I bought it.' She pushed open the door and they entered.

It was cold and dim in the hallway and Stella suddenly felt nervous. She continued through and the villa opened up to reveal a large room with a curved ceiling and a fireplace.

'It turned out pretty well hooking up with Luca on the yacht. I gave him a detailed list of the kind of property I was interested in and he said he'd let me know if something came on his radar that fitted the bill.'

'And this one did?'

Stella nodded. 'It certainly did.'

They wandered around in silence. Stella's heart thumped as she watched Fern take in the spacious, white-walled rooms filled with pale winter light streaming through patio doors and windows. Although it was empty of furniture, there were splashes of colour in the floor tiles and the duck-egg blue painted doors.

Stella turned to Fern. 'What do you think?'

'It's... it's beautiful.'

'You haven't seen the best bit yet.' She led the way through a covered terrace to a colonnaded walkway with raised flower beds on either side. Even in winter, the beauty of the garden shone through, the promise of spring colour and scent just a few months away.

Fern stopped halfway along the walkway, her face morphing into a frown as she turned to Stella. 'I don't understand. How much did this place cost?'

'Two point five million euros,' Stella said, trying to keep her voice steady.

Fern's frown deepened. 'But you won a million. How...?'

'I actually won twenty-seven and a half million.'

'Are you kidding?' Fern sat down with a thump on the low curved wall of the raised border. She shook her head. 'You told me you won a million.'

'I know how it looks; something else I've hidden from you, but actually, apart from Luca, I haven't told anyone the full truth, not even Chloe or Jacob. You're the only other person.'

'It's a lot to take in.'

'Almost everyone now knows I won the Lottery. A million is a number people can cope with and comprehend. The amount I've really won is, well, insane. It's taken me all this time to even begin to get my head around it and to make smart decisions about how to spend it and what to invest in.'

'People are going to start questioning things with you splashing money like this. You're not going to be able to keep it secret forever.'

'I know.' Stella joined Fern on the wall and shivered as the cold seeped through her skirt and tights. 'Can you imagine, though, how lush this place will be in summer?'

'It'll be incredible. You did say you wanted a place in the sun. So, you have a holiday home on Capri.'

'No, I don't.' A lump had formed in Stella's throat and her eyes blurred with tears. 'You do. I didn't buy it for me. It's yours.'

She watched Fern carefully as the words sank in.

Fern opened her mouth, closed it again and shook her head. 'No. You have to be joking?'

'I'm serious, Fern. This place is yours.'

Fern scrambled to her feet and paced along the paved path to the wall at the end of the garden with its view over Anacapri. She turned and walked back. Her breath fogged the air. She stopped in front of Stella and fixed her with a stern gaze. 'If you're doing this to buy back my friendship, you don't need to. Yes, things have changed between us, things that we may never be able to fix, but you're still my friend. You're like a bloody stupid infuriating sister, Stella.'

Stella looked away as she fought back sobs. Her jaw clenched and she swiped at her eyes. 'You're too good, Fern. You know that right? I'm sorry for every bit of hurt I've caused you.'

'I'm not condoning your behaviour, but your actions made me not only see sense but changed my life for the better. Paul was toxic and I'm well rid of him.'

'I know you are,' she said quietly. 'I'm just sorry it went that far.'

'What's done is done.'

'But seriously, I'm not doing this in an attempt to win you back.' She stood up and looked at her best friend of nearly thirty years. 'This is something I want to do for you, because you deserve it and because I can. I have more money than I know what to do with and by investing wisely, I'm set for the rest of my life. Chloe and Jacob too. This place is yours to do what you want with. I want to see you happy, Fern. I've made horrible mistakes that I can't erase. I'm all too aware that money can't buy happiness, but this place might give you the freedom to change your life for the better. To follow your heart and take a chance on love, if that's what will make you happy.'

EPILOGUE

FERN – THREE YEARS LATER

Fern twisted her hands together as she watched the tree-lined lane. She had no idea why she felt nervous, but she did. Perhaps it was because she wanted people to fall in love with the place as much as she had.

She glanced behind her at the farmhouse. The stonework was an earthy mix of pale grey, rust-red and apricot tones, while the restored wooden shutters framed the windows. The building and surroundings evoked a sense of peace. All she could hear was the breeze whispering through the branches and chilled hits on Spotify playing from inside.

Although La Casa dei Sogni, surrounded by forested hills, vineyards and the gentle green of open fields, felt far from anyone and anything, in reality the nearest town was within view, perched on a hill, its medieval walls honey-lit at night, a beacon in the darkness. Matteo's Tuscan retreat was only a short drive away too. Fate had brought them together at Il Ritiro d'Arte and Stella's gift had led Fern on quite the adventure.

Fern had been floored by Stella's unexpected gesture that cold December day on Capri. Although she'd been basking in love from her first couple of nights with Matteo, Fern's head and heart had remained in turmoil when it came to her friend. Their friendship had seemed damaged almost beyond repair. She was uncertain how she could ever trust her again, but to be given a villa... Stella had implored her, saying it was because she wanted to do something life-changing for Fern, because she deserved it and because she was sorry. Fern had wanted to refuse it; she hated the thought of owing Stella. But Stella wouldn't take no for an answer; the villa was Fern's and she could do what she wanted with it. The gesture proved to be the start of something special for Fern and a second chance for Stella, her generosity the beginning of a difficult journey to try to piece back together their friendship.

Leaving Capri for the second time had been even harder, yet there was no uncertainty about Fern and Matteo's feelings for each other, and Fern returned home free of Paul and the constraints of an unhappy marriage. He'd admitted adultery and while he'd kept the business, she'd received a lump sum payment. It was a clean break, with neither of them having ties to each other beyond the girls. She'd spent Christmas with Amber and Ruby, the last one in the family home, and after a huge amount of soul-searching, Fern was finally clear on her future.

Without a doubt, the villa had changed her life. Capri was a place she'd like to go back and visit, but it wasn't where she'd wanted to live. She'd fallen in love with Matteo, but she needed purpose in her life and to do something meaningful. Her idea of moving to Wales to open a B&B grew. With the family home sold, Fern had jumped at the chance of a summer in Tuscany when Matteo invited her. And that was when Fern had first laid eyes on La Casa dei Sogni.

The rustling of leaves brought Fern back to the present. Standing in the shadow of the farmhouse, she shivered. It was a bright spring day; the row of dark green cypress trees that lined the lane were bold against the pale-blue sky. The air was cool and fresh and she could smell the Bolognese that she'd made that morning. There would be lots of mouths to feed later, but Fern loved the idea of her Tuscan home being breathed into life with the arrival of other people.

'There you are.' Amber's voice filled the stillness of the afternoon as she crunched across the drive. 'I've been looking for you everywhere.'

'I thought I heard a car.'

Amber glanced at her watch. 'It's going to be another half-hour at least until they get here.'

Fern breathed out slowly. 'I'm just worried I've forgotten something.'

'That's why we're doing a soft launch, Mum.' Amber hooked her arm in Fern's and laughed. 'And there's absolutely nothing to worry about. The place is perfect. Come on, I've made tea. Let's at least wait with a cuppa.'

With a last glance at the empty lane, Fern followed Amber inside. She knew everything was fine and she wholeheartedly agreed that the place was perfect. After seeing and falling in love with the stone farmhouse during her summer with Matteo, it had become clear what she wanted to do, and where. The Capri villa, although beautiful, had been chosen by Stella, while the Tuscan farmhouse had stolen Fern's heart. Stella had said she could do whatever she wanted with the villa, so, with her mind made up, she had put it up for sale. Everything had then begun to slot into place. The eventual sale made Fern a multi-millionaire overnight. With Ruby graduating and getting her first nursing job in Bristol, Fern had bought a three-bed apartment on the harbourside for her to live in, and when Amber had swapped the bright lights of London for a digital marketer job in Bristol, she'd moved in too.

The exchange on the Tuscan farmhouse had been finalised the

summer before, so Fern had spent the last few months renovating it. Not that it was in a state of disrepair, but with the money she'd made on the Capri villa sale, she was able to turn a tired-looking farmhouse into a boutique B&B that managed to be luxurious while retaining its rustic charm.

Her dream of a tiny B&B in Wales had grown into a Tuscan escape, a place far removed from the worries of everyday life, nestled in the beautiful countryside within reach of medieval villages and the historic city of Siena. Long days had been spent painting, tiling and tackling the garden, offset by equally long evenings having dinner with and talking to Matteo. The nights were far from lonely with them together at his Tuscan retreat or surrounded by peeling wallpaper and the smell of paint at Fern's farmhouse. Fern didn't mind being on her own when he returned to Capri. Her days were filled with hard but satisfying work and long chats and video calls with Amber and Ruby, plus she began to get to know the locals. And, of course, Matteo would pop back for fleeting visits. The nights of crying herself to sleep were long gone.

It had been Amber's idea to do a soft launch – a week with Fern's friends and family before paying guests arrived for the second week of the Easter holidays. After a cup of tea, the peace was broken by the welcome sound of Chloe and Ruby's laughter as they emerged from one of the taxis. Fern's heart filled with joy. Ruby's paramedic boyfriend got out next, his eyes roving over Fern's new home. She had only met him once, and had found him sensitive and well-mannered and, most importantly, he doted on Ruby.

Fern opened the car door for Edith and helped her out. Edith held Fern at arm's length, her smile making the corners of her eyes crinkle, before she pulled her into a tight hug. Edith had become a close friend. She was the mother figure Fern had always craved, but their friendship was what she treasured most – someone Fern could bounce her ideas off during their long phone calls.

'It's good to see you.' Fern's words were muffled against Edith's shoulder.

'You too,' Edith said, releasing her.

Across the other side of the taxi, Stella met Fern's eyes and smiled. There was always an initial awkwardness whenever they saw each other, as if they had to work out how to behave around each other, but they'd find their way, they always did.

Jacob emerged from the taxi and towered over his mum, but at nearly seventeen, he'd grown into his lankiness. Fern was glad they were here. All families had their ups and downs, and Stella and her children were like that: family.

The taxis sped off up the lane, and 'oohs' and 'ahs' rang out as Fern ushered everyone inside. Amber headed into the kitchen to put the kettle on again, allowing Fern to show off her new home. After months of hard work, it felt good to have the place filled with people. Only Matteo was missing.

* * *

With bags taken to rooms and drinks made, Fern left everyone in Amber's capable hands. The open-plan living room was the heart of the house, a space to relax in, with a wall of books at the far end, a sofa and armchairs around the fireplace in the centre and a dining area close to the kitchen. Fern's lemon tree painting that she'd started at Matteo's retreat hung on the wall, a constant reminder of just how far she'd come, both in her painting and sketching, which she'd continued as a hobby, as well as her personal life. It wasn't perfect by any means, but it had been the beginning of a whole new chapter of her life.

Fern liked how the kitchen was separate, yet she was still able to hear the chatter drifting through. It was a proper farmhouse kitchen with a large wooden table in the centre and a range oven where a fireplace had once been. The mushroom-coloured walls and stripped wood floors were warmed by the sunlight streaming through the French doors. Two large dishes of lasagne were ready to go in the oven and the table was covered with chopping boards, bowls and salad. It wasn't long ago that Fern had considered cooking to be a chore, but now she was embracing the idea of feeding her family and eventually guests. She'd also hired a local woman to help with the cleaning and washing, and she had Amber working on the marketing side of the business from the UK. They were a team and their strained relationship had healed. Everything had come together perfectly.

'Hey,' a familiar voice said.

Stella was leaning in the kitchen doorway with a mug of coffee in her hand. 'Just wondered if you needed any help?'

'I don't think so. It's all under control.' Fern pulled on the oven gloves. She glanced at Stella. 'You can keep me company though, if you like.'

Stella smiled and perched on the stool on the other side of the table. Fern put the two lasagnes in the oven, then chose a large ripe tomato and started slicing it.

'How are the renovations coming on?' Fern asked.

'Let's just say I'll be glad when they're done and I can have the house to myself.'

'No regrets though?'

'About the house? No, none.'

The changes in Stella's life were less drastic than the ones in Fern's. After eventually revealing the full truth of her Lottery win to friends and family, she used some of the money to buy a large, detached house in the countryside within commuting distance of Jacob's school and her job in Bristol, although she'd handed her notice in over a year ago to set up her own interior design business. She had a holiday home too and somehow, slowly and sensibly, had successfully navigated the minefield of becoming rich overnight.

'Do you remember when I promised you that our forties would be the best decade of our lives?' Stella said, watching Fern as she sliced another tomato.

'Yeah, on the spa weekend when you told me about your Lottery win; I didn't believe you at the time.'

'Do you believe me now?'

Fern layered the slices of tomato with mozzarella in a bowl. 'It turns out you were absolutely right.' She drizzled over olive oil and looked at Stella. 'But are you happy?'

Stella folded her hands on the table. 'I'm getting there. I'm happy because Chloe and Jacob are. Jacob's doing well at school and is pursuing his love of football. Chloe's still finding her feet, but there's plenty of time for her to figure out what she wants to do. She's talked about going travelling with a friend. I think it will do her good. Jacob wants to spend a chunk of the summer with his dad, so I might go out to the villa in Spain.'

Fern nodded and put a large handful of rocket into a wooden bowl. Stella was more subdued than she used to be. Fern wasn't sure if it was because she'd mellowed with age. Despite the massive changes in her life, there was an underlying sadness. As far as Fern knew, she was single. She didn't really know if she still hooked up with random men or not – Luca was occasionally mentioned, but it seemed to be only a casual, occasional thing, and she certainly hadn't committed to a long-term relationship with anyone. Fern hoped that one day she would meet someone, but only if he made her happy.

'Have you seen Paul?' Fern wiped her hands on a cloth and met Stella's eyes. It didn't hurt like it used to, talking to Stella about him. He was out of her life and she was so much better off; his behaviour and Stella's betrayal had been the catalyst for Fern's life changing for the better. Despite all the hurt and upset, in a weird way she was grateful.

'No, I haven't. The girls are on speaking terms with him though?'

'Yeah, they've all found a way to move on.' *Just like I have*, Fern thought.

* * *

At dusk, Matteo arrived with a box of wine and was greeted with a cheer. He drew Fern into his arms and kissed her. Her longing for him hadn't diminished in the nearly four years since they'd first met; her feelings had simply grown. He was welcomed warmly, first by Amber and Ruby who adored him and couldn't be happier he was with Fern, and then by Edith who gave him the biggest hug and ushered him into the garden.

A long wooden table, made from reclaimed and restored scaffolding planks, took pride of place on the terrace at the back of the farmhouse. The outside space and the view had ultimately sealed the deal for Fern and as she sat there now, surrounded by her friends and family, she could hardly believe it was real. This was her life. All of this was hers, from the sweeping lawn edged by trees where fireflies would emerge at dusk in late spring, to the olive grove at the end of the garden. It was a fairy tale place, and a dream come true. Gone was the view from her kitchen window of their old family home onto a patio and fake grass. Here the kitchen had double doors that opened out onto her own slice of Tuscany.

As her eyes trailed across the smiling faces around the table, she acknowledged that she couldn't have asked for a better day. At the far end, Ruby and her boyfriend were looking loved up, with Chloe and Jacob on either side of them. Jacob was still eating – Fern had lost count of how many helpings of lasagne he'd had – while Chloe was looking sleepy, with her hands clasped around her glass of wine. Stella and Edith were deep in conversation – there was too much chatter to make out what they were saying – and Matteo was listening intently to Amber. She beamed as she told him about her marketing plan for the farmhouse. Matteo reached beneath the table for Fern's hand and clasped it in his lap. A feeling of absolute contentment washed over her. Everything was as it should be. She'd rid herself of a toxic marriage; she'd opened her heart and learnt to trust again. She was stronger and happier than she could remember ever being.

* * *

After tucking into dark chocolate Florentines and coffee, Fern hooked her arm in Edith's and they strolled away from the others down the grassy slope. Edith used a walking stick and her pace was slower than the last time Fern had seen her, but her spark and positivity remained.

'The place is wonderful, Fern. Even better than I was imagining.'

'Does it tempt you to take the plunge and move to Italy?'

'I have too many friends back home to uproot myself now. Moving countries was something I should have done right after retiring, not now I'm heading into my late seventies. And anyway,' she said, squeezing Fern's arm tighter, 'why on earth would I put myself through the stress of selling my home and buying in Italy when I have places like this and Matteo's two retreats to visit.'

Fern stopped by the bench beneath a birch tree. It had a view to the farmhouse one way, and the other way to the olive grove. They sat and she clasped Edith's hand.

'Are you happy though?'

'Did I envisage that I'd get to my age and still be on my own?

No.' She chuckled. 'But that's life. It's a funny old thing. I'm not actually lonely. My life is filled with love. I have nieces and nephews and great-nieces and nephews. I have fabulous friends.' She gave Fern a knowing look. 'I have freedom and the means to travel and for the time being' – she patted the arm of the oak bench – 'my health.'

'Have you seen Maya?' Fern asked gently.

Edith pulled her shawl tighter and folded her hands in her lap. 'No. It's too hard. I hear about her through friends. She's suggested we meet, socially only, for a cup of tea and cake, as if we're simply old friends catching up.' Edith shook her head. 'I don't want to pretend and I don't want to put myself through that. Sometimes cutting our ties with the past is the only way to move forward, even if it hurts us deeply at the time.'

Fern put her hand over Edith's. 'I get that. Admitting my marriage was over was the hardest thing I've ever done, but when I made the decision, it was as if a weight had lifted. I hated him by the end, for the way he'd treated me, the way he'd talk to me. I hated myself too for letting him. Matteo opened my eyes to what love should really be.'

'He was worth the wait.'

'I love him, Edith. He's everything I've been missing my whole life.'

'And *you* are everything he needed. I like how you've followed your own path and have done something for yourself. Yes, being here has enabled you and Matteo to be together, but this is your project, your passion. You both have purpose and places you've created through love and hard work. And you have each other. That makes me very happy.'

* * *

The evening began to wind down. Edith headed to bed and Fern noticed that Ruby and her boyfriend had disappeared too. The lasagne had been demolished, along with at least a dozen bottles of wine. She couldn't wait to greet her first paying guests; spring would be busy, and her new venture would give her little time to miss Matteo when he headed to Capri to open Il Ritiro d'Arte for three months before he returned to Tuscany for the summer.

For the first time in her life, Fern had independence, money and a job she was proud of and thrived on. And she had love too.

The last of the plates had been brought in and stacked in the dishwasher. She spied Amber outside, wiping down the table. Over the past couple of years, she'd been Fern's rock; Ruby too. Fern couldn't have been prouder of them both; steadfast Ruby had graduated and been thrown into the deep end as a nurse in a busy A&E, while Amber had knuckled down and aced her business and marketing degree. Fern was grateful for her expertise when it came to tweeting, stories and Instagram live.

With everything cleared away, Fern stood for a moment in the shadows of the kitchen and gazed to where Chloe, Jacob, Amber, Stella and Matteo were sitting by the flickering fire. Music was playing, another bottle of wine had been opened and Chloe was dishing out playing cards. Fern would join them, but not yet.

She left the kitchen and went outside. After a sunny spring day, the April evening was fresh. Light flooded the terrace and the glow of the moon was enough for Fern to navigate her way past the trees to the fence that separated the garden from the olive grove. By day, the view was a patchwork of green, of vineyards, fields and tree-covered hills, while at night it was hard to tell where the sky started. The darkness was absolute, only broken up by the moon, the stars and the distant glow of a medieval hilltop village. It reminded her of Matteo's favourite spot at Il Ritiro Toscano, and it had become Fern's favourite spot in the whole world. The peace was all-encompassing, but she'd not once felt lonely, even surrounded by the endless space.

'I thought I might find you here.'

Warm hands slid around her waist. Matteo rested his head on her shoulder and she cupped her hands over his. Even in the quiet of the night, she hadn't heard him pad up behind her. The stillness was what she loved and the way any stress or anxiety evaporated here.

'You know me too well,' she said.

'You should get a telescope, set it up down here for stargazing.'

'I think guests would like that.'

'I was thinking more about you.' He kissed her neck and held her closer.

Fern closed her eyes and leant back into him, relishing his warmth and the comforting firmness of being in his arms. In her mind, she could still see the sky decorated with stars, but images of the last few years flashed by too, much of it filled with hard work and laughter. The people she loved most in the world were all here. Especially the man with his arms wrapped tight around her.

'It's been a good evening.' His deep voice filled the silence.

'The best.'

'Do you want time on your own or are you coming back inside?'

Fern breathed in the cool air. This area of the garden was filled with wildflowers, their colour breathing life into the landscape after the long winter, but it was too dark to see them. Now was the time for returning to the warmth, for refilling her glass with wine, for laughter and late-night chats, before heading to bed with the man she loved.

Fern took Matteo's hand and they walked together back across the long grass to the farmhouse. Firelight flickered through the downstairs windows, reaching out invitingly into the dark, welcoming them back. It was everything she'd dreamed of and more. She squeezed Matteo's hand tighter, relishing the feeling he evoked. She remembered being at his Tuscan retreat for the first time and the distance between them after their first kiss, when they were unable to act on their passion for each other. Now she was free, living on her own terms, following her heart.

Fern pushed open the door of La Casa dei Sogni and drew Matteo inside. This was her life, filled with happiness and love.

ACKNOWLEDGMENTS

With all that's been going on in the world during 2021 and particularly at the beginning of 2022, writing romantic fiction set in beautiful locations has been a true escape for me and I hope it proves to be an escape for you too – uplifting and heart-warming armchair travel, this time to the stunning island of Capri.

Villa Giardino, plus the two art retreats in Anacapri and Tuscany are a figment of my imagination, however, they were inspired by real-life places. I owe Chiara Vicinanza my thanks for being so generous with her time and answering the many questions I had about Capri, which enabled me to add detail to the story. With her mother's family living on the island and Chiara herself owning Villa Eden (that she rents with Airbnb) in Massa Lubrense on the Sorrento coast, she was the perfect person to help with my research. Any inaccuracies are mine alone!

This is my second book with Boldwood (there are more to come!) and it has been wonderful to work with such a fabulous team, from supportive fellow authors to the publishing powerhouse of Amanda Ridout, Nia, Claire and Co, and in particular my fabulous editor Caroline Ridding, whose insightful edits, along with Jade's and Candida's suggestions and attention to detail, have made the book as good as it can be. Thank you all.

A big thank you to the fabulous book blogging community for helping to spread the word and to my author friends and non-author friends! A special mention to Helen Pryke for always being so wonderful (and for kindly checking the Italian phrases for me), and to Paula Worgan for being the most brilliant supporter of my books from the very beginning (and for curating her very own Kate Frost bookshelf!). Once again, a heartfelt thank you to Judith van Dijkhuizen, who's not only a lovely friend but always the first person to read an early draft of my books.

Last but not least, Nik, Leo and Mum, thank you as always for your encouragement and love.

MORE FROM KATE FROST

We hope you enjoyed reading *An Italian Dream*. If you did, please leave a review.

If you'd like to gift a copy, this book is also available as an ebook, digital audio download and audiobook CD.

Sign up to Kate Frost's mailing list for news, competitions and updates on future books.

https://bit.ly/KateFrostNewsletter

One Greek Summer, another escapist tale from Kate Frost, is available to order now.

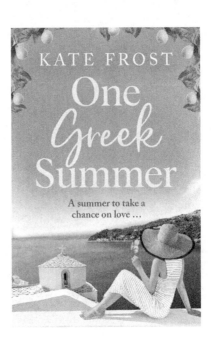

KATE FROST

One
Greek
Summer

A summer to take a
chance on love ...

ABOUT THE AUTHOR

Kate Frost is the author of several bestselling romantic escape novels including *The Greek Heart* and *The Love Island Bookshop*. She lives in Bristol and is the Director of Storytale Festival, a book festival for children and teens she co-founded in 2019.

Visit Kate's website: http://kate-frost.co.uk/

Follow Kate on social media:

facebook.com/katefrostauthor

twitter.com/katefrostauthor

instagram.com/katefrostauthor

bookbub.com/authors/kate-frost

Boldw🌕🌕d

Boldwood Books is an award-winning fiction publishing company seeking out the best stories from around the world.

Find out more at www.boldwoodbooks.com

Join our reader community for brilliant books, competitions and offers!

Follow us

@BoldwoodBooks

@BookandTonic

Sign up to our weekly deals newsletter

https://bit.ly/BoldwoodBNewsletter